Starting from Now

'Themes of love, loss, grief, family ties and animal activism are explored in this engrossing read focusing on regional Australia . . . McDonald's characters are meaty and convincing and she has a skill of depicting rural life and the sense of community that is often embedded in country areas.' *Weekly Times*

'McDonald continues to introduce engaging and enjoyable new characters throughout this interlinked series . . . The author's own experience gives readers a true sense of "life on the land" and the fragility of rural Australia and its communities.' Debbish

'McDonald delivers another top notch novel, her best yet, in *Starting From Now*. A story of family, duty, rural crime, journalism, activism and advances in farming enterprises, all wrapped up in a shroud of mystery. *Starting From Now* is a highly commendable novel from a talented Australian storyteller.' Mrs B's Book Reviews

Fleur McDonald has lived and worked on farms for much of her life. After growing up in the small town of Orroroo in South Australia, she went jillarooing, eventually co-owning an 8000-acre property in regional Western Australia.

Fleur likes to write about strong women overcoming adversity, drawing inspiration from her own experiences in rural Australia. She has two children, an energetic kelpie and a Jack Russell terrier.

Website: www.fleurmcdonald.com
Facebook: FleurMcDonaldAuthor
Instagram: fleurmcdonald

OTHER BOOKS

Red Dust

Blue Skies

Purple Roads

Silver Clouds

Crimson Dawn

Emerald Springs

Indigo Storm

Sapphire Falls

The Missing Pieces of Us

Suddenly One Summer

Fool's Gold

Where the River Runs

Without a Doubt

Red Dirt Country

The Shearer's Wife

FLEUR McDONALD

Starting From Now

ALLEN&UNWIN
SYDNEY · MELBOURNE · AUCKLAND · LONDON

This edition published in 2020
First published in 2019

Allen & Unwin
83 Alexander Street
Crows Nest NSW 2065
Australia
Phone: (61 2) 8425 0100
Email: info@allenandunwin.com
Web: www.allenandunwin.com

A catalogue record for this book is available from the National Library of Australia

ISBN 978 1 76087 860 3

Set in Sabon LT Pro by Bookhouse, Sydney
Printed in Australia by McPherson's Printing Group

10 9 8 7 6 5 4 3

Prologue

The three men slipped through the trees, ghostly in their night-vision goggles, white police procedure overalls and masks.

From the outside, they all looked the same: men dressed for a forensic examination of a murder scene. If there were security cameras in the clearing, no one would be able to tell them apart. But inside the overalls one man was large, with a receding hairline and pot belly. Another one was tall, slim with ginger hair and beard. The third was thin, agile and clearly in charge.

They stopped at the outer rim of the clearing, looking around and listening to make sure none of the employees were still present. Earlier, from their hiding spot in the bush, they had watched the cars leave for the day, but they couldn't be certain someone hadn't been left behind to protect the equipment.

The three men had done this before. They believed animals should be safe and forests left unlogged. The natural world needed to be protected. Otherwise their children and grandchildren would inherit a planet that could not sustain itself. The men would never understand why the logging company had been granted a licence to knock down the trees growing within the Gippsland forests, but they knew for certain that the people who were ruining the environment had to be stopped by any means possible. Not only was it the beautiful trees they stood to lose, but the native flora and fauna. These forests were home to the tiny marsupial, the Greater Glider, which were listed as vulnerable. And, although not a threatened species, the trees were also the home of the red-wattle bird and yellow-tailed cockatoo. Of course, there were the more common native animals like kangaroos—they needed to be conserved as well. Even though the men's group focused on animals—that was what they called themselves, Voices for Animals—they extended themselves to stopping logging because it hurt animals in the process. In their minds, the two causes crossed over.

The men's plan was to disable all the machines so the logging wouldn't be able to get started in the morning. The delay would hopefully be long enough for their urgent application against the state government to be heard and a temporary injunction put in place to prevent the logging. They hoped. But even if this didn't eventuate, at least the machines wouldn't rumble to life tomorrow morning.

Gerard was carrying the toolbox. He didn't know how to use the tools and neither did Colin. But the leader did.

'Good to go,' Colin whispered and waved them on.

Sure-footed thanks to their night-vision goggles, they entered the clearing. None of the men would admit it, but their hearts were beating in time with their ragged breathing and adrenalin was coursing through their bodies.

With another glance around, Gerard jogged to the first of the machines and pulled the keys out of the ignition. He pocketed them and moved on to the next one.

Colin shadowed the other man and waited for instructions. The leader took some wire-cutters from the toolbox then popped the bonnet of the first bulldozer.

'Need a light here,' he said in a low voice.

Colin saw the man had lifted his night-vision goggles and he did the same. He took a small torch from behind his ear and shone it onto the engine.

A small snip and it was done.

'Easier than having a vasectomy,' the leader had joked when he'd told them his plan. 'A quick snip and the machines won't start in the morning.'

Colin had thought it was an excellent idea, which was why he'd volunteered his services. At home his wife and daughter would be sitting in front of the television, waiting anxiously for him to come home. This was more important, though. He'd sat down with them both before he'd left and explained what he was doing was for the future of the world. For them, for his grandchildren.

Colin trod softly through the clearing to the next bulldozer, the moon reflecting off the cab window. He watched as the other man placed the pliers on the wires and cut.

It was simple, he marvelled. His one hope was what they were doing would make a difference. That was what he wanted to do; make a difference to everyone's future.

'Next one.'

They moved methodically from one machine to the next. Colin looked at his watch. It had taken them less than twenty minutes and there was only one left to go.

He heard the pop of the last bonnet and then swearing as the pliers rattled through the engine, sounding very loud in the dark clear night, before landing heavily on the grass.

'Shit.'

Colin went to help, shining the torch under the tractor. The other man shimmied under and grabbed the pliers, before quickly disabling the machine. 'I'm just going to take a coupling fitting off the back of this one,' he said. 'I've got a place to on-sell it to. In fact, I might go back and remove a few other bits and pieces. I bet a starter motor would be worth a few hundred.'

'Go for it. Might as well make a profit from these bastards while we're at it. Can go into our fighting fund.' Colin wandered around the front and stood with his back to the loader. The stars were incredibly beautiful tonight. There was a movement off to the side and, slipping his goggles back on, he saw a kangaroo staring at him through the trees.

See? he thought. *This is the whole reason the forests shouldn't be knocked down.* He felt the familiar surge of anger at the thought of these animals losing their homes.

He slowly sank to the ground and sat there, legs out in front of him and his arms behind his body propping him up, watching the roo. He could see the animal's nose twitching. It could probably smell them and was trying to work out whether they meant danger.

He smiled as the roo took a small hop towards him, unaware there was a human close by. Suddenly there was a loud metal bang as the bucket of the loader, which was about one and a half metres in the air, fell to the ground.

From deep in the forest, a loud cry from the alarmed birds echoed through the night, and the roo raised itself to its full height before bounding away in fear.

'Shit,' the other man said loudly from the back of the tractor. 'Sorry. I've fucked it up back here. Lost the hydraulic oil that holds the bucket up.'

Colin stared in dread at the bucket that had come down on his legs. He hadn't even realised he was that close to the tractor. Now, he was pinned to the ground. Colin reached out to try to shift the bucket—a futile movement, he knew. It was larger than he was and its steel was at least a few centimetres thick. But he had to try! It shouldn't be on his legs. How was he going to get out, now the hydraulic pump had been taken off the machine?

It was strange, he thought. *Surely this should hurt?* He couldn't feel anything. Reaching down, his hand came away wet. He could smell it. Blood.

'Mate?' Colin's voice was panicked. 'Jeez, I'm bleeding.'

'What do you mean, you're bleeding?' The leader came out from behind the tractor. 'Did you scratch yourself on something?'

'Front. Tractor.' He wanted to squeal with fear, but his head was fuzzy now and he couldn't work out how to move his tongue.

'What? Oh, fuck!' The man raced to the front of the tractor where Colin was pinned underneath the bucket. He knelt down and realised there was blood seeping into his jeans and onto the ground beneath him.

Colin tried to grab at his arm, but his hand felt heavy and he couldn't make contact.

'It's okay, mate. It's okay. *Gerard!*' He turned and yelled over his shoulder. 'Ring an ambulance. Now! For fuck's sake. Colin, mate, hang in there. We'll get you out.'

The man got up and tried to lift the bucket. It was a dead weight. 'Help here, Gerard. *Quick!*'

'Shit, what's happening?' Gerard asked, finally arriving and seeing his friend lying in a pool of blood, with his head thrown back and his face pale, not just from the glow of the moon.

Racing back, the leader looked at Colin, whose eyes were shut now, his face white and bloodless. 'No, no, no!' he muttered as he ripped off his shirt and tried to stem the blood flow. Deep inside, though, he knew it was futile.

'You gotta keep this going,' Colin whispered. 'Make sure you fight the good fight. For me. For our kids and the future.'

Gerard was standing back, fear on his face.

'It's okay, Col, you'll be all right. The ambos are on their way, aren't they, Gerard? Just hang in there.'

'It's not . . .' Colin stopped talking and there was nothing but deathly silence in the clearing.

'Col?' the leader whispered. 'Col?' he looked at Gerard. 'Fuck, what've I done?'

Chapter 1

Zara Ellison looked around the Melbourne courtroom. The public gallery was nearly full, and the lawyers were seated at the front of the room, looking deadly serious.

Outside, a crowd of demonstrators were waving placards and shouting slogans. As if their protest was going to influence the jury's findings. The protesters wanted to shut down the forestry company. One of their own had been killed during a covert mission that had been designed to cause mischief rather than anything too destructive. The accused was also one of their own. According to them, if the forestry company hadn't been harvesting trees, then the men wouldn't have had to demonstrate and no one would've been killed.

In one way, the death of the protester, Mr Colin Grawd, had been fortunate for the activists. The logging had been stopped while his death was investigated. Although, a month later, Zara had reported in one of her stories that they were hoping to start again once the court case had been concluded. Not just the protesters and families of the deceased and the accused were hanging on the verdict; the word on the street was that the logging company had lost millions in downtime since Colin Grawd's death. This had pleased Voices for Animals, according to their spokesperson.

At the start of the case, the court had heard that Gerard Hooper had been the one who had disabled the machines and removed the hydraulic pump from the rear of the tractor in order to profit from its sale. The charge was manslaughter. The Crown lawyers had spoken of Colin Grawd as an impressive man of integrity. He had long been involved in animal rights, which often crossed over to environmental causes. He had a unique ability to bring people together to work for a common cause. None of his integrity or good character had helped him, though, when the loader bucket had fallen on his legs, severing them. He'd bled out for a cause he'd inadvertently managed to stop. For the time being.

In Zara's mind, a man of integrity shouldn't have been trespassing on someone else's land, but she was a journalist and kept her opinions to herself. She was very clear on never letting her perspective come through in her writing, which was why she was one of the most respected journos for the *Farming Telegraph*. Last year, she'd been shortlisted for a Walkley News Report Award. She'd ticked all the boxes, making tight deadlines, completing research, showing great storytelling and writing ability, but she hadn't won that category. What she had won was the Feature Writing Award for a story she'd written about the personal journey of a farmer who'd been paralysed from the waist down when a boom spray, which had been jacked up, had fallen on him. His determination to keep farming, and the adjustments he'd had to make so he could, had been described with empathy and skill. Lachy Turner, her editor, had been so proud of her that night that she thought he'd been going to burst!

She didn't give a lot of thought to awards—that wasn't why she wrote—but it was nice to be recognised. Perhaps this story would rate a mention somewhere too.

With a keen interest in this case, Zara had travelled from South Australia to attend the trial. She'd also spent a lot of time researching the people involved. The investigation she'd done was in-depth—she never wrote anything that couldn't be substantiated by at least two sources. Zara had spoken to many people off the record and found that Colin Grawd was a serial protestor. He wasn't one of the rent-a-crowd who so often turned up at these types of protests—he was hardcore. An extremist.

He liked breaking the rules.

Why the lawyer for the defendant hadn't brought that up, she wasn't sure. He could've made a case around the fact that Colin broke the law regularly. He trespassed, did things that weren't legal. Surely that would help Gerard, who didn't seem to have done anything like this before. Well, not that she'd found out about yet.

The hallway door opened and a few more people entered, expectation on their faces. Among them was a tall, thin man with a balding head and a ponytail. He took a seat in the back row, where he'd sat for the past week, and put his hand to his face to adjust his sunglasses. He wore them constantly, which is what had caught Zara's attention when they'd left the courtroom on the first day. Wearing sunglasses inside was strange; although at first she'd thought they were prescription. But she'd seen him later that day rubbing his eye. Before he put his glasses back on she'd noticed that his eye was damaged somehow—it was milky. Now Zara suspected he was blind in that eye.

The man, whom she'd given the name Cloudy Eye, had been an avid follower of the case, but she hadn't been able to work out what his interest was. She hadn't managed to link him with either the defendant or the dead man, and he didn't seem to know their families. He kept to himself, listening intently and leaving the courtroom as soon as the judge's gavel had fallen for the day. That in itself had piqued her curiosity. Why would a member of the public be interested enough to sit in on five days of evidence without a particular reason?

She knew he wasn't a journalist—he didn't have an identification tag like the one she wore around her neck, and he didn't take notes. She didn't know his name and wanted to get a photo of him to see whether she could identify him when she was at the office, but the use of mobile phones wasn't permitted in the courtroom. She made a mental note to get a photo when they were leaving court after the verdict. Perhaps someone at work would know who he was.

Her smart watch vibrated, and she looked at it. Lachy had sent her a text. Quickly she got up and went out into the hallway, before digging her phone out of her bag.

Tapping on the message, she saw: *Result yet?*

Zara glanced at her watch. It was close to deadline.

Not yet.

Going to get it in time?

Not sure. They're not back. We've been told they're coming, and lawyers are in place.

Shit! Hope for the best.

Zara put the phone back in her bag. Nothing she could do about it, but she understood the urgency of getting the story into this week's *Farming Telegraph*. This case could set a precedent in the law around activists trespassing on private property.

As she started back to the courtroom, her phone buzzed again. *Jeez, Lachy, nothing's changed in two minutes*, she thought, glancing at her watch.

Not Lachy this time. Her mother.

Zara hesitated. She didn't really want to look at the message while she was working, but her brother had had an oncologist appointment today, following the last round of scans. They were all hoping that the tumours in Will's bowel had shrunk.

Call when you can.

'Shit!' That didn't sound good. *Or*, she thought, *maybe it's great news and we'll be able to celebrate tonight.* She really hoped that was the case. Will was her only sibling and they were very close. In relationship and age. Zara's mum, Lynda, used to joke that the thirteen months between Will's birth and Zara's had been the only time their house had ever been quiet.

Will was the quiet one; Zara had been noisy from the moment she'd entered the world, or so her mum always said. Will was calm and considered, and Zara valued his gentle counsel and friendship.

It had been a long two years since her brother had been diagnosed with cancer. The shock of someone so young having bowel cancer had turned into a determination that he would beat the disease. Zara refused to consider any other alternative, particularly as the diagnosis had come so soon after their father's death in a car accident.

Zara clenched her jaw and pulled open the door to the courtroom before the images of her father dying in the car could hijack her emotions.

Work, she told herself. *Think about work.*

Her heart hammered against her chest as she sat down. Not wanting to think about that dreadful time or the outcome of Will's appointment today, she shut her eyes and took a few deep breaths. The grief was still raw, and emotion overtook her when she least expected it.

People in the courtroom suddenly stirred and her eyes flicked in time to see a door at the back opening silently and the foreperson leading the jury into the dock.

An air of expectation hit the room, and the low chatter and rustling suddenly stopped. Zara grabbed a pen and notebook from her bag. She scanned the faces of the jurors, trying to work out the verdict. They were all expressionless except for the girl on the end. It looked like she'd been crying, and her face was red. Zara wasn't sure if the tears meant a guilty or not guilty verdict.

'All rise.'

There was the noise of lawyers' chairs scratching on wooden floors. Everyone else stood too. The heavy door opened and the judge strode into the courtroom.

'Be seated.'

The judge waited for the noise to settle down before turning to the ladies and gentlemen of the jury. 'Have you reached a verdict?'

The foreperson was a grey-haired man, who looked to be about fifty. 'We have, your Honour.' He held out the verdict to the bailiff, who handed it across to the judge.

Reading it, the judge nodded and handed it back.

'We the jury find the defendant, Gerard Hooper, guilty of manslaughter.'

There was a cry from the public gallery and Lily, Gerard's wife, burst into noisy sobs.

'How could you do this?' she yelled at the jury. Her friend tried to calm her, but Lily shook her off. 'He's a good man!'

Zara swung her gaze to Colin's wife, Christy, and teenage daughter, Sophie. Christy was crying with what Zara assumed was relief; Sophie had her arm around her and stared at Gerard, hate etched on her face.

Ignoring the outburst, the foreperson read on. 'We the jury also find Gerard Hooper guilty of trespass with the intent of causing harm.'

Guilty on both charges. This was a fantastic result for farmers!

Zara could imagine the headline. It would be on the front page of the *Farming Telegraph*. *ACTIVISTS WARNED: STAY OFF OUR FARMS*. Zara knew the paper's deadline for printing was very close, but she needed to wait to see what the judge had to say before she texted Lachy. Then she'd try to get a comment from both wives, the lawyers and even some of the protesters.

While she was on the ground doing that, Lachy would ring some of the peak farming bodies and get a statement from them, but it would be too late to get the whole article in this week's paper. Just the bare facts. They'd have to run a big feature on the story next week. But she also knew Lachy would be angling to be the first paper to get the story up on social media, so it was still urgent.

She'd have to get her skates on.

'Thank you to the jury. You are now dismissed,' the judge said in his deep voice. 'Sentencing will be next week.'

'Your Honour, we'd like to appeal—'

'Do it through the proper channels, Mr Hudson.' The firm tone broke into the lawyer's address. 'Court dismissed.'

The gavel fell and among the bustle and noise Zara heard the bailiff say, 'All rise,' and, with a flurry from his gown, the judge was gone.

Zara gathered her bag and jostled against the others trying to exit the courtroom. She pulled out her phone as she went. Other reporters were doing the same. It was a race as to who could break the news first.

Guilty on both counts. Sentencing in a week. Remanded in custody until sentencing. Lachy would be able to fill in the blanks and at least get the news on the front page of the paper. She knew he'd had the artwork ready for either outcome.

Outside, Gerard Hooper's lawyer, Mark Simpson, stood on the street and faced the journalists. 'We are disappointed with this outcome.'

Zara tried to use her elbows to push through the crowd, her phone recording what he said.

'Of course we'll appeal. Gerard Hooper is innocent of the manslaughter of Colin Grawd—they were friends and colleagues. In a democracy, everyone has a right to voice their opinion, so the trespassing charge is ridiculous. We intend to fight this.'

The protesters were swirling in behind him, chanting, 'Free Hooper! Free Hooper!'

'He's not innocent.'

Snapping her head around, Zara looked for the speaker who had managed to be louder than the activists.

Sophie Grawd stood alone on the footpath, her pale blonde hair pulled back into a ponytail, her arms crossed. Her face was red—whether from rage or another emotion, Zara couldn't be sure.

The journalists turned and hustled towards her. All except Zara. She stayed back and watched, her phone still recording. She would try to talk to her without anyone else around.

'Why do you say that?'

'Do you miss your father?'

'What would you like to say to Gerard Hooper?'

Zara stood a little way away and watched as microphones and phones were pushed in Sophie's face. She saw fear in the young woman's expression but, to her credit, she stood her ground.

'My father was killed by Gerard Hooper,' she stated clearly. 'I guess it was accidental. I'm sure that Gerard Hooper didn't intend for it to happen. However, the fact remains that I come home every day to a house that my dad isn't in anymore. My mum gets into an empty bed every night. I don't care how or why or what happened that night. All I know is that Gerard was in the driver's seat when that bucket dropped on my dad and now my dad's not here. He's in the ground. Gerard Hooper has to take some responsibility for that. I can't express my family's thoughts any more clearly.'

More questions were flung at her, but she turned and almost jogged back into the courthouse.

The group of reporters turned their attention back to Mark Simpson, who stood with a stony expression on his face.

'What is your response to Ms Grawd's statement?'

'Do you think she's right?'

'What is Voices for Animals' stance on the verdict?'

The questions came thick, fast and loud. Zara backed out of the forceful crowd. She was sure there wasn't going to be anything other than standard answers from Mark Simpson. He was a fox caught in the spotlight, trying like hell to escape unscathed. To Zara, Sophie seemed like a much more interesting person to interview right now.

Walking quickly back into the courthouse, she scanned the lobby but couldn't see her. She flashed her press pass at security and loaded her handbag into the security scanner, before walking through the X-ray machine, then headed back to the courtroom. With any luck, Christy would be speaking with her supporters in the corridor and Sophie would be with her.

The hallways of the courthouse were quiet now, just the occasional person walking along the passage. Most of the other courts were still in session.

Zara spotted Sophie coming out of the toilets and made a beeline for her. 'Hey,' she said as she approached, 'I'm Zara Ellison. You're Sophie, right?'

'I'm not talking to any journalists,' Sophie answered. 'I said what I had to say out there.'

Zara stopped and put her hand on Sophie's arm. 'I don't want to interview you,' she said. 'I just want to tell you how strong I think you are, for speaking up the way you did.'

Sophie shrugged. 'No choice. It's what I believe.'

'How's your mum?'

'We're coping.'

'Have you got family to help you?' Zara knew the answers to the questions she was asking, but was trying to establish a rapport with the girl.

'We'll be fine,' Sophie answered, and Zara noticed she avoided the question. 'I'm not talking to journalists.' She turned away.

'Okay, well . . .' Zara broke off. She really wanted to hand Sophie her card and ask her to call when she was ready to talk, but she didn't want to scare her off. 'Take care, okay? Look after yourself and your mum.' She turned around and started to walk away.

'Why do you care?' Sophie's question stopped her.

Zara turned around and held Sophie's gaze. 'My dad died when I was about your age. It's a horrible time to go through.'

'My dad didn't need to die.' The words shot from Sophie's mouth.

'I guess mine didn't either. But he did.'

'What happened?'

'Car accident.'

'So you didn't get to say goodbye either?'

Zara shook her head, hoping the visions of finding the crumpled ute would stay at bay.

Sophie looked at the floor, not saying anything.

'Look, Sophie, you don't know me from Adam, but if I can do anything for you, let me know.' Zara dug in her purse and brought out a card. 'My contact details are here.' Holding it out, she waited until Sophie took it, then gave her arm another squeeze and walked away.

'I'll tell you one thing,' Sophie called out to her as she left.

Zara stopped and looked back. 'What's that?'

'I think there was someone else involved.'

Taking an involuntary step towards Sophie, Zara sucked in her breath. 'What makes you say that?'

Sophie shrugged. 'Isn't rocket science. Neither Dad nor Gerard had ever had anything to do with tractors before. How is it that someone who doesn't know shit about machines can take the hydraulic pump off the back of a tractor?'

Chapter 2

'Zara! What other news have you got?' Lachy appeared at his office door, looking dishevelled. Maybe he'd slept at his desk again. There were a few coffee drips down his white shirt and what looked suspiciously like tomato seeds on his tie. 'Got the front page to print before deadline. We'll run the full story next week but start feeding out snippets on social media.'

'You eat at your desk again?' Zara said, reaching out to flick the seeds away and looking fondly at her mentor.

'If I didn't, I wouldn't get to eat.' Then he held his hand up, before stroking his large stomach. 'No comments on that last statement, thank you.'

Zara grinned. She knew Lachy well enough from their six years of working together to know he didn't care that his shirt buttons were straining against the pulling fabric and no amount of chiding about his unhealthy habits would change him.

'So, any other news?' Lachy asked again.

'Not yet. I've planted a few seeds.'

'Who with?'

'Sophie, Colin Grawd's daughter. I think she wants to talk, but I couldn't get anything out of her today.'

'What makes you think she'll talk to you?' Lachy quizzed.

She shrugged, knowing he wanted to hear her thought process—that was how he got the best out of his staff. Getting them to talk through their ideas, testing them for any holes or to see if something could be done better. It was Lachy's way of guiding the younger journos, mentoring them. He figured his job as the editor was to create good journalists, ones who researched well, reported facts and wrote tight, interesting articles. He'd used the same method ever since she'd turned up at his office for an interview, straight out of university.

'We're similar ages and, like I said, I think she's wanting to talk to someone.'

'I thought she was a lot younger than you.'

'Yeah, maybe she's twenty or so. We're in the same decade! But her dad has just died in a terrible accident and I can relate to that. We have something in common.'

'It would be a great story.'

'Of course it would. You've taught me well, you know!'

Lachy laughed and smoothed his tie down over his stomach. 'I'd like to think so.' He paused. 'You'll have to make it fairly quick, though. It'll be old news before long.'

Zara nodded. 'I'll give it a couple of days, then see if I can get in contact with her.'

'Right, I'll leave it with you. You don't need an old man like me looking over your shoulder.'

She threw him another fond look and headed to her desk. The open-plan office was filled with noise—phones ringing, keyboards clacking. There were three journalists conducting phone interviews, their fingers flying across the keyboards as they paused to ask questions then typed the answers. The other five journalists must be out in the field.

She looked around to see if Liz, her closest friend, was around. Zara spotted her deeply engrossed in a phone conversation. Her pretty, round face was serious, and her pen scribbled quickly across her notebook. Liz was the only one who wrote longhand then transposed her stories onto the computer. When Zara had teased her about being a dinosaur at the age of twenty-five, Liz had laughed and said she didn't care. 'I get a better feel for the story if I hand-write things first. And I like the connection of the hand to pen to page. You should try it.'

Zara tried to catch Liz's attention, but she was concentrating on her story.

'Hey, Zara, have you finished that piece on China buying the largest shipment of wool in three years?' called Michael, another reporter, as she walked past. 'I'm just off the phone from the state buyer for Elders and I've got something you might like to use.'

'Great, Michael, thanks. Can I get back to you in five?'

'Sure.'

Zara sat down at her desk with a sigh. The adrenalin of hearing the verdict was ebbing away and she could feel the onset of a headache. She knew she had to call her mum, but she wanted to put it off for just a while. Ignorance was bliss, after all, and she felt sick at the thought of what her mum might tell her.

Rubbing her temples, she rummaged through her top drawer looking for some Panadol. Punching two out of the foil, she put them in her mouth, then reached for her water bottle. It wasn't there. Swallowing hard, she managed to get the pills down her throat without the help of a drink. She looked around for her bottle. Another strange thing on top of some other weird incidents in the office lately. During the last two months small things had been mysteriously disappearing from her desk, but when she'd asked the others if they'd noticed anything odd, no one had. It was an open-plan office, so if someone was playing silly buggers, someone would have noticed. But no. Nothing.

Odd.

The red light was flashing on her desk phone. Messages.

Grabbing a pen, she tucked the receiver against her ear and shoulder and punched the code for her message bank.

'*Zara, Bonny Murray from* Livestock Now *here. I'd love it if you were able to do a story on the convention we're running in a few months' time. Got a focus on lamb production. Thought it was right up your alley. Give me a call.*'

Writing down Bonny's number, she recalled that the last time they'd caught up for a drink Bonny had mentioned something about getting all the lamb producers together to have a conversation around births to market percentages, among other things.

'*Scott Founder. AgriMachinery. Call me, regarding new product release.*'

'Tosser,' she muttered, but dutifully wrote down his name. The last dealings she'd had with him were when they'd had a machinery sales guru out from America, and she'd followed Scott, his dealership and the American throughout the state as they'd road-tested the header in different shires and in heavy and light crops. It had been the final night and they'd all been in the pub together when Scott made his move. She'd come out of the ladies' room to find him waiting for her. He'd tried to push her against the wall and kiss her. 'You've had my attention this whole trip. I haven't been able to think of anything except you against me.'

'Really?' she remembered saying. 'Is that why you were busting a move on Chris yesterday?'

Chris was a journo from a different rural paper; a very pretty young woman.

'Nah, she doesn't do it for me. But you do,' he'd answered without missing a beat.

'Gee, Scott, such a shame. You just don't do it for me.' She'd tried to duck out from under his arm, but he'd clamped down and pulled her to him. Thankfully Chris had come to her rescue, but not before she'd had to endure Scott's beery breath close to her face as he whispered what he'd like to do to her if only she'd come back to his room.

She shuddered at the thought of Scott. Maybe she'd ask one of her male colleagues to deal with him. Slamming down the receiver, she reached for her water bottle and remembered it wasn't there. She sighed heavily, got up and walked quickly to the kitchen, where she grabbed a glass of water and downed it in one gulp.

'Oh, there you are!' Liz popped her head around the door. 'I wasn't sure you were back yet.'

'Only about ten minutes ago. Have you borrowed my water bottle?'

'Why would I do that?'

'I don't know. Just asking. Mine's missing. I wish I knew what was going on,' Zara frowned. 'That's the second time this week something has gone missing from my desk!'

'Mr O'Grady, my nana would say. Whenever anything went missing or something strange happened in the house, she'd blame him.'

'And who is Mr O'Grady when he's at home?'

'I dunno! Someone she made up to account for her bad housekeeping, I think. If there was an empty coffee cup on the table, she'd swear he'd shifted it from the kitchen sink, or if the ironing had built up, it was because Mr O'Grady had taken it out of the cupboard and put it back on the ironing board. If the floor wasn't swept, same deal. She was weird like that.'

'Well, he's being annoying! Last week it was my good pen and coffee cup, and the time before, those little green stones I have on my desk as good luck charms.'

Liz leaned against the door and crossed her arms. 'We're going to have to mount a search because my four favourite highlighters have gone.' She grinned widely, before lowering her voice. 'Just joking. I haven't had anything go missing. Maybe Mr O'Grady's come to haunt you and you alone.'

Zara laughed and refilled her glass.

'What happened at the trial?'

'Guilty on both counts,' Zara answered, sinking down into a chair at the table and running her fingers across her forehead.

Liz gave a low whistle. 'That should set the cat among the pigeons.'

'In a good way.'

'I'm really glad that was the result. About time someone stood up to these people. Your case was all about trespassing on forestry land, but more and more it seems activists think they can trespass on private property and cause havoc. They're putting the stock and the people in danger. These are not just farms, they're people's homes, where there are kids. Not to mention the risks to biosecurity. There is so much wrong here. You know, when I was home on the farm over the weekend, Mum and Dad said they've been getting phone calls in the middle of the night, and when they answer, there's no one there. It's like someone is checking to see if they're home, or they're harassing them or something.'

Zara shook her head. 'I'd really like to know what their end game is.'

Liz looked at her quizzically.

'The animal rights activists. I know today's court case was about what should happen to people when they trespass, but all of the farmers who have stock have been watching the case closely because of just what you're talking about. I heard about a farmer in Queensland who had five or six of them come in the driveway of his farm and just start taking photos of his feedlot. I'm sure they don't understand they could be putting the animals' lives at risk by not going through proper protocols.

'So, let's just say for a moment all the farmers do throw their hands in the air. They say, "Mate, you've got us beat. We're giving up farming. Leaving our farms. You do what you think is right with these animals we've been caring for." What's going to happen to the stock that's left? Who's going to take care of all those animals? I bet groups like Voices for Animals won't. Or, if they try, they won't be able to do it properly. There'll be millions of animals in a worse position because of what the extremists are trying to achieve.'

Liz nodded. 'That's a good point,' she said.

'It's one thing to make sure animals are treated humanely. That's got to happen, without a doubt. But to trespass on private land is absolutely unacceptable.' Zara's phone buzzed in her back pocket and she took it out. 'Shit,' she muttered, turning the screen around to show Liz. 'Mum.'

Liz reached out and touched her arm. 'It'll be okay.'

'Hi! Mum, sorry I haven't got back to you.' Zara made her voice as cheery as she could. 'It's been crazy here, waiting for the verdict and—'

'It's not good news,' her mother broke in.

Zara's breath left her body and her shoulders slumped. 'Oh.' She felt Liz put her hand on her shoulder.

'The cancer has gone into his liver. The treatment hasn't worked.' Silence. All those weeks and months of the two-hour drive to and from Port Augusta to access chemo treatment, and it hadn't worked. Not to mention the four-hour drives to Adelaide to see the specialist.

For once Zara didn't know what to say. She felt numb. The doctors had warned this could happen. The bowel was close to the liver, so if the cancer was going to spread, that was a spot it could end up. And then the whole thing would get tricky.

'Oh no, Mum.'

There was a silence, then a little gasp and Zara realised her mother was crying.

'Is there more?' A feeling of dread began to drip into her stomach. There couldn't be more news. Other than to say when the next round of treatment would start. Or when the next operation was. What the next plan of action would be.

'Zara? Zara, where the hell are you? I need you to . . .'

Lachy's voice filtered through the mist that seemed to shroud her, but she couldn't respond. Liz patted her shoulder and left to speak to Lachy.

'Three months,' her mum answered in a strangled voice. 'That's all we've got. Three months.'

Chapter 3

Zara looked around the bare rooms of her new house. It was only two weeks since that phone call from her mum, telling her it was time to come home.

Not just time to come home, she was *needed* at home.

'I need you here,' was what her mum had said. 'I can't do this by myself.'

Zara didn't remember much about the rest of that day. Only that Liz had put her in the car and driven her home. She'd stayed, ordered takeaway and sat with Zara while she alternated between crying and ranting about the unfairness of it all.

'He's only twenty-seven! How could this happen? And especially after we've lost Dad. What, are all the Ellison men cursed or something?

'I still dream about it,' Zara said, hiccupping with sobs. 'I've never told you, but I was coming home from uni for the weekend and Dad texted to say he was going to be in

Barker when I came through. He wanted me to call in and have dinner with him. It was his and Mum's twenty-fifth wedding anniversary and he wanted me to help organise a surprise for her. He was planning to take her to Singapore.' She stopped there and had another cry. 'Will was supposed to be there as well, but in the end Dad had to enlist his help to keep Mum busy, because she wanted to come in and have dinner too.' She wiped her face and groaned as if in pain, leaning forward with her arms wrapped around her. 'Will,' she muttered, 'why has this all happened?'

Liz rubbed her back and started to pack a bag for her, while Zara stayed sitting on the bed, tears running down her cheeks.

'He wasn't there,' she told Liz, finally looking up at her. 'Wasn't at the pub when I got there. I tried to ring Will and Mum but I couldn't get them, so I drove home. I thought maybe the plans had changed.' She shook her head as Liz stopped folding the clothes and sat down beside her again. 'Wishful thinking. When I drove around a corner near home, I found Dad.' She wiped at her eyes. 'I saw his ute on its roof. Crushed in on top of him . . .' Her voice trailed off and she sat staring into the distance, and really there was nothing more to say. Her dad was dead, and her brother was going to be dead too very soon.

'Will's my safety blanket,' she told Liz. 'The first person I call when things are going right—and when they're not. Dad's death brought us closer together, all of us, not just Will and me, but Mum too. We've got the "fam bam" WhatsApp group going, sending each other text messages and jokes. We hear from each other every day . . .' Her voice trailed off again and, finally, she couldn't talk anymore.

Liz suggested they call Will's doctors, as her mum had told her to; they could explain directly to Zara what was happening. So Zara made the calls, holding Liz's hand for support. They both listened on open speaker, Liz asking more questions than Zara, who couldn't seem to find her voice. Her friend took in more than Zara could, wrote notes and then, together, they went over what they'd learned and why the prognosis for Will was so bleak.

The last MRI scan had shown that the cancer had grown through the bowel wall and attached itself to the liver. There were also spots in his lungs. The doctors had offered him another round of stronger chemo, but they weren't hopeful it would slow down the disease's progress. Will had made the hard decision to opt for quality of life rather than quantity. He wanted to die at home. On the farm. On Rowberry Glen. The logistics of that were mind-blowing.

Zara hung up the phone and stared at Liz. 'How could he give up?'

'You can't ask that,' Liz had said. 'It's his choice. You can never ask that.'

During the drive to Barker this morning, she'd still wanted to rage at Will.

'We're the Ellisons. We don't give up! We've heard the stories of our great granddad. He never gave up. He could've lost the farm during the Depression, but he kept working away, trapping rabbits, shearing, working wherever he could get a job—sometimes far away from home. But

he kept doing that because he wanted to keep Rowberry Glen. Granddad did the same. Even though he was in bad shape when he came back from the Vietnam War, he still fronted up to start farming again. And Dad? Well, he never gave up either! When interest rates were sky high, with a big debt, he tightened his belt and knuckled down. Methodically working his way through the lean times. He came out the other side. There were plenty of times all of those men could've given up, but they didn't. So why are you?'

Liz was right, though. That was a question she could never ask. It was Will's decision, but she wished he'd talked to her about it. She could've told him how much she needed to him to fight. Needed him to live. And that was when she realised he wasn't going to, no matter how hard they prayed or wished or hoped. It had gone past that.

It had taken her the whole two weeks to get organised. To negotiate a new contract with Lachy, so she could work from Barker, without having to attend editorial meetings every week. To clean out her desk and her apartment, redirect her mail. She owned her apartment, so it could sit empty until she came back to Adelaide—after all, it wasn't going to be long, according to the doctors. And she'd need to stay there when she did have to go back to the city for meetings.

In among all the kerfuffle and reorganisation, her missing things had mysteriously turned up on her desk that last morning she had been in the office.

Thinking about it as she drove, she couldn't work out what had happened, but there had been a handwritten note: *Sorry. I was playing pranks on you. I hadn't realised what was going on in your personal life. Sorry again. I'd hoped you'd realised it was me doing this.* She had felt creeped out so she had told Lachy about it.

'Don't worry,' he'd told her, patting her on the shoulder. 'I'll look into it.'

Of course, she'd also had to find a house to rent in Barker. Not that it was too hard to decide on one. There weren't many to choose from. She'd decided as she'd lived by herself for so long now that it didn't matter how close she was to her family, she still needed a bit of space.

Today she'd driven the well-worn road from Adelaide to Barker and, after visiting Will in hospital, turned her car into an unfamiliar house in a familiar town. A town she never thought she'd end up living in again. Never wanted to end up living in.

When she'd left for boarding school, she'd promised herself she'd never stay for too long in Barker again. There was too much excitement in the outside world. The small, quiet country town didn't suit her. Her mum had always said her wings were too big to stay and, once she'd become a journo, her job had enabled to her to spread those wings wide.

The trip she'd done with the *Farming Telegraph* to America to report on cattle feedlots seemed like a lifetime away, when in reality it was only six months ago.

'It's not forever,' she whispered to herself. 'Just until Mum gets back on her feet.'

Will, by contrast, had never wanted to leave Rowberry Glen. When he'd made the trek to boarding school, twelve months before she had, he'd struggled with city life. He hadn't liked not having space or freedom. For a boy who had ridden motorbikes and mustered sheep like a man, becoming a student wearing a tie, shorts and long socks, sitting in a classroom without a view, had been a difficult transition. His saving grace had been Zara's presence, when she started at a boarding school across the city, and footy. He'd lived for the weekend games. As soon as year twelve had finished, he'd pulled on his work boots, put on his hat and headed out the door to the paddocks. He hadn't shifted since.

Dragging her thoughts back from the past, Zara looked at her new home. She spun around the empty kitchen, looking at the walls that needed a good wash. She moved into the lounge, then walked through the rest of the house. It was cold and smelled musty. Her mother had told her it was the only house they could get on short notice.

Maybe once her furniture arrived it would be okay, she coached herself. *A lick of paint, even.* Then she scoffed at herself. *There wouldn't be time.*

She wasn't a farmer but she'd grown up on a farm and she knew that between caring for Will, writing for the *Farming Telegraph* and helping on the farm, there would be no time for anything else.

The thought of working on the farm again sent a strange rush of emotions through her. As kids, she and Will had helped their dad—Will more than she, Zara was happy to admit. Lamb marking had been one of the more fun times of farming—her job, when she was little, had been to count the lambs' tails on the ground at the end of the day. That way they'd know how many lambs they'd marked. Even as she'd grown older and been given more complex jobs, she'd still liked climbing into the pens with the lambs and patting their cute little furry faces. Will always got tired of her getting in the way. While he was trying to catch the lambs to put them in the cradle, she would be trying to pat them.

A sad smile crossed her face as she remembered her dad finally getting annoyed too. 'If you really have to pat them, Zara, for goodness sake go and see if there're any orphans and bring them home.'

So she had and Lamb Chops had joined the family, quickly becoming everyone's favourite. By the time she was six months, Lamb Chops had had the kelpies bluffed and would eat their pellets when they weren't looking. As time had gone on and she'd had to be put out in the paddock with the other ewes, she'd learned to stand at the fence and baa until someone came and scratched her head. Then she'd taught the other ewes to follow her down the drafting race when it was time to draft again. Lamb Chops had lived to the ripe old age of twelve, and she'd been buried in the beautiful sunny spot next to the creek, near the graves of all the dogs who had passed on.

Pulling her thoughts back to her new house, Zara real-ised the thick white walls had hairline cracks starting at the ceiling and wending down to the floor. They would have to stay a dirty white for the time being. She wished the windows were bigger; many of the rooms were dim because the sunlight couldn't filter through.

Zara guessed the house had been built in the early nineteen hundreds, like a lot of the houses in rural South Australia. Maybe there were stories here.

There were wooden floorboards all through the house and there was a fireplace in the lounge. She'd need wood; the winters here were bitter. She could remember having to go out and chip the ice from the dogs' water bowls, and sometimes, after a particularly cold night, the pipes in the house would freeze and the shower wouldn't run in the morning.

Going back out to her car, she looked around. Her house was one street back from the main road and there were five houses on one side and five on the other. Hers was surrounded by a thick wire fence. The front yard had a small stretch of lawn, then a garden bed holding a single bravely flowering geranium and lots of red dirt.

The familiar street and view of the silos at the end of the road made her pause.

She really was here.

Will really was dying.

Her mum really couldn't do this without her.

With only her mum to do the farm work and look after Will, she knew she would be needed in the next week or so because seeding was about to start. Well, it was if it rained.

It seemed to her that it was unfair to expect people to continue with their lives as normal when life was anything but that. But, as her father used to say, life goes on.

Zara wanted to yell and scream at the sky and tell the universe that what was happening to her family was beyond what anyone should have to endure. Her father was dead and now her brother was dying!

Since her dad had died, her mother and Will had run Rowberry Glen well together. Their lives were settled and stable. They had a routine—Will checked the sheep and did the heavy work, and Lynda helped out in all the other areas. That was until Will had become too weak to manage the farm work. There'd been talk of employing a workman, but she didn't know if that had happened yet.

Will still lived in the same house as their mum, as there weren't any other houses on the farm. Zara knew it hadn't bothered either of them, because the farmhouse was large and almost in two sections. Will had his side and Lynda had hers. Zara recognised, though, that Will had been lonely. One night he'd told her he'd signed up to a dating site, then the next day he'd been embarrassed and tried to take down his profile. Not before a couple of the women in town had seen it, and he'd been teased mercilessly at the pub the next time he'd gone in. Zara had tried to tell him that it was very common to try to meet someone through dating sites, but his embarrassment had stopped him from trying again. Everyone in town would've known he'd found someone through the internet.

'Who'd want me anyway?' he'd said in his pragmatic way. 'I've already had cancer, and I've not got a lot to offer anyone.'

'That's wrong and you know it,' Zara had exploded at him. 'You're kind, caring and funny. Not to mention good-looking . . . apparently,' she'd added. 'Not that I'd know!'

They'd laughed but Will had never mentioned it again.

The shock had been immense when he'd had his first bout of cancer two years ago. A healthy young man, with his life in front of him. It had been stage three and an operation had removed lymph nodes in his groin. The doctors had been hopeful, even though the cancer had grown through nearly all the layers of the colon. There had been rounds of chemo, low blood counts and another operation. Will had spent weeks in hospital in Adelaide—the surgery had been too major for the Port Augusta hospital, which would've been closer to home. But it had meant Zara could visit him after work every day. It had been tiring and draining for them all; Lynda had come on weekends or when she'd been able to get away from the farm. Someone still had to be checking the sheep and making sure everything was running smoothly.

Back then they'd all been filled with hope, thinking that Will could beat the disease. After all, the doctor had told them that of all the cancers, bowel cancer had one of the highest survival rate if it was found in time.

And now, well, they knew the truth. It wasn't curable for Will.

The rumble of a truck engine, then the beeping of a reverse warning caught her attention. Glad of the distraction, she waved to the removalists and helped them back into her driveway.

'Long way from Adelaide, love,' said the driver, jumping down from the cab and stretching. 'Not sure why you'd want to be shifting back up here.'

'Sure is, Pete,' Zara answered, not wanting to tell him they were her thoughts too. 'It's a long way from anywhere.'

'Right, where are we headed?'

'Bedroom is first on the right and kitchen down the end of the hallway,' she told them.

'No worries, love. We'll get you set up in no time.'

The men worked quickly to unload the bed and tallboy and, while they were doing that, Zara grabbed the linen off the back seat of her car. It wouldn't take her long to make up her bed. She kept thinking about Will, who was in the local hospital today. Only three streets away. When she'd seen him this morning, he hadn't opened his eyes, just gripped her hand and squeezed it before saying in a low, weak voice that he was glad she was there. He'd needed a blood transfusion, to increase his red blood cells. Zara knew from experience that once he'd had the transfusion he'd be less lethargic and hopefully would be able to go home by this afternoon. Blood seemed to have a magic effect on him.

Still, James, the doctor had been on the ward when she'd arrived and he'd said in a low tone that Will having three months was looking less and less likely.

Zara had wanted to cover her ears and sing 'la la la' very loudly. The news couldn't get much worse.

'Hi, sweetie, how are you getting on?'

Zara looked up at the sound of her mother's voice and smiled when she saw her framed in the doorway. Will had got his height from their dad, whereas Zara had inherited her mother's short stature. Standing at only five foot four, Lynda was slight with prematurely grey hair pulled back in a ponytail. Her hands were wrinkled and dry from the hard work on the farm, but Zara loved the way they could still smooth her hair back from her face when she needed comfort.

Lynda looked tired, drained and sad.

Zara stopped making the bed and went over to hug her. 'How are you holding up? How're things at the hospital? I saw Will this morning, but you hadn't come in yet.'

'I had to talk to the contract seeding bloke before I came in,' she said. 'The business doesn't stop, just because we're having problems.' She ran her hands through her ponytail, worried. 'I don't know whether to put that crop in or not. It's so dry and if we get a big wind the whole farm will shift. Just another thing to think about.' She sighed and glanced around. 'Looks like you're getting organised.'

With a half-laugh, Zara said, 'I've only been here about an hour. And the guys have only just arrived. I'd offer you a cup of coffee but I have no idea where the kettle is, let alone any cups.'

'There's a box in the kitchen labelled "kitchen gear",' one of the removalists said as he walked by.

'Ha! There you go. That's service,' Lynda said. 'Let's get the kitchen unpacked. At least you'll be able to cook.'

'I think it's more important to have somewhere to sleep! Let's stay in the bedroom, since I've already started here. I'll buy you a coffee to save opening boxes in every room.' Zara went back to the bed and tucked the sheet in before unfolding her doona.

'And where do you think you're going to buy coffee from?' Lynda asked as she opened a box and pulled out coathangers. Methodically she stacked them in the wardrobe, while Zara placed pillows and cushions on the freshly made bed. 'Don't forget you're in the country now.'

'Surely someone makes coffee?'

'I'd invest in a coffee maker, but Kim at the roadhouse always makes a good brew.'

Zara filed that piece of information away before saying, 'So how did you find Will? Has the blood transfusion made any difference yet?' She hated asking that question.

'A bit brighter. It always amazes me how quickly that works. How lucky we are people donate blood. He'll be home again, resting, soon. I'll pick him up on the way back. James was happy to let him go home.' Lynda came over to Zara and took her hands. 'Thank you for coming back. This is going to be such a horrible time and I really couldn't do it without having you here.'

'I wouldn't have let you go through this by yourself, Mum,' Zara answered. 'We'll muddle through. Just like we did when dad died. I hope this doesn't sound awful, but at least this time we've got warning. We know it's going to happen.'

'I know. I haven't decided if that's a good or a bad thing. Anyway, just having you here is going to make all the difference. I was thinking about that this morning. Any questions I've got about the breeding and wool and things Will handled, I should be asking him now. But I don't want to. It makes it so—' her voice tightened as her eyes welled with tears '—so final.'

Zara thought her mum wanted to say something else, so she waited, but there was nothing more. In the end Zara patted her shoulder and began unpacking clothes from the suitcases, Lynda working silently alongside her.

An hour or so later, the removalist who'd driven the van stood in the doorway. 'That's the last of it, love. The fridge is plugged in and we put the washing machine in the laundry, if you can call it that. It's a room out in the back garden.'

'Thanks, guys. Really appreciate everything you've done. It's been smooth sailing with you around.'

'Glad to help. Catch you later. Good luck!'

Zara turned back to Lynda. 'Come on, I'll quickly show you around, then you go and see if Will is able to go home. I can unpack a bit more, then I'll come out.'

The back door was sticky, but after a couple of good yanks it opened, and they walked out onto a large cement verandah covered with a grapevine. From there a large area of lawn sprawled all the way to the back fence, with a little outhouse down there too.

'Look at this mulberry tree,' Lynda said, stopping to finger a stem of a large tree near the side fence. 'Gorgeous. I love mulberries at Christmas. With lots of cream and ice cream.'

'You'll have to come and pick them. You know very well I'm no gardener,' Zara answered.

Next to it was a weeping willow, which shaded nearly half the garden.

'It'll be a beautiful place to write,' Zara said. 'I can set up a table there.' She pointed to a shady spot where the leaves from the willow nearly touched the ground. 'Even if it's really hot, I think that would be a great spot to sit and get my stories straight.' She paused. 'Or drink wine.'

'It's certainly pretty. Much better than the front.' Lynda pulled open the door into the outhouse and Zara peered over her shoulder. 'Make sure you keep this door shut. You'll get snakes in otherwise.'

Zara went inside and ran her fingers along the concrete double laundry troughs against the wall. 'I haven't been away so long that I've forgotten everything, you know.'

'Just a gentle reminder.' Lynda smiled at Zara. 'Right, I'll go and see if I can collect Will and see you a bit later. Okay?'

'Sounds like a plan.' Zara suddenly realised it would be nice to be back closer to her family, despite the awful circumstances.

Chapter 4

Dave drove silently towards Barker, Kim sitting alongside him in the passenger's seat. He knew she was annoyed.

It took a lot to get Kim aggravated, but she was certainly riled right now. Out of the corner of his eye, he could see her winding her hair around her finger again and again. A clear sign of agitation. He'd heard her take a couple of deep breaths, as if she was going to say something then thought better of it.

It would come out soon enough. And he could wait, because he was sure her frustration was aimed at him and it wouldn't be pretty when she talked about it.

The long-awaited visit back to Western Australia, to see his family and work through some of the angst and hurt due to his banishment from the family farm many years ago, hadn't worked out that well and he knew Kim thought he was partly responsible.

He felt like a churlish teenager as he thought, *You don't get it.*

Redirecting his mind, he wondered what had been happening in Barker during the time he'd been away. It had only been three weeks, but he felt like he'd been gone years.

Jack had texted a couple of times but had not told him too much of what had been happening. *You're on holidays and there hasn't been anything I haven't been able to handle*, had been the response when he'd asked what was going on. Dave grinned to himself as he thought about the message. He'd been quietly and gently put in his place!

Jack had, however, sent a photo of Bob, the old kelpie Dave had inherited when a farmer he'd helped had died. In the picture Bob was curled up in his bed under Jack's desk and the caption was: *Not missing you.*

Dave had sent back a smart reply: *Good spot for stinking you out.* Bob was known for his revolting farts.

When they'd left, Dave and Kim had patted the old dog goodbye, not sure whether he would be there when they came home, he was so old and decrepit. Still, it seemed he was still kicking, and Dave was pleased about that. He hadn't had a pet in a long time, and he'd been surprised at how much he enjoyed Bob's gentle company at his feet most nights. Even though he stank the house out often!

The town entrance came into view and he smiled. There was no place like home. It didn't look like anything had changed much; not that he'd expected it to. This was Barker and nothing changed in years, let alone weeks.

'Looking forward to sleeping in my own bed tonight,' he said, looking over at Kim. 'Are you?'

She nodded.

Dave raised his eyebrows. Oh. Things were bad.

He flicked the blinker on and turned the corner into their street. As their house came into view, he felt contentment washing over him. He was home.

Perth was a lovely place to visit, but Western Australia wasn't home anymore. To Dave home was two eyes and a heartbeat. Kim. But home also meant the house they'd bought together in their town.

Unwittingly memories of the last three weeks with his family resurfaced. Dean, his brother, had got his arm caught in an auger five months ago, and although he'd been released from hospital, he and his wife, Mandy, were living in Perth while he went through rehab and learned to live with an arm that didn't work. Their mum had come down from Northam and stayed in a little unit near Scarborough. Every day they had walked on the beach and talked, but Dave, no matter how he'd tried, hadn't been able to rid himself of the anger he felt every time he saw both his mother and Dean. As far as he was concerned, they were both traitors.

'Someone's moved into that house at the end of the street.' Kim finally broke her three-hour silence. 'Look, there's a car in the driveway.'

'Don't recognise it.' He paused as he read the number-plate. 'Must be someone new in town. Wonder who it is. Maybe Jack knows.'

'I'll go over and take a cake later. Make them feel welcome.'

Dave put a hand on her leg and patted it. 'I knew you'd do that.' He pulled up in the driveway and switched off the engine.

He got out and popped the boot while Kim went and unlocked the house. He could hear her inside opening windows and doors to let in fresh air.

Carrying the cases inside, he placed them both on the bed and unzipped them.

'So, are we going to talk about what happened in Perth?' Kim's voice came from behind him.

He didn't turn around. 'What do you mean?' He took out his dirty washing and put it alongside the case.

'While we were there, you weren't behaving like you.' Kim came around and sat on the edge of the bed.

Dave avoided her eyes. 'I don't know what you're talking about. You asked me to go over there and see them. I did just that.'

'Dave, sweetheart, they were trying to mend fences. You kept putting them back up again. Sometimes—' She broke off and her hand snaked back up to her hair and she began twisting it again.

'What?' This time he looked at her. Defiance was burning in his stomach. Surely Kim of all people should understand, although how could she? Being turfed out hadn't happened to her. He wanted her to understand that the minute the city skyline had come into view all the hurt and anger from being thrown off the farm hit him so hard he could barely breathe. The injustice of what his father had done, and the fact his mum, his *own mother*, and brothers hadn't stood up for him; well, the unfairness was beyond what he could bear. The betrayal by his family made him want to hit out at someone.

Dave had thought he'd dealt with all those emotions years ago. Clearly he hadn't, because he'd been unprepared for how he'd felt. That had made him angry with himself on a different level.

'You behaved like a spoilt child most of the time. At dinner, you'd sit there with your arms crossed, not inviting conversation. I'm surprised they put up with you for as long as they did.' She paused. 'Your family are lovely, Dave. Especially your mum. I can see so many similarities between you and her.'

'I'm nothing like her.' The words came out before he could stop them.

'You are,' Kim insisted. 'You're both kind and thoughtful. Loving. She listens the way you do. She communicates the way you do. And Dean, he's similar. He tried to talk to you so many times while we were there, and you wouldn't talk back. You kept the conversation on impersonal issues—the weather, the news. Things that didn't matter, when he was trying to fix something that did. I really think you need some counselling.'

'I'd never not back a child of mine. Even when their mother and I divorced, I backed Bec and Alice to the hilt. If they needed me, I was there.' Dave stared at her, wondering why she couldn't understand. 'And you can shove the idea of counselling. The best therapy I've ever had is at the elbows of my workmates, at a bar. They understand.'

'Dave—' Kim started.

'No.' He put his hand up, not wanting to continue the conversation. 'Enough. I thought you would've been able to see things from my point of view. You usually can. They stole the life I wanted. The farm. All the things I wanted to do and be.'

He watched as Kim frowned. 'Don't you like your life now?'

'What?' He was momentarily confused. 'Of course I do! I wouldn't want to be anywhere else.'

'So what you're angry about doesn't actually matter anymore. You wouldn't be here in Barker or with me if you'd stayed on the farm. Sure, you had a kick in the guts, but you've got on and made the best of what you've been given. If you keep this anger inside, it's going to end up eating away at you—you'll get sick. You've got to deal with it. You say you can't understand why I don't see your point of view, but you know what I don't understand?'

Dave opened his mouth to answer, but she didn't give him a chance to speak.

'I don't understand how someone who is such a great communicator, who loves helping people sort out relationships, can be so stubborn and pigheaded about his own. You really should take some of your own advice, Dave.'

Dave stood there for a second not saying a word. He knew he had to control himself so as not to say something he'd regret later. Finally, he turned on his heel and walked out of the room, saying, 'Some wrongs can't be made right just by saying sorry. I'm going to see Jack.'

❧

'Look what the cat's dragged in!' Jack got up from his desk as Dave opened the door. 'You didn't ring and say you were back. Welcome home!'

Dave held out his hand and grinned at him. 'I'm glad to be back. Holidays are fine for about three days and then I want my desk and a case. What's going on?'

'Not much, my man, not much. Been really quiet.'

Bob gave a hoarse bark and limped out from underneath Jack's desk.

'Ah, g'day there, old fella,' said Dave, squatting down to pat him. 'You been stinking Jack out?'

As if on cue a puff of foul-smelling air reached them, and both men rolled their eyes.

'Nice to know some things don't change!'

'Certainly not with Bob,' Jack agreed, reaching for a piece of paper to fan the air.

'So . . .' Dave sat down and put his feet up on the desk. 'Surely there's been something going on? You've got to justify your wages somehow! What about the dangerous driving case against Frank Syme? Did he lose his licence?'

Bob let out a heavy sigh, and flopped to the ground next to Dave's feet and closed his eyes.

'Nope, just a suspended sentence. Bloody stupid, 'cause I see there's rubber around the place again, but I just haven't been able to catch him. I'd love to impound his ute.'

'The JP wasn't thinking clearly that day,' Dave said. 'Sometimes they make our job that much harder, don't they?'

'Hmm, sometimes. But I guess it's our job to catch him at it, isn't it?'

Dave nodded his agreement.

'You know, one interesting thing that's come to light—and you'll love this—is the reporting of drones.'

'Drones?' Dave put his feet down and leaned towards Jack.

'I've had reports of drones being flown over some of the farms. The first time I dismissed it, thinking it could've been an enthusiast with a new toy, but I've had three reports now. Maybe it's something more. What do you think?'

'Could be someone learning to fly a drone and not realising the rules. Keep an eye on it, though. They shouldn't be flying over private property. That's illegal. Is there anyone new in town? The house next to us has been rented out, maybe they're here with an alternative motive?'

'Like what? That's one suspicious mind you've got there.'

'I'm supposed to have a suspicious mind,' Dave retorted. 'I don't know, but maybe someone is flying it to see what they can steal, or maybe they're trying to spy or perve or something. I think three reports of a drone flying where it shouldn't is more than an enthusiast with a new toy.'

'Yeah, you're probably right,' Jack agreed. He got up from the desk and went to the filing cabinet. 'These are the reports: times, places, all that sort of thing.' He put them down in front of Dave. 'But you know what would be handy here?'

'What's that?'

'A local police Facebook page. We could put up the rules on drones and other things. You know, keep people in the loop with what's going on.'

Dave laughed as he picked up the reports. 'I've got no problems with that. I know there are loads of stations doing it, but that'll have to be your baby, Jack. My old brain doesn't know how to cope with that sort of thing.'

'Leave it with me. I'll get it sorted.'

'How's Joan?' Dave asked. The long-time station secretary kept him and Jack well in hand.

'She's had a few days off. Been sick with the flu, but she rang this morning and said she'd be back in tomorrow.'

'Just so long as she doesn't share it around! Don't feel like getting sick when I've just got home.' With that he remembered the look of shock on Kim's face as he'd left the bedroom not fifteen minutes before. Involuntarily he groaned and ran his hands over his face.

'That doesn't look like the gesture of a rested man,' Jack observed.

Dave shook his head. 'I just snapped at Kim and I shouldn't have.'

'What?' Jack leaned forward, a look of bewilderment on his face. 'You two never argue. What's going on?'

Clenching his jaw, Dave considered brushing off the question. Kim's words came back to him: *I don't understand how someone who is such a great communicator, who loves helping people sort out relationships, can be so stubborn and pigheaded about his own. You really should take some of your own advice, Dave.'*

He really shouldn't shelve this any longer.

'Shit. Look, it's my fault. I let my emotions get the better of me. You know, I've said to you before, as coppers we need to train our minds to be strong. Dealing with the stuff we do, things we see. If we don't, we'll lose ourselves, get wrapped up in the horror of our job. And if we get to that point, we need to be able to talk about it.' He stopped, but his fingers continued tapping on the desk. 'I let this crap with my family get the better of me, and when Kim called me on it, I reacted. Badly. Took it out on her when it's my problem.' In a way, Dave was glad he could talk to Jack about how he felt. A long time ago, he'd worked with a copper called Spencer, who had made it easy for him to open up; he'd tried to do the same with Jack. But he hadn't been able to express himself to his family or to Kim.

Silence filled the room.

'What happened when you got over there?' Jack asked quietly.

Dave shrugged. 'I honestly don't know. As soon as I saw the skyline, I just got angry. Like, white-rage anger. I haven't felt that for a long time. I thought I'd got past that type of lividness.' He paused. 'There was no going back from there.'

Jack nodded. 'But it's not Kim's fault.'

'No.'

Pause.

'You need to fix it.'

'Yeah.' Pause. Dave nodded, as if convincing himself.

'Yeah.'

Chapter 5

Zara turned into the driveway of her family farm.

Rowberry Glen.

The sign proclaimed it was the home of Brian and Lynda Ellison. Underneath in smaller writing it also said *Will Ellison*. There was a sheaf of wheat on one side of the writing and an outline of a merino ewe on the other.

Zara's name wasn't mentioned. She hadn't lived here since her last year of primary school.

Looking at the sign, it hit her again: soon, like Brian, Will wouldn't be here either. The two Ellison men struck down in their prime. *Were they cursed?* Zara wondered. It felt like it.

It would just be Lynda and Zara left. Mother and daughter.

And memories.

The sign had been a gift to Brian from Lynda, Will and Zara when she was small. Zara couldn't remember how old she was, just the feeling of excitement when Brian unwrapped it on his birthday and his exclamations of pleasure. That afternoon, after the home-made birthday cake, decorated with Smarties and chocolate sticks, all four of them had gone to the front gate and dug holes for the sign. Brian had used rapid cement to make sure the legs were secure, and then they'd poured a bottle of lemonade across it to christen it. She remembered her dad saying it was one of his best birthdays ever.

Swallowing hard, she pushed her foot down on the accelerator and drove on. To her right there were a few small hills that rose gently out of the earth, some prickly looking bushes growing on the slopes. There were outcrops of rocks and sheep dotted in among them. On her left ran a small gully; it was too shallow to be a creek, but occasionally, when it rained a lot, it ran with water. Small scrubby bushes lined the gully's edge, and every so often a towering gum reached towards the sky.

As kids, Will and Zara had played in the rockpools with the sheepdogs who had been their constant companions. Now the gully lay dry, but the sheep found shade there during the heat of the day.

The grass was bleached golden and devoid of any goodness, and there were large bare patches of ground where nothing grew. The land was parched and, as Zara knew from her work as a rural journalist, most of the state was waiting impatiently for a steady, soaking rain. Last year's rainfall had been below average and now it was mid-April and everyone was hoping this year wasn't going to be the same. Just looking around at the property, she hoped her mum would decide not to put the crop in right now. The land wasn't ready for the invasion of tynes, no matter how 'nil-till' they were.

The tall trees surrounding the farmhouse came into sight as she rounded the corner. The dam, where she had taken her horse for a drink every day, was right next to the front gate and she slowed to a stop. The house paddock was empty of the two horses they'd owned most of her childhood. Zara hadn't been living at home when Starbuck and Winkey had died, and there didn't seem any point in getting another horse when she wouldn't be home often enough to ride it. Her mum didn't ride anymore and Will preferred the ute or motorbike.

She started to get out of the car to open the gate, but the gate jerked and started to swing open by itself. Frozen for a moment, she looked around trying to see how this could possibly be happening. Then she saw a camera perched high up in a tree and some type of opening mechanism.

Will must've rigged up an electric gate! How clever.

She drove through and waved up at the camera. She wondered how much he could see from the house.

Following the purple dirt track, she went over a ramp before rounding the small bend into the house yard. Zara parked near the garage but, before she could get out, she was greeted by three kelpies running around her car, barking and trying to jump in as a welcome.

'Sit down, you lot!' she growled good-naturedly, trying to pat all of them but instead managing to get her hand in the mouth of one of them. 'Yuck.' She wiped the saliva on her jeans and continued to walk towards the house, while Trixie, Shadow and Boof ignored her command and competed for her attention.

Inside she called, 'Hey! I'm here. What's with the gate? You turned into Big Brother or something?'

'In the office,' Will called back.

He certainly sounded stronger. Not a lot, but better than he had this morning.

Zara put down her satchel containing her computer, notebook and recorder and took a breath before walking down to the office.

'Whatcha doing?' she asked with a smile. Will was dressed in his normal gear and, other than being pale and gaunt and having lost not only his hair but his eyebrows as well, he looked like he was ready to go to work.

'Mucking about,' he answered, getting out of the chair and coming over to her.

As Zara put her arms around him, she had to control her emotions. His shoulders were bony, while his stomach protruded and was abnormally hard. His face was puffy from the steroids. In the last month, it seemed to her, he'd become weaker and even thinner. There wasn't much of him left to hug. She knew from Lynda that he wasn't eating much. It made him feel sick and she guessed this was from the positioning of the tumours around his stomach. It made her angry, but she couldn't show that to Will.

'What's with the gate? No one warned me about that!' she asked again, letting go of him.

'Great invention, yeah?' he said, sitting back down.

Zara noticed he puffed a little as he did so. Again, she said nothing.

'I bought it online. Look, here.' He tapped at the computer and brought up a screen, which was similar to footage from a security camera. She could see the front gate in one shot, two different troughs in two different locations, and the last screen showed the dam.

He pointed to the front gate. 'There's a sensor that sets off an alarm when a car pulls up at the gate. I check who it is and then open the gate to let them through. If I'm not here, the gate can still be opened, and I get a record of numberplates.'

'Oh, so you couldn't see me waving to you? Just the numberplate?'

'I saw you, but it also takes a photo of the numberplate.' Will looked pleased with himself.

Zara frowned. 'What's with the cloak-and-dagger stuff? Are there problems with trespassers? Is there something I should know about?'

'Not at all, unless you count the Jehovah's Witnesses who visit once a year. Nah, I originally bought it so I could monitor the troughs and water points. When I was having treatment, as much as I wanted to jump in the ute and get outside, there were days I just couldn't, and in summer up here, that's no good. Mum could've done it, but she was looking after me and I didn't want her under any more pressure. I had all the paddock cameras fitted in the last six months, but only just got the gate one. Didn't think to tell you about it.'

'I've heard of large stations with this type of technology,' Zara answered as she pulled up a chair and sat next to her brother. 'Does it work as well as they say? I've always had some concerns that you can only see what's in the frame of the picture. You won't see stock that might be weak or sick outside the camera's view.'

'It's certainly not the be all and end all. The most fertile thing on a farm is the owner's feet, that's for sure. But just for making sure the water is okay, that the pump is working and so on, it's pretty good. So here . . .' He hit another couple of buttons and brought up another screen. 'This is the trough in the paddock we call South Nine. Remember, over on the boundary of John and Bec Hamilton?'

'Yeah,' Zara nodded. 'I haven't seen them in ages.'

'Last week this pump ended up with a tankful of dirty fuel. Don't know how that happened, but it did. So, it sets an alarm off here in my office to say there's a problem. I dial up this screen and see the trough is empty. Of course, from here I can't see what the problem is, other than there's no water. That's when I can say to Mum that we need to go for a look. So, we both went out there, worked out what the problem was. I was able to drain the tank, but then Mum organised another load of diesel, got a jerry can and,' he looked up and grinned, 'Bob's your uncle! Sorted. The fuel company was most apologetic!'

'And that made your life easier?' As she said it Zara wanted a hole in the ground to open and swallow her whole. *Made your life easier. What a stupid thing to say.*

Will didn't seem to notice. 'It did, because it meant I didn't have to get out there and drive around checking, using up the little energy I have in places that didn't need me that day. I still try to do a stock run every week. I go out for an hour or so every day—you know, break it up. I'll start close to the homestead, then the next day head out further, and so on.'

'What made you think of this?' Zara sat back and ran her hand through her honey-coloured hair, pulling it up into a ponytail with the hairband she had on her wrist. Then she leaned forward again, reading the words on the screen. 'It's got the time and date down here,' she said, pointing to the bottom right-hand corner. 'Is there anything else that helps?'

Will shrugged. 'Look, you can get much more expensive gear than I've got here. I watched a video online of a camera that will zoom in and stay with the vehicle as it's moving around the yard. It must've had some kind of swivel and zoom on it, but I don't need that. Just enough to check the water.'

She tapped a few keys and watched as the screens changed from one trough to another. The picture was a live feed and she could see sheep coming and going from the trough; it looked strange without any sound. 'Well, I think it's a bloody great idea!'

'Mum likes it too.'

Silence filled the room and Zara tried to think of a way to fill it.

'Mum mentioned this morning about whether or not to start seeding. What do you think about that?'

'The same as she does. It's too dry.'

'You're not going to start yet?'

'Nah, and if it hasn't rained by May, I don't think we will this year. Just run the sheep—it's still busy with stock. You've got to feed, shear, crutch. All of that. But no point in putting the land under any extra pressure, or spending the money to start seeding, if it's not going to rain . . .' His voice trailed off as they both realised he probably wouldn't be there to see the shearing or crutching.

Another silence. What was wrong with her? She and Will always had things to talk about.

'Have a look at this,' Will said as if he sensed her unease. He tapped at the mouse and brought up a Word document.

Zara leaned forward and looked to where he pointed.

'I've been writing down all the breeding of the ewes, mating times, where the water pipes are, all that sort of thing. I'm trying not to forget anything because once I'm gone it'll be up to you and Mum to explain everything to a workman or do it yourselves.' He ran his finger down the screen. 'See here,' he pointed to a map that was embedded in the file. 'The red lines are the underground water pipes; the green dots are the tanks, and the blue rectangles are the troughs. I've marked where the joiners are, just in case something bursts one day. Hopefully you won't have to dig too far to find them.' He stopped and took a breath.

Zara could see he was getting upset. She leaned over and put her hand on his arm. 'This is great, Will. I'm so glad you're doing it.'

'You both need to know.'

'We do. Mum does and whoever comes to help her out does too. But, Will, I don't know that I'm going to be here that much.' She broached the subject that had been playing on her mind. It had been clear from a couple of their conversations that her mum was expecting she'd stay in Barker after Will's death.

That wasn't something she'd intended at all.

'What do you mean?'

'Well, I've got a job in the city. In Adelaide. I can come and help, but . . .' Her voice trailed off. She didn't want to say that she was going back after he'd died.

Instead, Will said it for her. 'You're not staying for good? You're going to go back after it's all finished?'

'Well . . . um.'

'I thought you were coming back for good. To help Mum run the place?' He gave a shrug. 'Maybe that's my bad. I just assumed. Of course you've got a job and that's important.'

Zara shook her head. 'Do you really think I'd make much of a farmer? Come on,' she said, to lighten the mood. 'Don't you remember the time Dad sent me to muster the shed paddock and I ended up getting in the rams instead of the ewes? Not only the wrong bloody paddock, but the wrong sex too!'

Will laughed. 'And I also remember something about bogging the chaser bin in creek sand during the harvest and having to drag it out with the other tractor! Yeah, you're right, you'd probably be a liability.'

'Hang on there, I don't think I'm that bad! But I'm better at writing about it than doing it.' She rubbed her finger along her jeans, feeling awful, despite the light-heartedness, that they were having this conversation.

Will sighed. 'Seriously, though, you're right. You've got your own life to live after this is all over. Mum knows that too.'

Zara thought about her life in Adelaide. The cocktail parties, the dinners, the travel to saleyards and overseas. Interviewing industry leaders. Seeing the rise of women in farming. Her little unit at the top of a four-storey building; the way the leaves from the trees outside the windows created shadows that danced across the wooden floorboards. She didn't have ties, no boyfriend or major stresses. Well, a deadline could be a stress but that was all part of the job. What could Rowberry Glen offer her that she didn't already have?

The words 'a family' filtered through her mind.

Chapter 6

Zara pulled up in the driveway of her new house just as the sun was beginning to set on her first day in Barker.

Her mum had tried to get her to stay for dinner, but she'd been keen to return to her unpacking. Plus she'd found it confronting being at the farmhouse, surrounded by photos of happier times when her dad was alive and her brother was well. It was to be expected, she thought, but there was such a dark blanket of grief wrapped around the house, even though there had been the occasional laugh, that she'd been glad to be able to escape just for a little while.

She was angry with herself for feeling like this. She wanted to be able to be there to support her family. To stop thinking that Will was any different because he had a death sentence. To be able to hang out with him and talk and laugh as they used to do. The last two years had snatched that away because she found herself watching her words and behaviour. Not wanting to say anything that would upset

Will or draw attention to the fact he was dying. And she was watching him all the time. Watching for shortness of breath or any sign of a temperature. Anything that might indicate he was deteriorating.

How did you behave normally around someone who was dying?

As she got out of the car, a flock of galahs swooped and soared overhead and disappeared towards the edge of town.

A door banged next door and then a voice said, 'Hello there, you must be our new neighbour. I'm Kim.'

Zara turned around and saw a woman standing on the doorstep. Her long, curly hair fell below her shoulders and her face was friendly and kind.

'I guess I am,' she said, slamming the door shut and walking towards the woman. 'I'm Zara. Zara Ellison.'

'Really?' Kim sounded incredulous. 'Well, now, haven't you grown up! You probably won't remember me. I have the roadhouse on the edge of town. Your mum used to bring you and your brother in to get hot chips on the way home from swimming lessons when you were small. I know your mum and Will. He used to pop in occasionally when he was in town getting things for the farm. Grab an iced coffee and sandwich. But I haven't seen him around for a while.'

'Oh, right. I think I remember. It's been a long time since I lived here. Actually, Mum mentioned you this morning— said you had great coffee at the roadhouse. I don't know why she didn't tell me you lived here.'

'When you have a husband who is a coffee snob, you learn to make good coffee. Come down and I'll make you one. So, what are you doing back here? Last I heard, you were a high-flying journalist.'

Kim came down the steps and walked across the yard to lean against the fence, and Zara could see she was wanting a long conversation.

'My brother is sick,' she answered. 'And I just moved in today, so I still have a heap of unpacking to do.'

'Ah . . .' A heavy sadness entered Kim's voice. 'Yes, I'd heard that Will wasn't well.'

Zara felt her throat close over. *Don't be too nice or I'll cry,* she thought.

'I'd heard he was having more treatment. Not good then?'

Zara shook her head.

'Well, what a beautiful thing for you to do. To come back here and help. How's your mum holding up. And Will?'

'We're all fine. Adjusting.' *What a load of shit.*

'Well, Dave and I are here if you need anything. Even if it's just help to shift some of the furniture.'

'Thanks.' Zara felt awkward accepting help from someone from her childhood who she barely remembered. 'That's nice of you . . .'

'Are you still going to be working while you're up here?' Kim wanted to know.

'Yeah, I've had a transfer from work, so I'll report on this area now. It won't be as busy so I can spend a bit more time at the farm and help out there.'

'I'm sure they're both really pleased you're home.'

A car turned into the street and drove slowly into Kim's driveway.

'That's Dave now,' said Kim. 'Come on and I'll introduce you.'

'I really should—'

'Won't take two seconds to say hello,' she insisted.

Zara felt like rolling her eyes. *Fantastic.* She'd managed to get a house next to the town chatterbox. Just what she didn't need.

'Hello, honey,' Kim said as a tall man with greying hair got out of the car. He was solidly built, Zara noticed, but had a gentleness about him.

'Hey you.' He leaned down to give her a kiss.

Zara could tell he whispered something in her ear, because a smile spread across Kim's face. Zara looked away uncomfortably. Public displays of affection were not something she liked.

'Come and meet Zara. She's Lynda Ellison's daughter.'

'Oh, g'day, Zara. Welcome to our street.' He walked towards her and held out his hand.

'Thanks. Nice to meet you,' Zara answered politely, shaking his hand. How had she ended up here when all she wanted was to go inside and unpack, a glass of wine next to her?

'Dave's the local detective,' Kim said, proudly putting her hand on his arm.

'Oh.' Zara's ears pricked up. 'That's great to know. I may have to come and interview you at some point.'

'Interview? Are you a journo?' Dave asked.

She nodded. 'I work for the *Farming Telegraph*.' Even as she told him this, she could see the distrust cross his face. *Wow, even in a tiny country town where nothing happened, the cops didn't like journalists.*

'I'll be happy to help you if I can,' he answered, though Zara had the distinct impression he didn't mean it. 'But we don't get a lot of crime out here.'

'No, I don't suppose. I guess it's fairly quiet, with not many people around.'

'Well, it's not always quiet,' Kim said. 'What about when Milly was attacked?' She turned to Zara and started to say, 'My niece . . .' but stopped as Dave put his arm around her shoulders and squeezed slightly.

'Sounds interesting,' Zara said. 'I'd like to hear about it.'

'It was a few years ago now,' Dave said. 'Not newsworthy at all.'

'Right. Well, I'd better get on,' Zara said. 'I've still got loads of unpacking to do.'

'Did you want to pop over for dinner?' Kim asked. 'I bet you haven't had a chance to do any shopping.'

'Oh no, thanks. I'll be fine. I'll scratch something together.' She turned and started to go back towards the house, but Kim's voice stopped her.

'How about this? I'll bring you over a home-cooked meal and you can eat it when you're ready, rather than with strangers when you're tired and sad.'

Zara's first reaction was to say no again, but somehow the words 'I'd really like that,' popped out. Her hands flew to her mouth. 'Sorry, I shouldn't have—'

Kim let out a peal of laughter. 'Of course you should have, sweetie! It's hard to make conversation with someone you've just met, especially when talking is the last thing you feel like doing. You go and get unpacking and I'll drop something over in a while.' She linked her arm through Dave's. 'Come on, I've got some news for you,' she said.

Zara watched them go. She didn't know anyone their age who were so clearly that much in love. There must be a story there. And maybe she'd pegged Kim wrong. Maybe she wasn't a chatterbox, just someone who liked to help people.

You're back in the country now, she reminded herself, before grabbing the keys out of the car and locking it. Then she laughed at herself. Hers would be the only locked car in Barker, she'd wager fifty dollars on it!

❧

The kitchen was unpacked by the time Kim knocked on the door with a container of something that smelled mouth-watering.

'Thai chicken curry and rice. And there's a fresh salad on the side. Enjoy. Sleep well and we'll see you tomorrow.'

Zara appreciated that Kim left so quickly, because her energy was beginning to desert her. She opened a bottle of wine and poured herself a glass, before leaning tiredly against the wall. She knew she should set up her office tonight too. Lachy would be on the phone to her first thing in the morning for the daily editorial meeting.

Closing her eyes, she imagined the bustle of the office: Lachy yelling instructions and phones ringing off the hook. Here it was quiet. Even the galahs had stopped screeching. She'd forgotten how silent the country could be; the stillness was almost unnerving. She took a deep breath and picked up her dinner and wine and moved into the office. The removalists had put the office desk under the window that looked out onto the backyard and placed the three boxes marked 'office' in the middle of the room. A bookshelf was pushed up against one of the walls and her filing cabinet was next to it.

Setting down her food and drink on the desk, she sat and took a mouthful of the curry. It was delicious and before she knew it she had eaten the whole lot. She hadn't realised how hungry she was. Turning to the boxes, she tugged at the sticky tape holding the flaps down. Inside were folders stacked neatly; she grabbed the top ones and started to place them on the bookshelves. One of them held all her stories for the *Farming Telegraph*. She flicked through it quickly and saw the last one she'd written on the court case involving the death of Colin Grawd. She stopped and looked at the photo she'd snapped of Gerard Hooper as he was walked to a police van. Her eye was caught by a man standing at the edge of the frame, looking intently at the accused. In fact, now she looked carefully, the two men were staring at each other.

Opening her computer, she went through her photo file until she found the one she was looking for, and enlarged it. She was certain it was the man who had attended court every day, the one with the deformed eye. Cloudy Eye. Who was he?

Changing screens to the Google search engine, she typed in 'man with milky eye, Melbourne'.

Good one, Zara, she thought. *You won't find much with that.*

The internet was much slower than in the city, and in the end she drank the rest of her wine and went back into the kitchen for a refill before the page had loaded.

She looked at the hits that Google had come up with.

Listeria infection.

'Ugh,' she said.

Crazy contact lens—great idea for Halloween.

'Interesting thought.' She scrolled down but couldn't see anything useful.

There was something about this man, she just knew it, but clearly she wasn't going to find out who he was through some random Google search.

Flicking through the rest of the folder, she thought with pride about the stories she'd written over the last three years. She really loved her job and meeting people through it: the federal agricultural minister, the president of the National Farmers' Federation, and many other leaders in the agricultural industry, Nuffield Scholars included. She'd even made friends with some of the people she'd encountered through work. Tammy and her husband, Stu Warren, were innovative pig farmers making waves across the industry with their forward-thinking practices. She met them when she was covering the new system they'd implemented in their shed. They'd installed a computer program called 'PigAmation', which could do everything from monitoring the climate inside the shed to controlling and recording the amount of feed eaten by each sow. Stu and Tammy had been the drivers behind the program, telling the software company what they had needed to measure and manage, and supplying some of the initial funding. The program had revolutionised the way feed was distributed, and streamlined measuring the progress of the pigs. All this had helped them understand their bottom line much more and showed where they could make adjustments and cost savings.

Zara and Tammy had kept in contact following their initial interview two years ago, after finding they shared an interest in crime authors and wine. Now they met for a drink or coffee whenever Tammy was in the city and discussed the new-release novels that had come out in the time since they'd seen each other last. It wasn't unusual to get a text message from Tammy in the early hours of the morning, saying something like, *OMG! Just finished Michael Robotham's new-y. You HAVE to read it!*

Don't suppose that will happen as much now, Zara thought. *At least not for a while.* Sighing, she continued to unpack the box. At the bottom was her favourite photo, carefully wrapped in a tea towel and tucked in between the covers of a folder. She placed it on her desk and stared at it.

It had been taken when she was sixteen. Zara had been competing at an athletics carnival and she'd won a gold medal for the fifteen hundred metres. Her dad was standing next to her, his arm around her shoulders, smiling broadly. He'd even told her that day he was proud of her. Something of a rarity. How could she have known then that a few years later photos like this one and her memories would be all she had left of her dad?

Brian had been a tough old bugger. That's how his best mate, Mick, had described him at the funeral. Tough but kind. Someone who loved his family. Someone who loved farming and animals. The community.

Zara agreed with some of that, but not all. He'd been hard on his kids, for sure, expected them to work and pull their weight. But if he hadn't been, neither she nor Will would have developed the work ethic they had. And yes, he'd loved his family, but she wasn't quite sure he was as community-oriented as Mick had described. He'd loved spending time on the farm, with Lynda and the kids, more than being part of a sporting group or local committee. The most community-minded thing she remembered him doing was cooking sausages at a footy fundraiser to send Will's team to Adelaide for a competition down there.

She made a mental note to ask her mum where Mick was now. It would be unusual if he wasn't around helping Lynda and Will in some form or another.

'Dad, what would you make of all this?' she asked out loud, slumping down into the desk chair. 'Why do I feel the way I do?'

As if on cue, her phone rang and she jumped.

Lachy.

'Settled in yet?' He rarely said hello.

'Still got a few boxes to unpack.'

'How're you faring?'

Zara paused. 'Okay.'

'Come on, Zara. I know you better than that.'

Reaching for her glass of wine, she took another sip and considered her answer. Lachy could read her like a book.

'I'm struggling a bit.'

'With the move or the situation?' Straight to the point.

'Probably both, but mostly Will, I think. I don't like the way I'm feeling. I'm pissed off with him.'

'What the hell for? Poor bastard can't help what's happening to him.'

'He's given up.'

Pause. 'How has he done that, Zara?'

'By not fighting.' Her voice rose in resentment. 'He's not having any more treatment. Maybe there would be a chance if he did! Why wouldn't he take every opportunity there was to get better, Lachy?' Tears started and she sniffed as her nose began running too.

Lachy's voice was gentle when he answered, 'Doesn't matter why, Zara. It's Will's choice and that's all that counts. At this point in his life, it's got to be about what he wants and how he gets it. Nothing else.

'Tell me, if this was you, would you want to spend your days in and out of hospital, feeling like shit, or at home, on the farm you love and with the people you cherish? I'll bet he hasn't made this decision lightly, and I'll also bet that he's thought about both you and your mum and the effect it will have on you.'

'But . . .'

'You know how I know that?'

'How?'

'Because Will's kind and considerate—like you. He would've thought about how you and your mum were going to cope. Tried to work out what was best for you too.' He paused. 'I think you'll find people in his situation do that all the time.'

Zara wanted to ask how he knew that, then she remembered that Lachy's sister had passed away two years ago from breast cancer. He'd taken unpaid leave for a couple of months before she died, to be with her.

'Zara,' Lachy said quietly, 'he needs to do this his way.'

Chapter 7

Zara pushed open the door to the police station. She wasn't sure how she would be welcomed after the shutdown she'd seen on Dave's face last night.

It had been Lachy's idea that she call in and introduce herself. As he'd reminded her, 'They might want your help at some stage.'

There was an older lady who looked vaguely familiar sitting behind thick glass, typing at a computer.

Zara took a quick look around and decided it was like every country police station she'd ever been into. On the wall were the usual domestic violence and kids helplines, along with those for Beyond Blue and Lifeline. There were wanted posters, and pamphlets offering help with drug and alcohol problems.

The lady looked up from the computer and shifted her glasses to the end of her nose, peering over the top of them. 'Can I help you?' she asked.

Summoning her friendliest smile, Zara handed her business card through the slits in the glass. 'Hi, I'm Zara Ellison, a reporter with the *Farming Telegraph*. I wanted to make myself known . . .'

'Ah, Zara. You're Lynda's daughter, aren't you? I remember when you were a tot. Nice to see you're home. Such a bad business about Will. I'm really sorry to hear he's so unwell.'

For a moment Zara didn't know what to say. When she'd made the decision to come back home, she really hadn't factored in that people would remember her and know about Will's illness. Laughable, really; she of all people should know how country towns worked. Everyone knew everyone and they all knew each other's business. She was sure her mum would've told her friends that she was coming home to stay for a while, and so it would've got around. What was confronting were the references to Will being sick. It wasn't like she needed a reminder.

Summoning her professional smile, she answered, 'I'm sorry, I don't remember your name, but your face is certainly familiar. And, yes, I'm back here for a bit.'

'I'm Joan and I certainly wouldn't expect you to remember me. I used to help out at the school, listening to you kids reading and the like.' Joan gave her a motherly smile. 'Now, how can I help you? I hope you're not here to report a crime; you've only been here such a short time!'

Zara shook her head. 'Nope, just here with my reporter's hat on. I'm still working while I'm here, so I wanted to introduce myself to the station. Let everyone know I'm around.

I met Dave yesterday. His house is next to mine.' She paused. 'Are there any other police officers working here?'

'There's a lovely young man by the name of Jack. I'll get him for you. Dave is our detective. Really great bloke. Couldn't get anyone nicer. We were lucky when he fell in love with Kim and decided to stay here in sleepy old Barker. Of course, Kim, well, she's the salt of the earth, would help anyone. Really top couple.' Joan stood up. 'I'll get Jack for you.'

Zara nodded her thanks and fished out her mobile phone to check her emails while she was waiting for the apparently young and lovely Jack.

She scrolled through and opened the one from Lachy. *Feeling better today?*

She tapped out: *I'm on the beat, so yes.* She'd just hit send when she heard a voice behind her.

'How can I help you? I'm Senior Constable Jack Higgins.'

Zara turned around and put her hand out. Jack was a tall, slim man, in his late twenties or maybe early thirties. His hair was cut short and his uniform looked like it had been ironed to within an inch of its life. She wouldn't have called him classically handsome, but he was good-looking enough. Not that she was looking.

'Hi, Jack, I'm Zara Ellison from the *Farming Telegraph*. I wanted to introduce myself. I'm going to be here for a while, so if you've got anything that you need to get into the media . . .'

'Thanks for introducing yourself, Zara,' Jack said pleasantly.

Zara braced herself.

'We'll certainly get in contact if we need to get anything out but, as I'm sure you're aware, we don't usually talk to journalists unless we have a reason.'

'I figured as much,' Zara said, 'but please let me know if I can help you in any way.'

'I'm sure we will.' Jack paused. 'You could like our new Facebook page, if that interests you? I've just started one under the name of Barker Police. Not that we'll be putting anything newsworthy up there, obviously, but you'll get any updates on what we're focusing on or gentle reminders of road rules.' He smiled.

'Excellent, I'll do that. Very forward moving of you. I follow heaps of police pages. Great way of connecting with the community.'

'Well, it's a good way to get messages out there,' Jack nodded. 'So, how come you've ended up in Barker? We haven't had a journo here in the whole time I've been around.'

'I'm only around for a while. I've just had a transfer out here for family reasons.'

Jack stared at her. 'Ah, I can see it now. I thought you looked like someone I knew. You must be Will Ellison's sister, yeah?'

Zara nodded, feeling like she had Will's name tattooed on her forehead.

'Sorry to hear he's so crook. I played footy with him when I first moved here. Hell of a nice guy. Must be really tough for you all.'

Unexpectedly a lump appeared in her throat, and all she could do was nod.

The door opened and a gust of cool wind blew through, bringing Dave with it.

'Bloody hell, that wind is off the icebergs,' Dave said as he combed his hair down with his hand. 'Ah. G'day, Zara. What brings you here?'

'Just came to introduce myself,' she said after clearing her throat. 'Let everyone know I'm around.'

'Good to know. Glad you've met Jack. How did you go last night? First night in the house and all.'

Zara heaved her shoulder bag up a little higher. 'No problems, although when the galahs got going at daybreak, I wondered what on earth the noise was.'

Jack laughed. 'Certainly are noisy buggers,' he agreed.

'Make sure you pop over for a drink sometime,' Dave said. 'I'm sure Kim would love to have a chinwag.'

'I will. And could you thank her for the meal last night—it was the most delicious curry I've had in a long while.'

Jack looked over at her. 'Mate, did you get Kim's chicken curry? God, that's good. I pretend I'm sick just so she brings it over to me.'

Dave looked at him. 'Really? I'm going to tell her that.'

'Yeah, it was fantastic. Just one more question.' Zara interrupted their banter and then watched as they both arranged their faces into neutral expressions. She wanted to laugh, they were both so alike. She bet Dave had spent a lot of time schooling Jack about how he should react to the media. 'Who's the local stock agent?'

83

Jack's face split into a grin. 'Going to introduce yourself there too?'

'That's what good journos do.'

Dave took his mobile phone out of his pocket and scrolled through. He scribbled out a number then handed her the piece of paper. Jack rolled his eyes at Zara—clearly Dave hadn't yet mastered the technology of sharing phone contacts.

'Karl Richards. That's his number. Young bloke, not been here too long. His office is next to the post office.' He nodded to her and turned away.

'Thanks very much. I appreciate your help.'

'Nice to meet you,' Jack said and followed Dave behind the counter. 'I'm sure we'll come across each other soon. It's not a very big town. And if you feel like it, share the Facebook page around.'

'You've done that already?' she heard Dave say as she exited out the door and onto the street, feeling vaguely disgruntled. Not that she had been received any less enthusiastically than she'd expected. Cops were always hard to crack. Lachy had told her that keeping the police on side was a good idea, and if she ever found any info that would be helpful to them, to give it over. 'You create a source for life that way,' he had said. Still, they had both been polite and they'd shared a couple of laughs. That was a good start.

I'll have to find something that would interest Jack, rather than Dave, Zara thought. *I think he's going to be too tough to crack, even if he comes across as a very nice man.*

Her hair blew back from her face as she walked against the wind towards the post office. Crossing the empty street, she saw a faded sign on a stone building proclaiming itself to be the stock agent's office. Karl Richards didn't seem to be associated with any of the larger stock firms like Elders or Landmark, but that didn't surprise her. In South Australia there were a lot of independent agents, which meant they all had to work hard for clients.

Inside, she was immediately hit by a musty smell. Instantly she was thrown back to her childhood, to when her mum, dad, Will and she used to visit her grandparents. Their house had been dark and always smelled mouldy, as if there wasn't enough sunshine getting in through the tiny windows and hard-to-open doors, and Zara was sure that was one of the reasons she loved letting the sunlight into the places she lived.

The darkness of the house had scared her as a young child. She'd been convinced there were ghosts in the passageway from the kitchen to the living room. She never walked that hallway, she always ran, especially at night, when her gran was cleaning up the kitchen and her pa had already retired to the lounge room to watch the ABC news and smoke his pipe. And she ran fast, just in case one of those ghosts could grab at her heels and drag her somewhere she didn't want to go.

A door slammed, bringing her out of her reverie, and she turned towards the noise.

'Well, hello there,' a male voice said. 'You're a sight for sore eyes. What's your name?'

Zara wrinkled her brow at the obvious flirting. 'I'm Zara Ellison, journalist with the *Farming Telegraph*.' She held out her card.

The owner of the voice came into view and in front of her stood a tall man with dark hair and even darker eyes. His skin was tanned, and he looked like he worked out a lot. Did Barker have a gym now? She doubted it, but this guy was seriously ripped.

'Well, Zara Ellison from the *Farming Telegraph*, I sure am glad to meet you. I'm Karl Richards.' He held out his hand and she took it.

In the first seconds of introductions she pegged him as a larrikin, someone who loved to chat, laugh and play jokes on people. His face was alight with fun. It would be good to know someone who could make her laugh while she was here. God knows, she'd need it as time went on.

'The local stockie at your service. And why are you here? Got some stock to sell? Or have some been stolen?'

'Why?' she asked instantly. 'Do you know of some that have been stolen?' Then Zara laughed. 'None of the above, but I've got some questions for you.'

'Shame. Fire away.'

Zara explained why she was there and then asked, 'Can you tell me if you've got any stories or anything of interest going on? Sheep or cattle feed trials, anything really. Who are the most innovative farmers around or, at least, who wouldn't mind talking to me? I need a couple of stories for next week's paper and I only arrived yesterday.'

Karl leaned over his desk and grabbed a map and a pen. 'Are you doing a penance or something? How come they've thrown you out into the sticks? Insulted the boss, maybe?'

Zara laughed again. 'Nup. I haven't been banished. I've come back for family reasons. You probably know my family. Are you the stock agent for Will Ellison?'

A grim look settled on Karl's face. 'Yeah, I am. And that's a shitty situation. Are you his sister? I've heard about you and I've read your work in the *Farming Telegraph*. I should've put two and two together.'

'That's me.'

'I've told both Lynda and Will that if they need any help with anything, no matter how small, to let me know. The guys from the footy club are always around to lend a hand as well. We discussed it at the last committee meeting. And I know Mick Sands has been helping a bit too.'

'That's my dad's best mate. I'm not surprised he's there. And thanks.' Shoving her hands in her pockets, Zara rocked back and forth on her heels. 'I'll let them know again,' she answered in a low voice.

'Now, back to the farmers,' Karl said, 'I think the best thing for you to do is come down to the pub tonight. We've got another footy club meeting and there're a couple of guys on the team you should talk to.'

'Sounds great! What time?'

'Make it seven. That'll give us time to get the meeting out of the way and then we can focus on how we can help you.'

Chapter 8

'Hey, I'm here,' Zara called into the empty kitchen of the Rowberry Glen homestead.

The heart of the house hadn't changed in all the years Zara had been alive, although the yellow curtains in the window were now faded, rather than the happy, bright colour they had been when Lynda had first put them up. Pots and pans hung from the ceiling over a floating kitchen counter, and the gas stove was in the corner, butted up against the door that led into the pantry. Indoor plants sat on every available surface, including on the cabinet full of plates and cups. The kitchen had always been the hub of the house: warm, inviting and friendly.

She called out again, 'Mum? Will?'

There was no answer and a trickle of worry gnawed at her stomach. The ute was parked outside, so they must be here somewhere.

She walked into the lounge and found that empty, then along to the office, but there was no one here either. She opened the door to what had once been her bedroom. Not that it was her room anymore—it had been cleared out when she'd left and was used as a guest room. The curtains were drawn and the bed was made. Through the dimness she could make out a wardrobe and dressing table; again, neither was hers, they were both new. All the posters of her idols—Keith Urban, the Red Hot Chili Peppers and Tim McGraw—were long gone. She shut the door and moved further on down the hallway; her mum's bedroom was the next one along.

Then, from further on in the house, towards Will's section, she heard a clunk.

'Mum? Will?'

'Down here,' Lynda called. 'In Will's bedroom.'

Zara hurried towards the sound of her voice. 'What's wrong?' she asked as she walked in.

'There's nothing wrong,' Will answered impatiently from the bed. 'Mum's panicking over nothing.'

'He's in pain,' Lynda said. 'I'm trying to convince him we need to go back to hospital.'

'We don't.' Will sounded angry but he looked grey and drawn. 'I'm fine.'

'But, love, you know what the doctor said. He can give you stronger meds. You don't have to put up with discomfort.'

'I know. But I also know myself. I'm all right. Just stop fussing.' The last few words came out as a yell and both Lynda and Zara took a step back.

Defiance radiated from Will, as if he was daring them to say another thing.

'Okay,' said Zara, thinking quickly about how to defuse the situation. 'How about we monitor you for a few hours and if you think the pain is excessive, we'll call the doctor?' She looked at her brother before adding, 'It's a compromise.'

Will sneered at her. 'I'm dying, I'm not stupid.'

Lynda gasped. 'Will!'

'Hey! That's enough. I don't care what you are, but don't be mean,' Zara snapped. This was so uncharacteristic of her quiet, patient brother.

Will's head dropped and the fight seemed to go out of him. 'Sorry,' he muttered. 'Sorry.'

Lynda dropped to her knees beside him and patted his arm. 'Sweetheart, there's nothing to be sorry about. I can't imagine how you're feeling.' She paused and Zara could see a look of indecision on her face. 'Will, honey, maybe we could ask that counsellor we met at the hospital to come out. He said that anger and frustration and fear are all normal. And there's help . . .'

Will shook his head. 'I don't need any help. What's the point? That I learn to accept what's happening? By the time I do that, I'll have been in my grave for years. The freaking counsellor can't help me deal with what I'm facing.' He leaned back into his pillows. 'God knows, there's nothing good that comes out of having terminal cancer.' He was silent and it seemed to Zara that they had all run out of words.

She sat down on the end of the bed as Lynda continued to pat Will's arm.

'We don't want to interfere,' Zara said softly. 'We just want to make this as easy as we can for you. I'm sorry if you think we're fussing. We don't like seeing you in pain.'

'It's only going to get worse,' Will admitted. 'I didn't tell you that, but the oncologist warned me on the last visit. I'll stick it out for as long as I can and then . . .' His voice trailed off and he took a shaky breath. 'This will sound odd, but I like it.'

Zara was burning to ask why, but she took her lead from her mum and stayed silent.

'If I can feel it, I'm still alive.'

Lynda dropped at the kitchen table and put her head in her hands. 'I want to cry, but I don't have the energy or the tears,' she said.

Zara sat down beside her and put her hand on her arm, realising again that it was a good time to stay quiet.

The ticking clock was the only thing that made any noise and it seemed too loud in the silence.

'He's not the only one asking why,' her mum finally said. 'I do it too, every second of the day.'

'Me too,' Zara admitted. 'I can't understand why he stopped the chemo. It feels like he's giving up.'

'Oh, sweetie, that bit I do get. Another question I ask all the time is why he got the cancer in the first place.

One night I googled the causes of bowel cancer. To see whether it was something I'd done or given him to eat. The website I looked at said there's often a family history of bowel cancer, but there's none in either of our families that I know about. But there's the red meat we eat and the beer he drinks. Drank.'

'Mum, you can't do that. You'll go insane! It doesn't matter what caused the cancer. It's there. Knowing what caused it won't change that. And I've never known Dr Google to be failsafe.'

Lynda continued as if Zara hadn't spoken. 'At night I go into his room and watch him. I just want to see his chest rising and falling. He woke up one night. Asked me what I was doing. I couldn't answer him, so I just got up and went back to bed.'

The three kelpies who had been lying at the front door suddenly set off a round of barking and Zara heard the crunch of tyres on gravel. She gave her mum's arm another squeeze and got up to look out the window. 'Who do you know drives a white Toyota?' she asked.

Lynda had stood up and was now at the kitchen sink, splashing water on her face. 'Everyone in the country has a white Toyota. It's probably Karl. He rang this morning to see if he could do anything. Or maybe Mick. He sometimes turns up about now.'

'I met Karl today. He seemed nice. And he offered to help then, too.'

'Karl is a lovely bloke. Your father would've called him a larrikin. He loves a good time.' She peered out the window. 'But that's not Karl's car. Actually, I don't know who that is.'

Whoever was driving pulled up right next to the garden fence but didn't get out. Zara wondered how they'd got through the front gate without Will opening it from inside the house, but then she remembered that it could also be opened manually.

Finally, the car door opened and a large woman with long curly hair got out and went to the boot.

'It's Kim,' Zara said.

'Kim who? Oh, that's Kim Burrows. Hmm, I wonder what she's doing here.'

Zara opened the door and went out onto the verandah. 'Hi,' she called. 'Get down!' she said to the dogs, who were jumping around Kim's feet.

Kim bent down to pat one of them. 'You can smell my old dog, can't you? Hi, Zara! I thought I'd pop out with some food, so no one has to cook.' She was holding a large basket and started walking towards the verandah with a large smile on her face.

'Oh!' Zara was taken aback. 'That's really kind of you. Do you do this for everyone?' she asked, thinking of her dinner last night. 'And thank you for the curry. It was beautiful and I appreciated not having to cook.'

'This is how we do things in the country. When people have hard times, the neighbours come out in force with food and help. But I also run a business catering for people who can't cook for themselves. A little like Meals on Wheels.' Kim stopped to drop a kiss on Zara's cheek then continued, 'I'm sure none of you really feel like eating, let alone cooking. I thought bringing a few meals might help make sure you do eat. Hi, Lynda.' Kim's gaze slid past Zara.

'Hello, Kim. It's been a long time.'

'You've had a lot to deal with. How are you?' Kim's voice was full of compassion as she put the basket down and hugged her.

'We're going along fine,' Lynda answered. 'Come in. I'll put the kettle on.'

Zara picked up the basket and followed the two women inside. 'I'll just check on Will,' she said, leaving Kim and her mum to chat. Maybe her mum needed to talk to someone who wasn't directly involved.

Slipping quietly into Will's room, she checked his face and saw his eyes were closed. She was relieved to see the gentle rise and fall of his chest, then she shook her head crossly. She didn't need to do what her mum did. She just needed to be here for him.

'I know you're there,' Will said quietly.

'So I am. Mum's got a visitor.'

'Who?'

'Kim someone. Burrows?'

'Oh, yeah. She's a good chick.'

'She brought food.'

Will smiled even though his eyes were still shut. 'That's what she's known for. Feeding the sick, dying and those in need. I guess between all three of us, we fit the bill.'

Zara didn't answer.

'Do you remember when we were little, we'd go and stay with Gran and Pa over on their farm?' Will asked.

'That's funny. I was only thinking about that today. I used to be scared a ghost would get me as I ran down the passage from the kitchen to the living room.'

Will gave a little laugh. 'There weren't any ghosts there, you big scaredy-cat.'

'Tell that to a five-year-old with a good imagination!'

'We did! Frequently. You never believed us.'

Zara let out a peal of laughter. It felt good. Will smiled a bit wider and opened his eyes.

'Why did you bring that up?' Zara asked.

'Just been thinking about things. Our younger days, when you were a brat and I was the goody-two-shoes. How you used to be able to con Dad into anything but not Mum. Then how you looked after me when I was at boarding school in Adelaide. I don't think I ever told you how much I appreciated that. All your visits and phone calls during the week. Crazy, considering you're younger than me, but you took to it much better than I did.' The anger he'd expressed earlier seemed to have dissipated and now he was reflective.

Zara shrugged. 'I understood how you were feeling, even though I liked school and you didn't. It was hard being away from Mum and Dad at that age. Trying to make new friends and fit into a place we didn't understand. All those stupid rules about wearing ties to dinner and skirts to church.'

Will huffed a little. 'It was the long socks with shorts that used to annoy me. I thought they were trying to turn us into toffee-nosed snobs.'

'Never a chance of you being a snob. You'd talk to anyone anywhere.'

'That's what you should do.' He was quiet for a minute, then he said, 'You know there are good days and bad days with this stupid disease and today is a bad one. They're not all like this, you know.'

'I know. You weren't in bed yesterday when I was here. The blood helped then, didn't it?'

'Yep.' The talking seemed to exhaust him.

'Will?'

'Hmm?'

'Are you in pain? Like bad pain?'

'Yeah, it hurts. In my back and abdomen.' He shrugged. 'Par for the course, I'm afraid.' He shifted in his bed and tried to sit up a bit higher.

'Do you want help?'

'I can do it.'

'Okay.' She paused and watched him struggle before giving up. 'Hey, can we make a deal?'

'A deal? That sounds interesting, especially in my state. I mightn't be around to honour it.'

'Oh, ha ha! Let's not even think about that. What I was going to say was, promise me you'll ask if you need help. I'll keep Mum off your back if you absolutely make sure that you ask for something when you really need it—whether it's pain management or doctors or whatever. If you ask, then I'll know you're serious.'

Will gathered the doona into his fists and squeezed tightly. Zara held her breath, hoping she hadn't upset him.

He finally nodded. 'I think that's a fair deal.'

She reached out her hand for him to shake, but he just took hers and squeezed it as firmly as he could. 'Thank you,' he said quietly, 'for understanding.'

Zara wanted to say she didn't understand anything, only that she loved him and wanted to make sure he was looked after as well as possible, but instead she squeezed his hand back. Perhaps some things were better left unsaid.

There was loud laughter from the kitchen.

'Hey, tell me about this Kim. She seems like a cross between an angel and the town gossip. Knows everything about everyone,' Zara said.

'Kim is the kindest lady anyone could ever meet. And Dave, her husband, he's great too. Kim just loves helping people, and I guess to someone who hasn't lived in the country for a while, it could seem like she's a bit of a gossip . . .'

Zara cocked her eyebrows at him.

He smiled and went on. 'But she's far from it. She runs the local roadhouse, as well as the business I told you about. You said she brought food with her today?'

Zara nodded. 'A huge big basketful.'

'That's Kim. Anything she's ever told in confidence doesn't pass her lips, which is why she knows so much about people. She'd never break someone's trust. I hear people talk about her often and it's always good.'

'Maybe I shouldn't be so hard on her. I felt a bit smothered yesterday when she introduced herself.'

'Can I point out very nicely, sister of mine, that you are exceptionally independent and don't like offers of help, so perhaps your reaction was your problem, not Kim's.'

Knowing he was right, Zara gave a rueful smile. 'I think I've just been told.'

'I like to think of it as informed!'

Chapter 9

Zara pulled on her R.M. Williams boots and gave her hair a brush, before tucking her purse and phone into her handbag. It was only a five-minute walk to the pub and it was five to seven. She didn't like to be late.

When she'd left Rowberry Glen earlier that afternoon, she'd had a quiet talk to Lynda. 'Will has promised he'll tell us when he needs something, Mum. Can you try not to . . .' She'd battled to find the right words. 'Look, I know you're a mum and mums look after their kids, but Will knows what he needs. And you never smothered us when we were growing up. You let us wing it, and if we got hurt, then you'd deal with us. You need to do that now, if you can. Please?'

Lynda had taken it surprisingly well. It seemed Kim's visit had been the tonic she'd needed, even if it had only been a brief respite. She'd also told Zara that she wasn't going to start seeding and that seemed like a weight off her shoulders too.

Zara had made a note: her mum couldn't stay at home and look after Will and the farm all the time. She needed a break. Downtime.

She walked briskly through the cool night air, changing her thoughts from palliative care to work. That excited her.

Music was playing loudly, and as she rounded the corner into the main street, laughter filtered through the air. Sounded like the pub was rocking tonight. *And it's not even Friday,* she thought. She'd rarely been to the Barker pub—by the time she was old enough to drink, she'd left for the city, although they had occasionally come in for lunch or dinner as a family when she was growing up. She remembered the pub being full of men leaning up against the bar, laughing and talking, cloudy from cigarette smoke, but no music ever playing.

They must've moved with the times, she thought.

Inside, she realised, other than the new jukebox, nothing had changed. The lighting was still dim, it still smelled like spilt beer and she thought she recognised the old man at the end of the bar, nursing a schooner of beer.

Zara scanned the room for Karl. She was looking forward to seeing him tonight. When he'd made her laugh earlier in the day, she'd been surprised at how good it was to feel light-hearted like that. And then, when she'd heard her mum laughing with Kim earlier in the day, she'd known it was good therapy.

She checked the bar area but couldn't see anyone she knew in footy gear, so she turned to order a drink.

'What can I get you?' The publican, who had appeared from the back of the room, leaned on the bar and tried to peer down her shirt without her noticing.

'White wine, thanks,' she answered, leaning back. No matter how many times she'd walked into a room by herself, she still hadn't got used to it, and she felt self-conscious. 'Is Karl here?'

'Out the back. You new here?'

'Something like that,' she answered, putting a ten-dollar note on the bar. She didn't want to be rude, but she didn't want to encourage conversation either.

'Whatcha looking for Karl for?' He put the glass down heavily and some of the wine sloshed over the side.

'I'd like to talk to some farmers about what's going on around here.' As she said it, she realised the publican would be a great source too. He'd hear all sorts of stories. Steeling herself, she held out her hand. 'I'm Zara. I work for the *Farming Telegraph*.'

'Danny Bowman.' His hand, when he shook hers, was large and chunky. 'What sort of goings-on?'

'Oh, stock trials, innovative farmers, that sort of thing.' She paused. 'You'd hear a lot of things that are going on around the community, wouldn't you?'

Danny leaned forward. 'You wouldn't believe the things I hear in here. But you gotta be careful about what you repeat, you know? I don't want to cause any trouble.'

'I'm sure you don't.' Zara took a sip of her wine.

'There you are!' Karl came out of another room and headed straight over. 'I've been telling the boys about you. They're happy to have a chat. I thought you might get caught out here with Danny.'

'Yep, just introduced ourselves.' She picked up her wine and followed him, glad to see a friendly face. 'I'll catch up with you in a while, Danny.'

'I'm not going anywhere.'

'Fellas,' Karl called out and clapped his hands. 'This is Zara. Be nice. She's used to people with good manners, not you ferals.' He turned to her and said, 'You'll probably know some of them from when you were growing up.'

As if on cue a short, thickset man came up and held out his hand. 'Zara, we were in school together. Harry Thompson. Not sure if—'

'Harry! Of course I remember. Hello,' Zara said, pleased she knew someone else. 'What are you doing with yourself?'

'I bought the metal fabrication shop a few years back. Make silos and feeders, stuff like that. What about you? Karl tells me you're a reporter. I always wondered what you got up to after you left Barker.'

'I like to think of myself as a journo rather than a reporter. Sounds strange but I think of reporters as people chasing the hard story rather than writing about facts.'

He nodded enthusiastically. 'Must be a great job. Sounds really exciting.'

'It has its moments.' She smiled. 'Tell me about the metal fabrication business.'

'It keeps me busy and the wolf from the door,' Harry started.

Karl broke in. 'Let's not monopolise the guest of honour, Harry! You live in town and can talk to her anytime. Zara, come and meet Brock Doyle. He farms about eighty k west of here. Runs sheep and planted a lot of saltbush a few years ago, which helps with his carrying capacity. He also has a merino stud.'

'Great. Nice to see you, Harry. Hopefully we'll catch up soon. I'd like to hear more about your business and what you're up to.'

'Sorry to hear about your brother, Zara. If we can do anything, let us know, okay?'

'I will. Thanks.'

'This way.' Karl pointed to a group of three men talking earnestly at the back of the room. 'You right for a drink?' Karl turned to check on her and she held up her nearly full glass in answer. He nodded.

When they had wound their way through the throng to the edge of the group, one of the men turned and held out his hand to Zara.

'Hi, Zara, Mark Cullen. This is Brock Doyle—Doyley—and Ian Wood. Great to meet you. Karl told us about you earlier. We know Will.'

'Most people seem to,' she smiled. 'Nice to meet you all as well.'

'So, what's going on out your way, Doyley?' Karl asked.

'Could do with a bit of rain.'

'As we all could,' Ian agreed.

'I'm spending so much bloody time in my ute checking waters, I don't seem to be getting anything else done,' Mark said. 'I'm going to shear the dry ewes and get rid of them. Need to lighten the load on the place. Not that feed is scarce yet, but you never know when it's going to rain. I was watching *Landline* last Sunday and the outlook for an early break isn't good.'

'Yeah, I was thinking about doing the same thing. I locked a few paddocks up, hoping I'd be able to use them in a few weeks' time, when the other paddocks get thin, but as soon as I did that, all the bloody roos came in and started feeding. It's better if it goes to my stock, so I've put a mob back in there. Roo shooter is doing all he can to help out, but the numbers are just too large. They're all coming down from the north because there's no feed up there either,' Brock commented.

'Tricky juggling everything to work just perfectly, isn't it?' Karl said. 'I've got a market for some dry ewes, so let me know when you want to get rid of them.'

Zara lapped up the conversation. It felt as though it had been ages since she'd been at work and talked farming. In reality, it had only been a few weeks. She had a thought. 'Listening to you talk about all the time you spend in the ute, Mark—when I was out at Rowberry Glen yesterday, I found out that Will has gone all techy and installed motion cameras and monitoring systems on the troughs. Would that help you save time?'

'Yeah, it's a great idea and I've been thinking about it too.' There was a pause as the men exchanged glances and immediately Zara's story antenna turned on.

'He seen anything weird going on out there, anything he's caught on camera?' Mark asked.

'Weird as in . . .' Zara left the sentence hanging.

'Drones. Has he got eyes in the sky as well as on the troughs?'

Zara shook her head. 'Not from what he showed me. So you've got problems with drones? What are they doing?'

Someone jostled against her and pushed her forward against Karl, spilling her drink.

'Oh God. Sorry, Karl,' Zara apologised, feeling the dampness of the drink seep into her shirt and seeing a stain forming on his.

'Shit, sorry,' the man apologised from behind her. 'Oh, it's you. G'day, Zara.'

Zara looked up and saw Jack standing there, his face red with embarrassment.

'Don't worry about it,' Karl answered, patting his shirt with a hanky.

'You play footy too, do you, Jack?'

'Sure do. Only just got here, though. Bit late tonight. Got busy.'

'Doing what?' Zara asked immediately.

'Do you journos ever knock off? You're not getting me that easily,' Jack answered. 'Anyway, it wasn't work. Gotta get on, fellas. Have a good night.'

They watched as he walked quickly towards the door, stopping only briefly to have a word with another man. He yanked the door open and disappeared out into the night.

'Jack seems a bit on edge,' Ian said.

'I reckon he's real busy. I heard Dave talking to my old man yesterday, saying they had a heap of reviews and reports that had to be finished by the weekend. Got dumped on them unexpectedly.'

'Freaking paperwork. Who'd work for the government?' Karl asked.

'I'm with you on that.' Mark turned his attention back to Zara. 'I know you're the one supposed to be asking the questions, but I'm going to ask you a few.'

'Fire away,' Zara answered. She knew if she could establish herself with this tight-knit group of men, she would have a great deal of knowledge and resources at her fingertips.

'No eyes in the sky, you reckon?'

'Not that I saw, but I can check. He's got motion cameras on the front gate as well. I think they record, so he can get numberplates from the footage.' She waited, burning to ask some of her own questions.

'And he hasn't mentioned anything like a drone? I mean, I know he's crook and all, so maybe he's not taking much notice.'

'He goes out with Mum as often as he feels up to it,' Zara answered. 'But that's not very often anymore. The office and his cameras are how he checks everything. He's still interested, of course, but his body isn't working well.

If he'd seen something, I'm sure he would've said. Where are you seeing it?'

'The drone?' Doyley asked. 'Above farms. Flying out over the stocked paddocks. I've had two or three farmers mention it to me recently.'

'How do you know it's not someone who's just got a new toy?'

'Mate, it could well be, but I don't like it when there's an eye up there spying on my family. If it's harmless, then piss off and do it somewhere else,' Ian answered heatedly.

'That's the trouble with activists trespassing and the like,' Zara said. 'You've got no idea if this is innocent or not. And if it's not activists, it could be people casing the place to steal things. It frustrates me that South Australia hasn't got a Rural Crime Investigation Unit anymore.'

'Isn't that the truth? If it's not one thing it's another. And I for one, even though I've got nothing to hide, believe that bastard shouldn't be checking out my farm. For all I know they might be taking kiddie pictures of my daughter.'

'Shit, what a thought,' Mark said, shaking his head.

'The activists have certainly been using drones to check out farms down south,' Zara said. 'One of the other journos in my office wrote an article on a drone that kept chasing cars down the road.'

'What?' Karl looked over at her.

'Yeah, it scared the crap out of a few women driving home at night. It would appear over the top of a hill and so the driver would see the lights of the drone. Then it would follow the car for as long as it could. Turned out it was an older man causing "public mischief",' Zara made the quotation marks with her fingers. 'That's what he was charged with. He didn't have any reason to do what he was doing other than he loved scaring people.'

'There are some fuckwits around, aren't there?' Doyley sounded incredulous.

Zara fished around in her handbag and brought out three business cards. 'If you've got any more information, can you let me know? I'd love to write something about this.'

'Sure. If we get it out there to the public, then everyone can be aware of it,' Mark said.

'That's one of the best parts of my job, being able to raise awareness. That's why I love what I do.'

Chapter 10

'Hi, Joan,' Zara said as she walked into the police station. She shrugged out of the jacket she'd put on to walk over. The clouds had come in thick and fast during the night and held the promise of rain. After hearing the farmers talk last night, she hoped the promise would be fulfilled.

'Zara, what brings you here so early this morning? Horrible day out there.'

'It wouldn't be so bad if it wasn't for the wind. It's whipping up a lot of dust, but it's also bringing the clouds in.'

'I wouldn't hold my breath for anything other than a dust storm,' Joan said. 'I've seen it time and time again. We get our hopes up and all that happens is we get our rainwater tanks filled with red dust. The water runs the colour of rust for weeks afterwards.'

'Hope you're wrong!'

'Oh, me too.'

'Is Jack in?'

'He is. Can I tell him why you're here?'

'I like the element of surprise,' Zara said and gave Joan an impish grin.

'He doesn't,' said Joan, picking up the phone to call through.

'What cop does?'

'Zara Ellison is here to see you, Jack.' She listened for a moment, then put down the phone. 'He'll be here in a sec.'

'How long have you been working at the station, Joan?'

'Longer than I care to remember. Seen out three senior sergeants. Dave's been here . . . oh, three years, I suppose. Seems like longer. He's the best one I've worked with. Jack's not bad either. Dave has trained him very well.'

'You must've seen a lot of cases come through.'

'Always that, love. People seem to think that the country is quiet. From experience I know that some of the wildest things happen in the country.'

'Wildest, huh?'

'Yep. And the other thing I know is nothing is impossible in the country. City people seem to think they're the only ones who have prowlers or drug dealers or murderers. We have all that too. In spades.'

'Hmm. Not sure that's something to be proud of,' Zara said, wrinkling her brow.

Joan gave a little laugh. 'Maybe not. I guess what I'm trying to say is it doesn't matter where you live. When it comes to crime, the same things happen in the country as in the city.'

'Maybe I should lock my doors at night.'

'I think you're silly if you don't,' Joan answered seriously.

'Are you scaring the newest local, Joan?' Jack asked.

Zara turned and saw the senior constable standing in the doorway. She wasn't sure how long he'd been there or how much he'd heard.

'Oh, I hope not!' Joan resumed her typing. 'Just telling it like it is.'

'G'day, Zara. Come on through this way.' Jack nodded at her.

Zara followed him to an interview room. It held two chairs either side of a steel table. At a quick glance she saw the table was bolted to the floor. She certainly wasn't having the welcome mat rolled out for her this morning.

She waited until they were both seated before saying, 'Thanks for seeing me.'

Jack spread his hands out as if to say, *Why wouldn't I?*

'Did you meet a few people at the pub last night?' he asked.

'Yeah, I did. I'm going to write a story about Brock Doyle's saltbush and how it's increased his carrying capacity, and I might do a profile of Ian Wood. I'm really just trying to find people who are interesting and do some profiles. I've found that people don't have to be doing ground-breaking things to make a good story, they just have to be interesting.'

Jack nodded and glanced at his watch. 'How can I help you today then, Zara? I don't think I'm so "interesting" that you'll need to interview me.' He emphasised the word 'interesting'.

Feeling annoyed, Zara frowned. 'You know, Jack, I'm not the enemy here, although you seem to think I am.'

'Look, Zara, I'll be honest. We haven't had a journo living in town and coming into the office regularly, ever. You've been in twice in two days. We've got work to do and nothing would be so exciting or attention-grabbing that you needed to come and see us every day. We're just not sure what you want from us, especially since there's really nothing going on around here that would warrant a story.'

'See, that's where I think you're wrong, Jack. I heard last night there's a drone being flown over people's properties. I would've thought that warranted investigating.'

'Who have you been talking to?' Jack leaned forward and put his elbows on his knees.

Zara felt the keenness of his stare. 'Oh, come on now. You know us journos never give up our sources. I'm just asking you to confirm or deny whether you've had reports of drones being flown over properties.'

Jack paused for only a moment before responding. 'Yes, we have.'

'And are you investigating?'

'There's no active investigation ongoing at this time.'

Stop being so arrogant, Zara thought.

'Can I ask why?'

'You can, but that's a question I'm not going to answer. Now, is there anything else I can do for you?' Jack stood up.

Zara had dealt with enough coppers in her time to know there was no point in trying to get anything more out of Jack. She stood up and fixed a smile on her face.

'Thanks for your help.'

'You're welcome. This way.'

Out on the street, Zara shook her head and looked back at the station. Either Jack had been badly burned by a reporter at some stage in his career, or he'd been schooled never to have anything to do with them.

It's not like I'm chasing a murder investigation, she thought grumpily.

Glancing up at the sky, she realised the clouds had started to break up in the south, which was where any rain would've come from. Now, on the horizon, she could see the dirtiness of a red smudge. Dust.

The wind whipped around her and she pulled her coat tighter and put on her sunglasses. Looking down at the pavement, she started to walk towards home, composing the start of a story in her head.

> When asked if there was an ongoing investigation into unusual drone activity in the Barker region, the *Farming Telegraph* was told no. No further information was forthcoming.
>
> However, for the farmers around Barker there is a sense of disquiet. Drones aren't new technology and laws on their usage have been in existence since 2002. However, the last few years have seen an increase in their use; often for good, but sometimes not.
>
> Farmers have found drones to be very helpful when checking water levels in tanks and mustering from the ground. Barker farmer Ian Wood told me . . .

Zara grabbed her phone and switched on the voice memo. 'Call farmers met last night for comment on usefulness of drone within the farming industry.' She switched it off and glanced at her watch. Maybe she could catch Danny at the pub before she went home. She really should be getting out to the farm, but it would only take a couple of minutes and hopefully she would have enough to write a story for this week's paper. Changing direction, she walked to the pub, wanting to get out of the foul weather.

She pushed on the door and found it was locked, but she could see Danny restocking the fridge behind the bar. Knocking loudly, she waved when he looked over.

'Too early to start drinking,' he said when he opened the door. 'Damn, that weather is revolting. Come in, come in, before I have to sweep the floor again.'

'Sorry to bother you early, Danny.'

'No bother. What's going on?'

'I just went to ask the police about a drone.' She told him a little of the conversation from the previous night. 'I wondered if you knew anything about it.'

Danny nodded. 'Sure do. I've heard that some people have reported it. Dave was away when the first report came in, and Jack wouldn't do anything about it just in case it was a local who'd bought themselves a new toy and didn't know the rules around flying it. Then I heard of others—three times over the following week, still while Dave was away. Not sure if they were all reported or what's been done about it since.'

Zara wanted to ask how he knew the first report had been made while Dave was away, and if he knew that much, surely he knew who had made the complaint. 'So, four people reported the same incident, or the police have been told about four different incidents?'

'Well, I don't know what's been reported to them, but I know of four different times. First one was out on the road to Adelaide. There's nothing really out there except the gun club and cemetery, so it really wasn't doing any harm. Except Mrs Pickett could see it from her window and got worried.'

'As you would,' Zara sympathised.

'The second time I heard about it was when old George Mayne from Mayne Meats came in for his usual Wednesday counter lunch. He said there'd been one buzzing near the meatworks. Never went over the top, but he could see it out on the road. It was glinting in the sun. He didn't realise what it was until he told his grandson about it. See, now, to me that says it's not someone with a new toy. Maybe, instead, someone who wants to stir up a bit of trouble by focusing on the meatworks. But who am I? Just an old publican who knows not much.'

'Sounds like a perfectly reasonable conclusion to me. When was the third time?'

'Out on Ridge Road. Rhys Aldridge said he was going down to get the mail from the roadside mailbox and he could see it hovering over his shearing shed. Said it made the sound of an oversized mosquito. Now, the interesting thing about this one is that his shed is right on the road, so the person who was driving it must've been close by, but he never saw anyone. I asked him straight out and he said no.'

'Maybe casing it for fuel or something?' Zara wondered out loud.

'Coulda been. Or checking to see if they were shearing and there was any blood on the sheep.'

Zara looked at him, impressed. 'Love your thinking, Danny. You'd make a good journalist, such an enquiring mind.'

Danny went red and turned to put another row of beer bottles in the fridge. 'I just like to listen and then I think about things. I read a lot too, you know, and I've heard your name before. I know you reported on that court case in Melbourne where that protester was killed.'

'Yeah, I did. You must know a lot about farming and what goes on then?'

'I know a bit. Anyway, that's what made me think there was more to this drone.'

'I think you're right. Can you give me the names and phone numbers of the people you mentioned to me today?'

Danny nodded. 'You haven't asked about the fourth one.'

'Tell me about it,' she encouraged.

'Out at Murray Neilson's farm. Buzzed his house, so whoever was flying it broke the law that time. The law says that you've got to respect people's privacy and you're not allowed to fly over people, like during sporting games and things, and—this one's really important—you've got to keep a drone thirty metres away from people.'

'So how did that break the law, do you think?'

'I don't think buzzing his house is respecting his privacy, is it?'

'Good point.' Zara put her bag back on her shoulder. 'Can I grab those names and numbers, Danny?'

Chapter 11

As Dave drove out to Rowberry Glen, he kept glancing at the sky. Jack had told him this morning that he'd overheard some farmers talking about drones in the pub last night, and then Zara had turned up asking questions. She was perfectly entitled to do that, but he wished she hadn't. Not for any reason other than he liked to investigate things on his own terms, without a reporter looking over his shoulder.

Jack had heard that Will had 'gone all tech' and so Dave thought it might be worthwhile having a chat. Maybe he knew something about this drone that was causing everyone grief. Anyway, as part of the community policing he was briefed to undertake, going to see Will wasn't anything out of the ordinary. Perhaps the young bloke would be pleased for the distraction. Even so, Dave knew he would have to tread carefully.

He pulled up at the front gate and watched as it opened automatically. *So great not to have to get out and open it, then again to shut it*, he thought.

He was greeted by a round of barking kelpies, then walked down the path to find Lynda standing at the front door.

'Hi, Dave, what brings you out? Kim was only here yesterday!'

'She told me last night,' Dave said with a grin. 'She enjoyed catching up with you. Must be a bit hard trying to run the farm and be here for Will.'

'A bit of girl time was exactly what I needed, but I didn't know until I had it. I'm just on my way to do a stock run.'

'Is Zara helping you out?'

'On the farm? She will once she's found her feet, but what we really need is a workman. Someone who's going to be here for a while. Zara won't stay after . . .' She stopped and tried to smile, while starting to put her boots on. 'Were you looking for Will or me?'

'Whoever is in charge of the technology and security cameras.'

'That would be Will.' She looked up. 'Is there a problem?'

'Oh no, not at all, just wanted to ask Will a couple of questions, that's all.'

'He's having a better day today. Yesterday wasn't good; he was in a lot of pain. But he's sitting up in the office this morning. I'll tell him you're here.' She held the door open and ushered Dave inside.

As he walked in, he looked at the photos on the wall. Pictures of happier times when there were still four in the family, when they were all healthy and full of life.

'You must like farming to have continued on after your husband died. Did you come from a farm?'

'Yeah, I grew up on the other side of Barker. About eighty ks from here. Closer to Spalding. Mum and Dad had a few thousand acres running cattle. Herefords. Of course, they're not the flavour of the month anymore. Angus seems to be the breed of choice. I was an only child, so when it became clear I wasn't coming home, my parents sold the farm and retired.'

'You didn't want their land?' Dave was surprised.

'Too far from here. We would've been forever on the road between places. Farming like that is okay for a while, but Brian had done it before and he wanted to buy land closer to Rowberry Glen.'

'Did he succeed?'

Lynda stopped in the kitchen and refilled the kettle before switching it on. 'He died before any land came up. Then we all decided there was enough land here to keep me and Will occupied and give us a decent enough income.' She shrugged. 'Life seems to be what happens while we make other plans, doesn't it?'

'A truer statement there never was,' Dave answered. He turned as he heard footsteps behind him on the wooden floorboards.

A gaunt man with a protruding stomach stood behind him, and it took all of Dave's training not to react to the change in Will. 'G'day, Will. Good to see you, mate.'

'Hi, Dave. What's going on?'

'I was passing and thought I'd call in to say hi. I'd like to hear about the new technology you've put in, if you're feeling like you can chat.' Dave watched as Will's face lit up.

'Sure. Be happy to.'

'Tea or coffee, Dave?' Lynda broke in.

'I'll have a tea, thanks.' Dave had already scanned the kitchen and realised there wasn't a coffee machine there. It would have to be tea for him today.

'Will?'

'Nothing, thanks. Dave, come down to the office and I'll show you.'

Following Will, Dave cast his eyes around, taking in the details of the house. There were medicine bottles lining one windowsill, and a bed in the corner of the sitting room. Beside it were farming magazines piled high. *Will must spend a bit of time there*, thought Dave. He saw how the window looked out over the rolling hills and creek and could understand why he did that.

'Why the interest, Dave?' Will had sat down and was pointing at a chair. 'Drag it round so you can see.'

'Thanks. I've always been interested in this type of technology. Wondered if it really was as good as everyone says.' He wasn't going to mention the community policing or the drone just yet.

'Ah, you could have a conversation with Zara about that. That was the first question she asked me! Like I told her, it can't replace a farmer's footsteps, but it certainly has its place. Check this out.' He tapped a few icons and brought up a screen. 'This trough has been running low for a little while. Mum went to check it yesterday and found that there was a blockage in the float—a water beetle. So even though it was still flowing, the water had been reduced. I could see that the trough wasn't full but it wasn't low enough to set off the alarm.'

'Can you move the cameras around or are they fixed?'

'These are all fixed. I didn't think I needed the ones that panned around, because we're not going to use them to check the sheep. Only the water.'

'Ah, so you can't see anything more than that picture?'

'Nope.' Will took a shaky breath and his jaw clenched. After a moment he let out a slow breath. 'Was there a reason you wanted to be able to pan out?'

'I was curious to see what was visible to you,' said Dave, noticing but not commenting on Will's spasm of pain. He figured that in Will's situation, he'd want to be treated as normally as possible. 'I've had a few reports of a drone flying over some farms and I wondered if you'd seen anything with your cameras.'

Will shook his head. 'No, sorry. What you see there is what you get. I spend a lot of time not able to sleep, so I watch these screens a bit. There's infra-red lowlight on them and the most exciting thing I get to see is a fox coming in for a drink.' He paused. 'But I've heard about the drones.'

There was something in his tone that made Dave want to ask what he had heard, just as Lynda came in and put the tea on the desk. 'I'll see you later,' she said. 'Should only be about an hour.'

'Can you go by the house paddock trough as you leave?' Will asked. 'Then I can show Dave exactly what I can see from here.'

'Sure. Dave, can you thank Kim again for me. I very much enjoyed her visit yesterday. And the meals she brought.'

'I'll tell her,' he promised. 'See you later.'

Once Lynda was gone, Will adjusted his stance at the computer and reached into a drawer in the desk. He brought out some pills, popped two and swallowed them with a sip of water from the glass on his desk.

'Is it bad, mate?' Dave asked.

'It has its moments.'

'There anything I can do?'

Will shook his head. 'Just got to take it as it comes. I get really tired and the pain is getting worse. I haven't told Mum or Zara yet, but I feel different. I feel like it's creeping up on me real quick. I've got to force myself to get up every morning. I'd rather just stay in bed and sleep. And the medication makes me foggy.' He stopped. 'Maybe it's not the medication. Maybe it's just everything progressing. Who fucking knows? I'm torn between needing to give up because I'm so exhausted at having to fight every day, and being terrified to give up because I don't want to die.'

Dave wasn't sure what to say to that. Instead he clasped him gently by the shoulder and gave it a squeeze. 'I wish I could say something to make it a bit easier for you.'

Will shrugged. 'It is what it is.' He tapped on the mouse and brought up another screen. 'Keep your eye here.' He pointed to the end of the trough. 'You should see Mum turn up there in a minute.'

He stopped talking and looked at the screen, so Dave followed suit and asked, 'What do you know about the drones, Will?'

'Just that they're about.'

'You don't sound surprised.'

He was quiet for a while before saying, 'I'm not sure, but I may have had something to do with them being here.'

Turning to look at him, Dave didn't say anything, just waited. But there was nothing forthcoming.

'Will?' Dave asked.

Will's voice was low when he spoke again and it was nothing to do with his previous cryptic comment. 'Mum wants me to see a counsellor. To work through what I'm feeling. I dunno, to somehow accept what's happening. I haven't told her I've already seen one but she couldn't help me. I mean, no one can tell me I'm not dying, can they? So what's the point? Just need to move on and let happen what's going to happen.

'Yeah, I get tired and I need morphine to help me do the things I want to do, but you know what bothers me the most? What have I done in my life that has any type of meaning? I don't have kids; I don't even have a girlfriend. Nothing I've done will be remembered by anyone.' A ragged sob escaped him. 'I won't be remembered by anyone.'

Dave patted his back while Will cried for a few minutes then noisily wiped his nose.

'Jeez, sorry. I don't know where that came from.'

'Doesn't matter, mate. It needed to happen.'

Dave wanted to ask about the drones again, but felt it wasn't the right time. How could he quiz a man who was upset about dying? He'd come back tomorrow.

There was a movement on the computer screen and Will pointed, still taking shuddering breaths. 'There you go. That's what you'll see on my screens.'

Dave looked and saw the numberplate, wheels and half a grille of the ute. Then laughed as Lynda leaned down and waved into the camera.

Will shook his head. 'My mother is a card when she wants to be.'

'You know, Will,' Dave said, 'I believe your life has lots of meaning. And the meaning comes through the relationships you have. With your mum, with Zara. The boys at the footy club. All of those people are going to remember you because you impacted on their life. I think you're being very hard on yourself thinking your life doesn't have meaning. It has, more than you know.'

Kim sat down at the kitchen table and opened a new recipe book. A smell came wafting up from underneath the table. 'Oh yuck, Bob. I wish you'd stop doing that.'

'He can't help it, you know.' Dave's voice came from behind her.

'You're home early,' Kim said, surprised. She stood up to give him a kiss.

'I've got to apologise,' he said. 'I should have done it long before now.'

'You did apologise. That same night we had the argument.'

'I know, but I'm not sure I really meant it. I do now.'

Kim gave a soft laugh. 'I don't know if you should've admitted that.' She pulled on his arm and drew him over to the couch. 'What's made you change your mind?'

Dave sighed. 'I've been out to Rowberry Glen.'

'Oh. Such a lot of tragedy out there,' Kim answered, patting his thigh.

'Absolutely. Makes me sick to the stomach. That poor family.' He took another deep breath. 'Will said today he felt as if his life didn't have any meaning because he didn't have kids or a girlfriend. And I read between the lines that he felt as if he hadn't achieved anything. Bloody hell, he hasn't had a lot of time either.'

'He hasn't.' Kim pushed her hair back from her face. 'What did you say to him?'

'Well, now, here's the funny part. I said that his life had meaning because of his relationships with other people, with his family. His relationships were his achievements.' He didn't say any more, just let the words hang in the air.

'And do you think your family would say the same thing about you, Dave, if you were in the same situation?'

'No,' he answered honestly.

'Do you want to fix that?'

Dave could hear the tentativeness in her voice and wondered how he could've let things deteriorate this much. 'Of course I do, but I'm going to need some help.'

'You know I'll do anything for you, my love. All you've got to do is ask.'

Chapter 12

It was the end of the week when Zara finished off her opinion piece for the *Farming Telegraph* with Ian Wood's comments:

> 'Why the lack of investigation? Surely the drone's appearance in the last few weeks is worthy of concern and, as farmers, we are worried that people could be using such equipment to monitor our farms. Whether it's to check we're using good farming methods or it's with the intent to steal from us, or even if it's neither of these things, they shouldn't be allowed to fly across our land. I call on the Barker police to take notice of what is going on in their backyard and do something about it.'

She attached the article to an email and sent it to Lachy.

The window rattled as another big gust of wind hit it, and she could hear particles of dirt being flung against the glass by the gale.

Getting up, she went to stand in front of the window. The end of the street could hardly be seen, there was so much dust flying around. *Good thing it was nearly evening and most people would be tucked up in their houses*, she thought. *It wouldn't be too good on the roads with the lack of visibility.*

Her phone dinged with a text message. Lachy.

Good piece. How are things looking at home? All okay here.

Typing quickly, she said: *Haven't got out to the farm today. Been busy with the story. Like the distraction.*

Dropping her phone onto the couch, she sat down and switched on the TV, letting her head fall back against the headrest. She was exhausted and, as she'd said to Lachy, she hadn't even been to the farm. When she'd spoken to her mum earlier in the day, Lynda had told her that after Dave's visit and a good day yesterday, Will had slept all today. It was unlike him not to even try to get out of bed.

Zara had a horrible feeling that time was running out more quickly than any of them expected. Really, she should go out there tonight.

Her email dinged and she looked at the name in her inbox. Liz! She laughed as she saw the subject line: *White or red . . . That's if you remember me.*

There was a photo of Liz with a glass each of red and white wine in front of her, at a bar. *Cheers from our fave bar. Missing you like crazy. Hope you're coping. Love you. xxx*

Quickly she typed out: *White for me tonight, please. All okay here. Missing you too. Try and call you tomorrow. Any office gossip? Is Mr O'Grady still pinching people's things?*

Nah, must've just been focused on you. Some talk it was the cleaner and he just liked your stuff. I'm not convinced though. Sounds a bit weird.

Zara read the message and had to agree.

She was about to type out another message, when her phone rang. She jumped and felt a surge of pleasure as she saw Tammy's name on the screen. Her friends were clearly thinking of her tonight. 'Hey you! Haven't spoken to you for ages. What's going on?'

'Oh, Zara, I've been meaning to call you for ages. How are you? How are things with your brother?' Tammy sounded breathless, as if she had been running.

'Where are you?'

'Just walking back to the shed. Stu needed me to check the generators to make sure the cooling system for the pigs is working properly. It was pretty warm here today, and tonight the wind has dropped right off and it's quite humid. Not good for pigs.'

'You can have some of the wind from here if it'll help,' Zara answered with a laugh. 'Can hardly see the end of the street for the dust.'

As if the wind understood her conversation, there was an extra-strong gust and the office door banged shut.

'That sounds awful. I'd prefer the heat and not the dust, if I had a choice. I saw pictures on Facebook of massive dust clouds coming in over Adelaide. Is it like that there?'

'I guess that's why you live south and I'm not usually living north! And, yep, it is. Revolting.'

'How's Will?'

'On the downward slide.' Zara ran her hands through her hair and sighed deeply.

'Oh shit, I'm sorry, Zara.'

'You know, someone told me once that when a person with cancer dies, there's a massive amount of relief. And I thought that was awful. Surely there should be grief and sadness, not relief. But I'm beginning to understand why. The relentlessness of it all is so difficult.'

'Is he bedridden?'

'Not yet. Most days he tries to get up and spend a bit of time in the office. Then he goes back to bed. He's sleeping heaps. And when I googled what the end might look like, that's one of the signs.'

'How long have you been up there?'

'Not even a week! Five days today.'

'Do you think he was waiting for you to get there so you could help your mum?'

Zara paused. She hadn't thought of that. 'I don't know.'

'I've heard of people managing to hold on until loved ones arrive and they get to say their final goodbyes. Maybe Will was waiting until you got there to help Lynda.'

'I guess so.' She stopped talking as that sank in. 'Shit. Maybe I should head out there tonight. I've been thinking about it, but with the dust and everything, I decided to stay home.'

'I'm not saying that's it, just a thought.'

'Anyway, let's change the subject. Let's talk about something happy.'

'Excellent idea! You start.'

'Now, just because I had the idea doesn't mean I have to start! Anyway, I haven't got much good news. Or at least fun news.'

'We've been having trouble with protesters out the front of the farm. Not that that's at all funny. Scary, more like it.'

In the background Zara could hear the occasional deep grunt of contentment and the hum of the farm's cooling system. They were gentle sounds and, knowing what a well-run piggery Tammy and Stu had, she was gobsmacked to hear the protesters had targeted them. 'What the hell are they doing that for? Have you got a journo down there covering the protest? I haven't heard anything about it.'

'Oh, don't worry, the cops have been out and are making sure they're all kept off the farm. There've been a couple of papers down here but, really, it happens so often now, the shock factor has gone, and we're just getting on with our work, whether there are protesters around or not. Bloody annoying, though, getting the kids down to the school bus and that. It's not great for them to have to see it all, but until someone trespasses on our property, we can't do anything about it. They're allowed to be on the road.'

'Oh, that's not fair, Tammy. Your poor kids. Poor you!'

'And none of this conversation is funny. Let's change the subject again.'

'Okay, well, here's something different. I went to the pub the other night, to meet some of the local farmers, and the publican tried to look down my shirt. I haven't had that happen in years.'

'Gross! What did you do?'

'I probably should have called him on it but I just let it go. Easier than making a scene.'

'Huh! The #MeToo movement will have you for not doing anything about it.'

'I think we've all lost the ability to laugh at ourselves, you know. A bloke having a bit of a look isn't such a big deal. It's the ones who touch and intimidate that need to be made examples of.'

'I can still remember how my boss tried to kiss me in the ute one lunchtime. Despite the fact he had a wife and three small children. That was in the first piggery I ever worked at.'

'Now, they're the ones who need to be called out,' Zara said.

Tammy gave a little laugh. 'Do you think we've solved the world's problems tonight?'

Zara snorted. 'I don't think so! Reckon there are a few we've yet to solve!'

'I'm just about home again, so I'd better go. Got to feed the kids and be up early tomorrow so we can get all the jobs done before sports day.'

'So good to hear your voice.'

'And yours. I hope things aren't too difficult for you over the next few months.'

'Tammy, between you and me, I don't think it will be that long.'

'Much love, Zara.'

'You too.' She pressed the disconnect button and sat there staring at the soundless TV, thinking about their conversation.

Then she got up and googled 'protesters and piggeries'. The hits were many and varied. There were newspaper reports and photos of people, some well dressed, some in ripped jeans and T-shirts with slogans like: *Pigs are our friends, not food* or *Don't eat your mate.*

A photo caught her eye and she enlarged it on her screen. One of the girls looked like Sophie Grawd. Interesting that she should be protesting after the death of her dad during a protest. Quickly she googled 'Sophie Grawd, piggery protestors'. There wasn't much of interest there: stories that Zara herself had written about the court case, a few close-up photos of Sophie and her mother. Then she saw a website entitled 'Piggeries, the other story'. Zara clicked on that and found it wasn't a story on piggeries as she'd thought, but a website run by activists called Voices for Animals, reporting their opinion about the cruelty of farming pigs, and she had opened the membership page. Sophie's name was in the public membership list.

That's interesting, Zara thought. *I'm sure that's the organisation her father was involved with.* She had a quick look around the website and realised it was a fairly mild activist group rather than a militant one. Their campaigns had been silent vigils outside abattoirs, praying for animals' souls, or standing quietly on the steps of Parliament House asking for the outlawing of farming animals for meat. They didn't seem to be confrontational or aggressive. That fitted with the little she knew about Sophie. She likely wouldn't want to be involved with anything potentially violent after the death of her dad.

Zara stood up, intending to take something out of the freezer for tea, but instead she found herself in her bedroom, packing a small overnight bag, and then heading out to the car.

❧

Zara knocked on Kim's door; her car was running and she was ready to go.

'Hello, sweetie,' Kim said as soon as she opened the door, then her face fell. 'Is everything all right?' she asked cautiously.

'As far as I know,' Zara answered, 'but I thought I should go and stay out with Mum and Will tonight. Give Mum a break. I didn't get out there today. So just thought I'd let you know that I mightn't be home for a few days. I think I'll try to work from the farm.'

'No problems. We'll keep an eye on the house for you.'

'That's kind, thanks. Not that it should need it. I'm only letting you know so you don't get worried if you don't see me coming and going.'

'No problems, thanks for telling us. Drive carefully, won't you? This awful dust . . .' Her voice trailed off.

'Will do. See you later.'

'Zara?' Kim called after her. 'We'll be thinking of you.'

She turned and nodded.

Thankfully the dust had begun to settle as she drove out to the farm. Most of the paddocks still had some type of feed covering them, but even in the short time she'd been back, she could see the dry feed powdering up and starting to break down. If she'd been the praying type, she would've been praying now, as she drove, for steady soaking rains. For things to be a little easier for the farmers this year than it was last year.

A movement off the side of the road caught her eye and she instinctively hit the brakes. Assessing that the white station wagon in the parking bay wasn't actually going to pull out onto the road, she put her foot down and glanced in the rear-view mirror as she drove past.

Bloody tourists, she thought.

She flicked on the blinker to turn into the driveway of Rowberry Glen and saw the lights of the house gleaming welcomingly in the distance.

Chapter 13

Lynda was just pulling up in the ute as Zara turned the ignition off in her car.

'Didn't think you were coming out tonight,' she said through the open window.

Zara got out and walked towards her mother, patting the three dogs running around in the back of the ute.

'I wasn't going to, but I had this feeling I should. What have you been up to?'

'Actually, I'm glad you're here. Could you please give me a hand? I've got three ewes bogged in the dam and I was just going to ring Mick to see if he'd be able to help me get them out.'

Zara was already walking around to the passenger's side of the ute. 'Mick Sands?' she asked. 'Dad's friend? I was going to ask you about him.' She slammed the door and watched as her mum put the ute into gear and took off towards the north end of Rowberry Glen.

'Yeah, but then I remembered he's gone away on holidays. To Canada.'

'He's been around?' Zara looked towards the west, where the deep blue was beginning to sink into the last of the sunset.

The dust and wind, which had raged so severely earlier in the day, had now settled. The gum tree leaves hung heavily towards the ground, as if the dust weighed them down. The sheep were beginning to come out from under the trees and bushes and slowly walk towards the trough, one after the other.

'Yeah, he helps if I ask. I try not to ring too often, though. I'm going to get to the point where I have to do it by myself, aren't I? The footy club boys have been fantastic—Karl, in particular, comes out and checks on us. Takes Will for a drive now and then. But I can't rely on people's good will and charity forever.'

'No, I don't suppose you can,' Zara agreed, feeling a slight twinge of guilt seep through her. Maybe she should think about staying to help out. It really was a big job for her mum, who was going to be turning fifty-six this year. She changed the subject. 'I wrote a story about drones today. Have you seen or heard of any around?'

'Drones? No!' her mum's head swivelled around sharply to look at her. 'Doing what?'

'Flying over farms. I wondered if you'd seen it happen.'

Lynda gave a little laugh. 'Darling, I'd be lucky to recognise a drone.'

'An oversized mozzie, according to one of the blokes I talked to.' Zara smiled as she said it. The thought of a mozzie on steroids made her want to laugh uncontrollably. It really wasn't that funny. Must be all the emotions running around inside of her.

'Hmm, I worry about the future of farming. What some people don't understand is that without us there isn't any food, whether you eat meat or just salad and veggies! Both lots come from farms.'

'Yep, no arguments with any of that from me,' Zara said as the dam came into view. 'So, three bogged?'

'Yeah. If you can slip out on the sheet of tin that I've laid across the mud, you can attach the rope and I'll pull them out.'

'Should've brought my rubber boots.'

'Huh,' Lynda hurrumphed. 'I wish it wasn't just the slop in the bottom of the dam, rather than inches of rain.' She reversed the ute onto the edge of the dam and then got out, passing Zara a rope.

Zara took off her boots and rolled up her jeans, before testing the tin to see how stable it was and crawling out to the first ewe, who was only stuck to the knees.

'I reckon you could have got yourself out of here, if you'd tried a little harder,' Zara said as she fastened the rope to the ewe, who threw her head back and tried to jump through the mud. 'Stop it! You'll just make yourself sink in further.' Zara crawled back across the wobbly tin and onto solid ground, before shifting the tin and giving Lynda the thumbs-up so she could hook her end of the rope onto the ute and pull the sheep out. When she was on dry ground, Zara went in and took the rope off.

The ewe lay on the ground, her legs tucked underneath her, looking stunned. Zara straddled her and grabbed a handful of wool on either side of her body and tried to get her to stand. Slowly, she managed to get her steady on her hind legs before helping her up on the front ones. The ewe stood there quivering before realising that underneath her feet wasn't slush and mud and that she had traction. With a couple of wobbly steps, she moved away from Zara and then started to run with an unsteady gait, over the top of the dam bank and into the gathering darkness.

'And stay away,' Zara called to the disappearing animal.

'Quick, let's get the rest out, otherwise it'll be dark before we've finished,' Lynda called.

Turning around, Zara grabbed the tin and laid it out across the mud to the next ewe. They repeated the actions twice, and when the last ewe had finally been safely guided away from the empty dam, the women looked at each other and held up their hands in a high five.

'Good job,' Lynda said. 'You haven't lost your touch.' She was silent for a moment and Zara could hear in her mind the question that was coming. 'You don't think you could . . .' Lynda broke off. 'Sorry, love, I shouldn't ask that. I don't want to put any pressure on you.'

Zara was silent for a moment as she tipped her head back and looked up at the stars beginning to shine in the inky blackness. The air was cool on her skin and just for a moment she imagined what it would be like living at Rowberry Glen—in the same house as her mother and working the same piece of land that had been in their family for generations. Could she do it? Did she want to do it? Then, she remembered the adrenalin rush from the newsroom as the deadline for print drew closer, and she sighed. 'It's a beautiful night,' Zara observed, not acknowledging what her mum had said. Maybe all that was better left alone while emotions were running high.

'Yeah, it is.' Lynda leaned against the side of the ute and looked up. 'I'll fence this dam off tomorrow. So the rest of the mob can't get in and cause any more grief.'

'Is there a trough in this paddock?' Zara asked. 'How will they get water?'

'Over near the gate is a trough. I'll have to mob them up and shift them there so they know there's water in it. That way they'll stay away from the dam but know where they can get a drink. I think sheep just see the dam embankments and assume there's water. It depends on what they're used to drinking from.'

'What's the long-range forecast saying? Is there any rain due?'

'Nah, not in the next two weeks anyway. And we'll need more than a few millimetres. We'll need a bloody deluge to fill these dams—to wet up the soil and make the water run off into them.'

'Doesn't it frighten you?' Zara asked.

'Doesn't what frighten me?'

'Well, I guess I know that I've got money coming in every week. My pay goes into my account no matter what I do. You have to make sure so many things are going right—the weather, the stock market, the wool market. Aren't you ever frightened that you might not make any money?'

Lynda looked over at her and, in the dim light, Zara could see a half-smile on her face.

'Zara, honey, there are many years we don't make any money. You should know that. We break even. During the good years, we make sure we keep money aside for the bad ones. We try and drought-proof ourselves—make sure the dams are all cleaned out, the hay stack is full, all of that sort of thing. Farming is a business, but it's also engrained in me. I can't imagine doing anything else. Or living anywhere else. This is my home, and all the stock and work that go with that are also mine. I love it.

'There're plenty of times I wish things were different, don't get me wrong. I wish your dad hadn't died and I wish Will wasn't sick.' She shrugged. 'But what can you do? These things are so out of my control. If I could wave a magic wand, I'd change all of that. I'd make it rain, I'd keep the wool prices high all the time. But that's pie in the sky stuff. As farmers you can't think like that; you just have to take everything as it comes and adjust accordingly.' She pushed herself off the ute and walked around to the driver's side.

'Don't you get lonely?' Zara wanted to know.

'When your dad died, I spent a lot of time sitting on the verandah looking at the sky. Sometimes I'd rant and rave and ask why he was taken away so suddenly and, at other moments, I just sat and remembered the times we'd had together. I wasn't as lonely then because I had Will. And this land speaks to me. You don't have to have an indigenous background to connect with the land. Rowberry Glen has its own personality that keeps me company.'

Zara stayed quiet. She could hear the murmur of the mob of sheep behind them and her mum's earlier words reverberated inside her head. *'This is my home, and all the stock and work that go with that are also mine. I love it.'* Her mum would be okay here after Will wasn't alive anymore. There would be horrible lonely times, she was sure, but her mum would be okay.

'Don't you ever want another partner, Mum?'

Lynda didn't answer. Instead, she got into the ute and started it. 'Come on, let's head home.'

Chapter 14

Dave wanted to go back out to Rowberry Glen and follow up Will's cryptic comment that he might be the reason the drones were around Barker. Try as he might, he couldn't work out what on earth Will could've done to cause them to be there. He frowned and scratched his head as he thought.

'What's wrong, sweetie?' Kim asked as she came into the kitchen. Bob was at her heels and he went over to his favourite place underneath the kitchen table and flopped down.

'I'm trying to work out if I can go and visit Will again today,' Dave said.

'Why couldn't you?'

'I don't want to put him under any pressure. I could see yesterday he was really tired. I don't know much about these things, Kim, but I can't see how much longer he can go on. His eyes are all sunken back in his head and—' he broke off. 'I don't know, he sort of looks like a living skeleton.'

'I noticed that when I was out there. And I don't know too much about this sort of thing either. You and I've been really lucky not to have been through this with anyone we know.' She sank down in a kitchen chair and put her head in her hands.

'You want a cuppa?'

'Yes, please, love.'

Dave switched the kettle on and got two mugs out of the cupboard before putting a tea bag in each. He didn't feel like coffee in the middle of the day.

'Why do you need to go back out there?' Kim asked, reaching down to pat Bob's head.

'He said something about the drones yesterday and I couldn't follow up on it. I feel like he knows something about them.'

Kim was silent as she continued to pat Bob. Finally, she asked, 'If it was a murder enquiry, what would you do?'

'I'd have to go out there,' he answered without hesitation. The kettle boiled, and he picked it up and poured steaming water into the cups and started to dunk the tea bags. 'This is different, though. It's not a murder enquiry and I can probably solve the problem without calling on a dying man. He would just make it quicker and easier.'

'I guess all you can do is make the decision when you get out there.'

Dave put the cup in front of her and sat down, just as a puff of foul-smelling air radiated up from under the table.

'God almighty, Bob,' Dave said as he fanned the smell away.

'What about Zara—do you think she might know?' Kim asked as she got up and moved away from the table. 'I don't know why that dog has to do that.'

'Zara is part of the trouble,' Dave answered. 'She's on our case to do something about the drones. I know she's written a story about them because she came in and spoke to Jack, who told her there wasn't an investigation going on and she wanted to know why.'

'And why isn't there?'

'Well, really, up until now, I haven't had enough evidence that there's a problem. But I have three reports and one unofficial sighting. And when those reports came in, we were still on holidays and Jack didn't want to stir up trouble with the locals in case someone had bought a new drone and didn't know the rules. If that was the case, we could've just found them and warned them off.'

'Have you asked anyone—'

Dave slammed down his cup and jumped up. 'You are brilliant!' He leaned down and gave Kim a smacking kiss before grabbing his jacket from the back of the chair.

'What did I do?' she asked, looking at him bemusedly.

'Jack started some Facebook page. Maybe we'll just put a call out over that and see what comes back. He told me that he'd already got fifty or so people on there. What are they called . . . followers? Likers? Followers sound like they're zombies . . .'

Kim laughed. 'Likers is a better word. I'll see you when you get back. And take the dog with you so I don't have to put up with him stinking the house out.'

❧

Dave raced into the station and called out to Jack.

'What's wrong?' Jack asked, appearing at the door.

'Nothing, but I've had an idea. We don't really know anything about that drone other than it's flying out over land and so on, do we?'

'That's right.' Jack reached over to a file and handed it to Dave. 'This is all the information I have.'

'Right, can you put a notice, or whatever it is you do, on that Facebook page and ask if anyone has bought a new drone and, if they have, to contact the station. And then can you get the rules that relate to drones regarding where and how they're allowed to fly and put that up there too? Can you do that?'

Jack nodded. 'Yeah, good idea. That's what this page is all about. Making people aware and asking for help when we need it.' He turned to the computer and tapped a few keys.

Dave watched as a screen came up declaring that the page was the Barker Police Community page.

'What do you want to say?' Jack asked, his fingers hovering over the keys.

Dave shrugged. 'Something like: *Have you bought a new drone lately? If so, please read these conditions of where you are able to fly them.* I don't know. What's going to get the most attention on Facebook?'

'How about . . .' Jack started to type. *Got a new toy? A new love of your life? Does it fly like a bird? Do you*

147

know the rules? If you have a new drone, come and see us at the station and we'll help you understand them.

'Whatever you reckon,' Dave said, reading over his shoulder. 'I know nothing about social media.'

'I know in Queensland the coppers use Facebook for lots of different things—issuing information on traffic congestion, call outs for witnesses, missing persons. Anything, really. They've got nearly a million followers.'

Dave laughed. 'I don't think our little Barker page will get to that extent, do you?'

'Nah, but the reach of that page is incredible.'

'Any news on Will today?' Dave asked.

Jack shook his head. 'Nothing from the footy club. On WhatsApp today, they said some of the fellas were going out to visit him later in the week to see if they could lend a hand with anything.'

'Has Zara come in this morning?'

Jack shook his head. 'No, and that's for the best, I think.'

'You can't blame her for trying. I'd imagine that an exciting story like drones casing out farms to steal things from would be a great distraction from what she's having to face.'

Jack looked over at Dave, the amazement clear on his face. 'And that's coming from a man who has a dislike of journalists and has always encouraged me to stay away from them.'

'Hey, I didn't say that I liked the idea, just said it would have to be a good distraction for her.' Dave stood up. 'Anyway, I'm going for a drive. Need to get some air. Might go back out and see what's happening at Rowberry Glen. Are there any responses on the Facebook page before I go?'

Jack refreshed the page. 'No. I wouldn't have expected there to be yet. I only put the post up a couple of minutes ago.'

Dave nodded and started to walk out as Jack's phone dinged. 'That your girlfriend?'

Jack turned to scowl at him. 'Bugger off,' he said as he looked at the screen. 'Oh, shit.'

'What?'

He read from his screen: *Will has contracted an infection and things aren't looking too good. We're on our way out to see him. Karl.*

Dave groaned. 'God, it makes me feel so helpless. A young man like that. And he was frightened when I was there yesterday, that much was clear. Sometimes the world sucks.'

'Got that right,' Jack said, still staring at the message. 'You know he's younger than me? Really puts things into perspective.'

'I'll text Kim and let her know.' Dave clapped Jack on the shoulder as he walked out. 'You'll be right, mate. Hang in there.'

Chapter 15

Zara opened the door to five men, all looking unusually sombre.

'Hi,' she said. She held open the door. 'Come in.'

'Hi, Zara,' Karl answered, walking in past her and leading the way down the hallway to the kitchen.

'Here to see Will?' She glanced at the other men as they filed past her. 'I know your faces but, I'm sorry, I don't remember your names.'

Karl nodded. 'We heard he'd got an infection; thought it was time to come out. You've got Jock, Ray, Ash and Charlie here.'

'Are you guys from the footy team? So nice you've come. I knew Mum had messaged you, Karl.'

'That's us.' There was a pause before Karl asked, 'So what's happening? Where's Lynda?'

'Just giving Will some meds so he can get up and talk to you, hopefully, although I wouldn't be sure he'll be able to come out. He woke up in the middle of last night with a raging temperature. We tried to get him to the hospital, but the doctor ended up coming out and giving him intra-venous antibiotics.' She paused. 'An infection when he's this sick isn't good.'

'No, I guess it's not.'

'Be back in a sec.' Zara slipped through the kitchen and down to Will's room. She saw her mum leaning over him with a glass of water and a straw.

'Hey,' she said quietly.

Lynda didn't turn. 'Hi,' she answered. 'Just getting some morphine and more antibiotics into Will. Then he should be able to get out to the lounge.'

Zara went around to the other side of the bed and sucked in a breath. Will had deteriorated even since last night. His eyes seemed more sunken and his face was ghostly pale and beads of sweat covered his forehead. She took a sponge and wiped it gently over his face. Her beautiful brother looked like a breathing corpse. *How did this happen so fast?*

'Do you want to get up, Will?' she asked. 'Maybe it's better if the boys come down here?'

'I want to get up,' he said. 'I'm not sure I can, though.'

'Does it hurt too?'

He nodded. 'Back and legs. And my head.'

Zara glanced at her mum. Head? Maybe, along with the infection, that was why he'd gone downhill so quickly. The cancer may have spread. They'd known this could happen.

'Will, honey,' Lynda said, squatting down to his eye level. 'Let's get the boys down here, yeah? You'll be much more comfortable and then you'll be able to enjoy their company more.'

Zara could see he wanted to argue. To get up. To not let this beat him. But he was tired and didn't have the energy.

'Okay,' he whispered.

Zara went back into the kitchen. 'Can you guys grab your chairs and go and sit with him in the bedroom? He's not up to getting out of bed.'

'Sure we can,' said the one Zara thought was Ash. 'Oh, and by the way, did you know there was a white station wagon parked next to your front gate? There were three people in it, but I didn't recognise them.'

Zara shook her head. 'I saw a station wagon out in the parking bay on my way out here. Thought they were tourists.'

Karl put his hand on Zara's arm. 'You okay? You're sounding tired.'

'I'm glad I came out last night. I wasn't going to. It's crazy! Yesterday Mum and I were pulling sheep out of a dam and now this has happened. Not even twenty-four hours later! He's so much worse than yesterday. I guess infections do that. And, yes, I am tired.'

Karl leaned forward and gave her a hug. 'You look like you could do with one of these.'

'So could Mum,' she said against his shoulder. It was nice to be hugged, even if it was just for a moment. 'You might get a bit of a shock when you see him,' she said as she pulled away. 'And I don't think you'll be able to stay for long.'

'Thanks for the warning. We'll make sure we don't,' Jock answered.

They filed off towards Will's bedroom and Lynda came out, tears in her eyes. 'He wants us to call the doctor.'

'Shit, really?'

'Yeah. He must feel awful. I know there's a morphine pump they can put in so he can self-administer. I don't know how it works but it's measured doses. I'll ring James and see if he can come out later. I don't know whether Will can have it with the infection or not.'

'Thank God he makes house calls. Surely at this point, it doesn't matter what medication he has, just so long as he's comfortable?'

Lynda nodded. 'James will get him comfortable. I've known him for years and he's been a huge support to us since we found out Will was palliative. I know you didn't meet him last night, when he was here, but you will soon.' She picked up the phone and dialled a number, which she clearly knew by heart. 'Hi,' she said softly and waited. 'Yeah. He's worse.' Pause. 'Pain in his back and legs. And tonight for the first time he mentioned his head.' Pause. 'Yep, did that.' Pause. 'I think so and his temperature is still high. I haven't been able to bring it down.' Pause. 'Tonight? Really?' Pause. 'Only if you really want to, James. I just thought we'd keep the pain relief up and let the antibiotics do their job.' Pause. 'Okay, well, whatever you think is best. See you soon.'

Pressing the button to disconnect the call, Lynda ran her hands through her hair and groaned. 'Shit, shit, shit! I hate this!'

Zara went and put her arms around her. 'I know, Mum.' She held her tightly for a moment, then asked, 'What's James going to do?'

'He thinks he should come out tonight and put in the pump. Reading between the lines, I think he wants to assess him and see what the deterioration is.'

There really wasn't anything to say to that.

'Do you want something to eat?'

Lynda shook her head. 'I think I want to go to bed and sleep for a week.'

'Why don't you do that? I'll stay with him tonight.'

'I need to wait until James comes.'

'Okay, and then you can take a sleeping tablet and go to bed. I'll be on call for him tonight.'

There was a noise behind them, and the boys were trooping back out again, chairs in hand. Zara was shocked to see tears on Karl's cheeks.

'We'd like to come back, Lynda,' he said to her as they placed their chairs at the kitchen table, 'but he doesn't want us to. We're hoping he's wrong. Maybe the antibiotics will get everything under control quickly but, just in case they don't, we said goodbye to him tonight.'

'Oh no.' Lynda's hand flew to her mouth.

Karl came forward and put his arms around her. 'More horrible than words can say.'

'But you need to know that anything you need, anything at all, just ring any of us whenever,' Ray said in a gruff voice. He brushed his hand roughly over his face.

Charlie went to hug Lynda, and Jock followed.

'Please make sure you call,' Jock said.

'There's probably nothing we need help with,' Zara said.

'Actually, there is,' Lynda said, wiping away more tears. 'Can someone run around the sheep for me this week? Doesn't need to be tomorrow . . .'

'I'll do it,' Ray said. 'I'll come tomorrow and then every second day from then on. Until . . .' He stopped. 'You don't need me any more.'

Lynda gulped. 'Thank you, Ray. Thank you.'

An uncomfortable silence filled the room, and the boys looked at the floor and then at each other.

'Guess we should get going,' Charlie said.

A set of headlights cut across the yard and flashed into the kitchen.

'That'll be James. He was quick,' Lynda said.

The footy club boys took that as their cue to leave and within minutes they had been replaced by a gentle, quiet man with glasses and a doctor's bag.

❧

It seemed like James was in with Will for hours, but when Zara looked at the clock she realised it was only one. Lynda was in with him while the procedure took place, and afterwards Will fell asleep peacefully.

'Are you going to have a cup of tea?' Lynda asked.

James shook his head. 'No, I'm going to give you a sleeping tablet and you're going to bed. The next few days are going to be tough.'

'Days?' The word slipped from Zara.

'Days,' James confirmed. 'He's breathless and he was a little confused tonight. He couldn't remember if his friends had been to see him today or yesterday. Of course all of that can be attributed to a high temperature, but is also quite common in the last stages. I'm so sorry but I believe that's where we are. His body isn't strong enough to fight the infection. The morphine will help with the breathing and the pain. I'd really like you to consider moving him to the hospital. The nurses there are wonderful and he would be comfortable.'

The two women looked at each other. 'I don't know, James,' Lynda said, then sounded decisive. 'No, at least not tonight. Let's see how he is in the morning.'

James seemed to know not to argue and pulled out a sheet of white tablets and gave them to Lynda. 'Take one tonight. Hopefully you'll sleep like a log and feel a bit better tomorrow.' He paused. 'Hearing is the last sense to leave us, so make sure you keep talking to him when you're with him. All the time. He'll be able to hear you and take comfort that you're with him.'

'Do you think he won't wake up again?' Zara asked in a panicked tone. It was all happening so much faster than anyone had anticipated.

'The infection and morphine will certainly make him sleepier than normal. He'll probably come in and out of consciousness. Any conversations you have may not make much sense, but he'll be comfortable.'

Lynda took the tablets and put them on the table. 'I'll walk you out,' she said.

Zara wasn't sure what the relationship between James and Lynda was, but there was a familiarity between them that went beyond that of doctor and patient. Or patient's mother. As a journalist, she'd learned to read people's body language well and it certainly looked like there was something going on between James and her mum. Zara frowned as they walked out into the dark together. Not that she didn't want her mum to find someone else. And she'd asked Lynda the question not twenty-four hours ago, but she hadn't answered.

Lynda had been alone for a couple of years and, with Will gone, she'd need companionship.

The urge to talk and giggle with Will about this new development hit her so strongly it took her breath away. She might never be able to do that with him again.

Zara went down into his room and pulled the lounge chair close to the bed, then sat down and took Will's hand in hers.

If he'd had hair, it would have been wet with sweat—his bald dome was shiny with moisture—she could see it glistening in the dim light from the lamp next to the bed. She looked around for a flannel, but couldn't see one.

Instead she settled for a couple of tissues and blotted the dampness away.

She tried to think of something to say but for once her mind was blank. And every time she started a conversation in her head it sounded stupid to say it out loud.

'Hey, Will, do you know anything about Mum and this doctor? I was watching them tonight and I reckon there's something going on between them. Do you know anything?'

There was no answer.

'He seems nice enough. It would be good for Mum to have a friend, wouldn't it?'

Silence.

'I don't know why she hasn't mentioned it before now. Maybe she was worried we'd get upset. I even asked her about wanting another friend last night, but she ignored me! I think it's great, don't you?' She paused. 'I mean, strange, but great. It sort of leaves a funny feeling in my stomach that she'd be with someone other than Dad, but she needs to move on with her life, doesn't she?'

From outside, Zara heard a car door slam and an engine start. Then lights were cutting through the darkness and making for town.

'Better change the subject, hey,' she whispered. She felt an inappropriate urge to giggle. 'It was nice the blokes from the footy club came and saw you tonight.'

Will moved a little and she felt his hand close around hers. She leaned forward. 'Hi, sleepyhead.'

'It feels good to sleep,' he whispered.

'If it feels good, I guess you should do it.'

'I gotta ask you something.' Will licked his lips and worked his mouth before speaking. 'I'm frightened. I don't have a choice about dying now, but I don't want to go without you or Mum here.'

'We won't leave you, Will. I promise. We won't leave you alone.'

He nodded. 'You want to know about Mum and James?'

Zara leaned forward. 'Hell yeah!'

Will tried to smile. 'I think it started when I had my first round of treatment a couple of years ago. They got to be friends because she was coming to the hospital when I was there, and they'd see each other regularly.'

'Why didn't you tell me? Has she ever said anything?'

Will shook his head. 'Not a word. And it wasn't my business to tell you. Not my news.'

'Ha! Isn't she a dark horse?'

'He's nice.'

'That's all that matters.'

'Who's a dark horse?' Lynda appeared at the doorway.

'You, apparently,' Zara answered, turning to look at her.

'Me? Why?'

'You and James.'

Lynda came into the room and sat on the edge of Will's bed. 'Me and James, what are you talking about?'

'You've got a boyfriend, Mum. It was clear as day out there.'

Lynda dropped her gaze. 'I have a friend,' she said.

'And we're both very pleased, aren't we, Will?'

Will nodded. 'I'm glad that something good has come out of me dying.'

'Will, what a thing to say!' Lynda gasped.

'It's true, though. You wouldn't have got to know James if it wasn't for me.'

Will closed his eyes, but he had a smile on his face.

Chapter 16

The laptop screen cast a soft glow over the bedroom. Will had been asleep for a couple of hours and Lynda for about the same time. Looking for something to take her mind off things and taking a sip of the tea she'd made, Zara flicked screens to see if there was anything happening at any of the troughs. Will had talked about seeing foxes at times he hadn't been able to sleep. Maybe the sheep would come in for a midnight drink.

She was trying to get her head around the news about her mum and James. She was pleased for them. Her mum had been on her own for a long time and was entitled to be happy. Even so, it felt like the final chapter had been closed on her dad. That left her sad and conflicted. It seemed to add to the grief she was feeling about Will. She was hurting, and she felt incredibly lonely. What she wouldn't do for some arms around her tonight. She remembered the feeling of Karl's hug and suddenly wanted to ring to ask him to come and sit with her. She wondered if Jack's hugs would be as good.

'Stop it,' she thought. 'You're just sad.'

Tiredly, she flicked through the different pictures, all grey and white, but there was nothing to see. Leaving the screen showing the front gate, she put the laptop down and got up to stretch. Walking down the hallway to get her blood flowing again, she glanced at the photos, then went outside. The dogs were lying on the front verandah and they each opened one eye to see who was there. Trixie thumped her tail on the ground at the sight of her.

Zara sat down on the steps and Shadow heaved himself up and came over to her, nosing in under her arm. 'Hello, you sook,' she said, patting his nose. 'What's happening out here tonight?'

She looked up at the clear night sky, thinking it was amazing that only a few hours earlier she couldn't have seen the bright sparkles for dust. The air was cold and clear and gave her a burst of energy. 'Come on,' she said to Boof. 'I think you should come inside with us. Will would probably like to have you there, too.'

As she stood up and started to walk back inside, she saw the glow of car lights on the horizon.

Strange. She watched as they slowed to a stop and stayed in one spot. A trickle of worry started through her.

Going back inside, she quickly went to the computer. A car was parked at the gate. And it was white. She looked at the time on the screen: 3.02 am. She grabbed a pen and scribbled down the numberplate details. Looked like a Victorian one. White with blue lettering. Realisation dawned that it looked like the station wagon from the parking bay. Who was it, and what did they want?

Without warning, the car backed out and drove away, leaving Zara wondering what the hell was going on.

❧

James called in early the next day, before he started work.

Zara was sitting at the kitchen table with her hands wrapped around a cup of coffee, feeling like her eyes were falling out of her head. Will had been settled most of the night but she hadn't wanted to fall asleep in case she didn't wake up when he needed her.

'Hello, Zara,' James said, putting his bag on the table. 'How was the night?'

'Long,' she answered tiredly. 'But both Mum and Will slept, so that was good.' She smiled at him. 'We talked about you last night.'

'Me? Now, why would you have done that?' The doctor looked a little flustered.

'Hmm, maybe because both Will and I have worked out you and Mum are friendly.'

'Ah.' He gave a small nod and Zara wasn't sure if that was confirming or acknowledging what she'd just said.

'We're glad, James. I don't know why Mum hasn't said anything, but both Will and I are happy for you both.' She kept to herself her feelings from last night—they didn't matter right now.

'That's very nice of you to say.' He looked a little relieved. 'Now, I best get on and see Will.'

'Mum's down there.'

James nodded and left the kitchen, smiling.

❧

Zara drove straight to the police station after James had left. Her mum was sitting with Will.

She didn't have time to say hello to Joan, only, 'Is Jack or Dave here?'

Jack appeared and seemed startled at her frazzled appearance. 'Jeez, Zara, are you okay? How's Will? He's not . . .'

'No, he's hanging on. Have you got a couple of minutes?'

'Sure, come through.'

He held the door open and led her to the interview room. Setting the laptop down, she opened up a file and showed Jack the image. 'This was taken at 3.02 am today,' she said. 'I also saw this car in a parking bay close to Rowberry Glen. You can see the numberplate.'

'And what was it doing to cause you concern?'

'Nothing really, other than being parked in odd areas at odd times. I just thought you should know, with reports of a drone being flown around. People who aren't local being out in the early hours is weird. You have to admit that it's pretty unusual for a car to drive back tracks in this country at that time of night, particularly with an interstate numberplate. I think it would raise concerns for more than a few people.'

Jack scrolled through the footage and wrote down the numberplate details. 'There's nothing illegal about any of that, just so long as they haven't driven onto your farm.'

'I know.' Zara felt her temper rising. The lack of sleep and her emotions were getting the better of her. 'Ash, one of Will's friends who visited last night, said it was parked near the front gate when they came in, but when I saw it, the vehicle looked like it was about to pull out of the parking bay. At first I thought they might've been lost, but then to turn up at the gate at that time of morning and stay there for a good ten or fifteen minutes . . . Well, I think that's bizarre.'

'I agree, it's certainly strange, but I can't investigate strange, Zara, and you know that.' His voice was gentle. 'Do you want me to come out and have a look around your place? Check that nothing's been stolen or anything?'

'They didn't come through the gate. I would've known and the other cameras around the place would have picked them up. Will tells me the one on the front gate is a motion camera, while all the others stream continuously. I don't think anyone has been on the farm. I just want to know what they're doing out there in the middle of the night. It's unsettling! Especially with everything else going on. I don't want any of us feeling unsafe.'

Jack tapped his fingers on the desk as he thought. 'Of course you don't, but there's also not much I can do other than make a note of it. If they haven't been on your place, they're not trespassing—'

'Jack,' Zara broke in. 'I'm not telling you this so you can charge someone. I'm just letting you know there is a vehicle around that isn't local and is doing weird things. Maybe you can just keep an eye out.'

'Can I keep this footage?'

'Only if you know how to download it. Because I don't and I haven't got a lot of time.'

'Okay. Zara, I wish there was something that I could do to help you through this.'

'There's not,' Zara answered shortly. 'There's nothing that anyone can do.'

Jack looked down. 'I'm really sorry.'

'Can't change it,' she said briskly, so the tears didn't start to fall.

'I'll just take this for a minute,' Jack said, standing and picking up the computer. 'I'll be as quick as I can.'

In the interview room Zara stared at nothing. The conversation she'd had with Will last night was going around and around in her head.

'I'm frightened . . . I don't want to go without you or Mum here.'

She could hear his voice, soft and whispery, feel the grasp of his hands on hers, and every word pierced her heart like a knife. *'I don't want to go . . .'*

Her brother was going to die. Not in months, as they'd told them. In days.

'Oh, Will,' she muttered, and the tears came hard and fast. This time she couldn't stop them. Laying her head on the table, she let them fall.

A hand touched her shoulder, but she didn't move. She heard a chair being dragged around next to her and a hand start to rub her back. The gentle, methodical, firm touch helped ground her. Bring her feelings back under control. Even though the tears continued to fall, they slowed. And slowed again, until they stopped. She left her head lying on the desk and her eyes shut.

After a while she opened her eyes and lifted her head, digging in her pocket for a tissue.

Jack moved away.

'Sorry about that,' she said, not looking at him. Embarrassment flooded through her.

'Don't be sorry,' Jack said. 'What you guys are going through is awful. No one should have to go through that. Especially with someone so young.'

'He doesn't want to die.'

'No one does.' He moved close again and patted her shoulder. 'When you are in this situation right now, you think it's never going to end. It's very hard to see past the moment you're in. But it does end. And there is life afterwards.'

'You lost someone?'

'My dad. When I was fifteen.'

'I lost my dad too.'

'I know,' he answered softly. 'Sometimes life really sucks.'

That made Zara smile. A handsome, burly policeman telling her life could suck.

'I'd better get back.'

Jack nodded. 'I've downloaded the footage and saved it to my hard drive. If I see the car around, I'll certainly have a chat with them. Now I've got the numberplate I'll be able to watch out.'

'Thanks, Jack. I just thought it was worth mentioning.'

'All information is good info, as Dave would say.'

Zara slapped her knees. 'Oh, can you tell Dave what's going on. I think Kim would want to know. And Mum might need a bit of support in the next little while.'

'Sure, although he was here yesterday when I found out from the footy club that things weren't good.' Jack hesitated and then said, 'I'll give you my number in case anything odd happens out there again. I don't want you having to worry about this on top of everything else.'

'That's really kind, Jack. Thanks.'

Jack smiled. 'I guess we got off on the wrong foot, didn't we? I don't like journos much. It's sort of ingrained in us as soon as we start training. And Dave has certainly instilled it in me, although he does always say, "Journos have their uses when we need to get information out there."'

'And you think we like you lot? You're hard to deal with when we want details for a story.'

'Then we've done our job,' Jack laughed. 'Friends?'

'Until the next story!'

'Sounds like a plan.'

Chapter 17

'What's happening?' Dave walked through the door of the station and found Jack staring at his computer. 'What've you got there?' He bent down to look at the screen.

'Zara Ellison brought it in earlier today.' He swung his chair around and looked at Dave. 'Will doesn't sound good, from all accounts.'

'I thought that might be the case when I saw him. Well, maybe it's not days, maybe a week or two. Infections hurry things up a lot.'

'Zara wanted Kim to know, in case her mum needed some support.'

'I'll text her again.'

'Anyway, this is what she brought in. Got three sightings of a white station wagon with Victorian numberplates.'

'And? It's not illegal for Victorians to be over here, is it?'

'Well, that's the problem. There's nothing concrete, but she saw them pulling out of a parking bay when she was on her way out there a couple of days ago, and the footy club boys said the car was parked right next to their front gate when they turned up to go and see Will.'

'Whose front gate?' Dave needed to be sure.

'At Rowberry Glen.'

'Go on.' He motioned with his hand for Jack to keep talking.

'Then it turned up in the same spot again at 3.02 am and stayed parked at the gate for about ten minutes. And, rightly, Zara's come in to let us know in case there's anything illegal going on.'

Dave looked at him out of the corner of his eye. 'Have you made a new friend?'

'Just think she's done the right thing here. Zara knows she's not going to get anything out of me for any of her stories unless I'm cleared to give information. We came to an understanding this morning.'

A half-smirk crossed Dave's face but quickly disappeared as a pen hit him.

'Anyway, what I was thinking was, perhaps if we see this vehicle we can pull them over and have a chat. See what they're doing here and so on. If we don't see it, maybe they've just moved on.'

'Have you run the plates?'

'Not yet. Thought I'd see what your thoughts were.'

'Won't hurt to run the plates, or have a chat if we see the car around.'

Dave went to his desk and sat down, opening his emails. 'Has there been anything come back on the Facebook page about the drone?'

'Not that I've seen. I did notice that Zara liked the post, which means she'd get a notification if anyone commented on it. Always the journo, even with everything going on.'

'Like I said to you before—distraction.'

'Don't forget to tell Kim.'

Dave rolled his eyes. 'Do you think I would?'

'More than likely if you get caught up in answering emails.'

'Jeez!' Dave took out his phone and sent Kim a text, then turned his attention to his emails.

The one from Steve, his boss, caught his attention.

Can you spare Jack for a couple of weeks?

Odd request, Dave thought, glancing over at Jack.

What for?

It would probably be a little while before he heard anything back from Steve, so he started working through the rest of the emails, responding or deleting as required.

'I'm going out,' Jack said after a while. 'Might have a squiz around for that car. It's not like there's anything else happening at the moment.'

'Roger that. Call me if you find it and I'll come out.'

'Righto.'

With Jack gone, Dave picked up the phone and dialled Steve's number.

'Dave,' Steve answered. 'How are things in Barker?'

'Busy, as always. The latest is reports of a drone flying over people's farms.'

'Drones! That does sound intriguing. You blokes always seem to get all sorts of things happening up there. Us here in the city, we get the drunks, druggies and murderers.'

'They could end up being interesting too. Now, tell me, what do you want Jack for?'

'I've got a little undercover job for him.'

Dave sat up. He knew what it was like to go undercover and there never anything 'little' about it. 'Like what?'

'We've got some inside information that a group called Voices for Animals is becoming more active. They're supposedly a peaceful group, but from our information it seems they mightn't stay peaceful for long. I think they're planning something big. I'd really like to get someone on the inside who might be able to tell me where they're going to hit next, just so we can be there and get control of the situation before it gets out of hand.

'There've been some nasty protests recently. I'm getting a bit of heat from higher up to shut them down before they start. Farmers are getting mad, the activists are angry, and it's a boiling pot of emotions that could end in disaster unless we keep on top of it. I don't have anyone on the inside. It just what we've gleaned from watching and more watching. That's why I want Jack.'

'So no intel, just pressure?'

'That's right.'

Dave ran his fingers through his hair and shut his eyes. 'Let me get this clear—you're wanting Jack on the inside of a group called Voices for Animals, even though you have no firm intel that there is any illegal action planned, only information from the coppers you've got watching the group? And that's it?' He rubbed his hand over his hair a few times, not sure how he was feeling about this. His spell undercover had been a long time ago, but he remembered it very clearly. After all, it wasn't every day he got shot in the shoulder.

'In a nutshell. Look, we've done a little investigation into this group and we feel there is something else to them. Something more sinister. There's a subsidiary that is much more extremist. Again, we've got nothing to base this on, except what we're seeing. They've just shown up in South Australia, been mostly making a nuisance of themselves in Victoria and New South Wales. Going onto farms, filming animals illegally, that sort of thing, then posting it online. They're creating fear within the farming communities.'

Victoria? There was a car in his area with Victorian numberplates. Filming animals? Drones in Barker. A few little pieces fell into place for Dave.

'So why do you want Jack?'

'Because you've taught him. You understand farmers and you've taught him to do the same. He knows what goes on in the agricultural community, so he'll be able to talk the language. You've been undercover so you'll be able to guide him.'

'Sure, for the farmers he can, but I'm not sure about the protesters.'

'That'll be his way in with the protesters,' Steve said. 'He'll be able to convince them he can get them onto farms, because he knows the language of the agricultural industry.'

Dave was quiet. 'When do you want him?'

'Sooner rather than later. Get him to grow his hair and look like a hippie.'

Dave laughed. 'I'll see if I can convince him to get a nose ring.'

'Plenty of them do.' Steve sounded serious.

'As do plenty of people who aren't activists. All right, send me some details and leave it with me. If he says no, I'll back him up, though, Steve.'

'That's fine.'

Dave put the phone down, pondering what he'd just heard. His phone buzzed.

Speak of the devil.

'What's up, Jack?'

'Got the car. I saw them driving down the main street and watched them as they pulled in at Kim's roadhouse, where she's put in these new bowsers. Now they're refuelling.'

'Okay. What I need you to do is come back here. I'll go and pick them up.' Dave got up and started walking out of the office to his car.

'What? I'll grab them. I'm right here.'

'Jack, listen to me. I need you to come back here. I've just got off the phone from Steve and there's something much bigger at play here. Come back to the station now.'

'Right. Do you want me to stay here and follow them in case you don't get here in time?'

'I'm getting in my car now. Come back here.'

'Right.'

'Can you run the plates?'

'Already done it. The car's registered to a Lee Jones from Victoria. No priors. No parking tickets. He's clean.'

'Okay. Is there anyone else in the car?'

'One woman, one male. Both still in the car, so I can't see their height or features.'

'When I bring them in, I need you to stay out of the way. I'll tell you why when I get back.'

'I'm pissed off.'

'I know you are, but trust me.'

Dave pulled up in his unmarked four-wheel drive and watched as a long-haired man went in and paid for the fuel. He was wearing a dirty T-shirt and ripped jeans. Just as Jack had said, there were two others in the car—a young woman in the front and a young man in the back. Dave guessed they were in their twenties.

The car pulled out, using the blinker correctly, and headed down the main street and out of town. Towards Rowberry Glen.

'There's an interesting coincidence,' Dave muttered. He picked up the radio and called Jack. 'Where were the sightings of the drone again? The south side of town?'

'No. Out the other.'

'Hmm, maybe it's the east side of town's turn now.'

Dave let them get down the road a little way before flicking on the sirens. The brake lights went on immediately and they pulled off the road and parked.

'G'day,' Dave said as the driver wound down the window and offered him his licence. 'Ah, done this before, have you?'

'No, never, but that's what they do in the movies, isn't it?'

The boy sounded young and innocent. He didn't look it.

'You're Lee Jones?' Dave asked as he looked at the licence.

'Yeah.'

'You're a long way from home. You two others from Victoria as well?'

They all nodded. Dave got out the radio and called Jack again. 'Can I have a licence check on one Mr Lee Michael Jones. DL number . . .' He read out the number and waited for a response.

'Do you want our licences too?' the girl asked.

'Not yet,' Dave answered. 'Do you know why I pulled you over?'

Lee shook his head.

'You ran over the white line. Could there be a reason you did that?'

'What? No. If you mean have I been drinking, no, not a drop!'

'Licence is clean,' Jack called back on the radio.

'Roger that.' Dave turned his attention to Lee. 'Then you won't mind if we breathalyse you?' He pulled out the yellow breatho and attached the plastic tube. 'Just blow in here until I say stop.'

Wide-eyed, Lee took a breath and blew.

'That's fine, thanks.'

Lee didn't register a blood alcohol reading.

'I'll just get you all to hop out of the car, thanks. I'm conducting random searches, looking for illegal substances.'

The three scrambled out and stood where Dave directed them.

He pulled on some gloves and then opened the glove box. He flicked through the numerous pens, notepads, chewing gum and Panadol boxes, but didn't see anything out of the ordinary. He lifted the centre console, but that was empty save for a few loose coins.

Then he saw a plastic bag corner sticking out from under the coins. He pulled it out.

Marijuana. Not much, but enough for him to have an excuse to impound the car and search it thoroughly.

He left it on the front seat, peered towards the back seat and noted there was a silver laptop in the middle, then went to the back and opened the boot. Sitting there in plain sight was a drone. Dave didn't know much about drones, but it looked pretty flash. He took a photo of it with his phone and texted it to Jack. *Jackpot! Can you get me info on this?*

He slipped the phone back into his pocket and picked up the machine, before holding it up to show all three. 'Anyone tell me why you've got a drone in the back of the car?'

They all looked at the ground.

A car coming from town flicked the blinker on and crossed to the other side of the road so it could pass safely. Dave glanced over and realised it was Zara. She must be heading home.

She looked over as she passed, but he didn't acknowledge her. He figured if she didn't have too much on her plate when she got home, he'd probably get a phone call. Curiosity would get the better of her.

'Come on, guys. You can't all be mute.' He looked over at the girl. 'What's your name?'

'Sophie. Sophie Grawd.'

'Well, Sophie, can you tell me what's going on here?'

'We weren't doing anything wrong.'

'I'll be the judge of that, if you don't mind. And you,' he turned to the other young lad, 'who are you?'

'Terry Wright.'

'Well, since I've not only found a drone, Lee, Sophie and Terry, but I've also found some cannabis, I'm going to have to impound your car for an examination. It may take a couple of days. Looks like you're going to be stuck here for a little while.

'I'm going to secure your vehicle and get someone to come and pick it up while I take you back to the station for a formal interview.'

Chapter 18

Dave ushered all three into separate interview rooms and left them sitting there while he went and found Jack.

'What have you got for me?' Dave asked.

'The drone's a DJI Mavic 2 Zoom,' he answered, his pen hitting each point written on his notepad as he spoke. 'It can fly up to eight kilometres away from the person controlling it and it has a flying time of thirty-one minutes.'

'How fast does it fly?'

'If the conditions are right—no wind and that sort of thing—it can go up to seventy-two kilometres per hour. It's a zippy little machine. And it doesn't make a lot of noise. They've worked hard on reducing the engine noise. Perfect for getting across farms without being heard. Being seen is a different matter.'

Dave scratched his head. 'So, I know I'm not that tech savvy, but don't they take photos? I can see a camera at the front here. Where do the pictures end up?'

'Downloaded onto a laptop somewhere, I'd assume. Did you find a laptop?'

'Yeah, there was one on the back seat.'

'My guess is that the images would be on that.'

'And is the camera a good one?'

'Yep, got the ability to zoom, as well as a wide-angle shot, and it adjusts its focus while it's flying. It'll have some good footage, I'd imagine. And they could've taken stills as well as video.'

'Right.' Dave had made some notes of his own and was now looking back over them. 'And the cost?'

'No change out of two and half g.'

'You'd wonder how these kids would be able to afford that, wouldn't you?'

Jack shrugged. 'Rich parents. Who knows? Maybe they've got jobs, but they look like students to me.'

'Well, they're in that age range, for sure.'

'Maybe they're not students, maybe they've got good jobs.'

'We won't know until we question them. Listen, the reason I pulled you out today was because Steve wants you to go undercover in an activist group. If these guys are doing what I think they're doing, then we can't take the chance they'll see your face. If you agree to take the job, that is.'

'What the hell does he want *me* for?'

'Because you can speak the farming language. All he wants you to do is feed info back as to where the next protest is going to be, so they can have numbers there to contain it. There's been some problems over east with the rallies getting out of hand.'

'And how the hell—'

Dave shook his head. 'That's all I know at the moment. Have a think about it and get back to me. But for the moment, stay out of the sight of these three, okay?'

Jack nodded. 'Do you want me to do a little research on them all?'

'There's nothing on the system?'

'They're all clean and they gave you their real names. I've checked all of the DLs.'

'Good job,' Dave said and dangled a set of keys in front of him. 'Go and pick up their car. Joan can run you out there.'

❧

Dave chose to talk to Lee first. After all, it was his car.

Lee was sitting at the table, his hands clasped in front of him.

'Do you need a coffee or anything?' Dave asked.

Lee shook his head.

'How long have you been up in Barker?' Dave asked, pulling out the chair and sitting opposite him.

'About two weeks.'

'And where are you staying?'

'In the chalets at the caravan park.'

'Ah, out with Mrs Jenkins. She's a good sort. And as far as I've heard, the rooms there are comfortable.'

'Yeah, they're not too bad. They fit our budget.'

'Bit short of coin?'

'We're students, so of course we are.'

'What are you studying?'

'Sophie and I are studying environmental science and Terry is doing law.'

'Highbrow careers. Good on you all.'

'We can do a lot of good by studying these subjects.'

Dave leaned back and looked at Lee. 'Good?'

'We need to know how to look after this planet and environmental science teaches us that. And law—well, there're always people needing help there, whether it's the new animal rights law or public interest. We've all got a concern with public interest. Making sure society knows what is going on behind closed doors.' Lee leaned forward as he spoke, the passion in his voice clear.

'That's an interesting comment, "Making sure society knows what's going on behind closed doors." Can you tell me what you mean by that?'

'Take farming,' Lee said. 'As people who don't farm, we have no idea what goes on beyond the boundaries of the fences. And I think we have a right to know. We feel it's our job to find out.'

Dave blinked. 'Wow. That's intense. But admirable.' He frowned and took a deep breath. His tone was curious. 'Tell me what you've been doing with the drone then.'

'Can I have my laptop? I can show you that way.'

'Sure.' Dave went to grab it, cheering up inside. He wouldn't have to get a warrant. It all seemed a little too easy, the way Lee was spilling his guts. But the kid was passionate about what he was doing and, when people were passionate, they often talked more easily, wanting to persuade others to their viewpoint.

'How's it going?' Jack asked when he went into the office.

'Singing like a canary. Where's the laptop?'

'Put it on your desk.'

'Have you had a chance to google any of them?'

'Not yet, just back from picking up the vehicle. I'm starting now.'

'I don't know how you'd do it, but can you find out if any of them are members of activist groups?'

'Onto it now.'

Dave went back into the interview room and put the laptop on the desk. Lee opened it and plugged in a password. Making some swift movements on the mouse pad, he brought up a short video.

Not able to tell where it had been taken, Dave watched as the drone flew over troughs, swooping down to capture the water level. It flew over mobs of sheep, after the farmer had been out trail feeding. It was clear they were gathering information on stock to make sure they weren't being underfed and had access to water. All of the stock looked healthy from what Dave could see.

And, most importantly, there weren't any people in the frames.

'What information are you getting here?' He wanted to be sure.

'We've been hearing reports of the area being affected by drought, so we want to make sure that all the animals are being looked after properly. Actually, we had a report that someone round here wasn't looking after his animals, so we came to check that out and decided to look at other farms while we were here.'

Dave crossed his arms. 'A report? From whom?' As he asked the question, he remembered Will's cryptic comment. *'I'm not sure, but I may have had something to do with them being here.'*

'I don't know who made the actual report, but we were told to look at farms in the area. One out on Golddine Road and the other on the highway into town. We've done both.'

'And what did you see?'

'The animals were in poor condition. We sent the images back to the people in charge and they'll decide what to do.'

Golddine was the road out to Rowberry Glen. Okay, so there was a bit more to this than Dave had thought. Who would've made the report to an activists' group rather than the RSPCA or the Department of Agriculture? Surely not Will. He wondered if he'd ever get to ask him now.

'Can you give me the name of the people you deal with?'

Lee looked sheepish. 'I actually don't know. I just get told where I need to go and I send the pictures back.'

Dave nodded. 'Thanks for being so honest with me. I'm going to have a quick chat to the other two and come back to you.' He got up to head out the door but stopped with his hand on the doorknob. 'Just one more thing. If you guys are students—and trust me, I've been there, so I know there's hardly any money even to buy a beer—how did you buy the drone?'

'It was supplied.'

'Who by?'

'Voices for Animals.'

Dave nodded and left the room. *Seems Steve was on the money.* Voices for Animals had started to turn up in places other than Victoria.

'Anything interesting?' he asked Jack, who was glued to the computer screen.

'All three are members of Voices for Animals. See, they're listed here on their website.' He pointed to Sophie's name first. 'Grawd, Sophie. Jones, Lee.' He slid his finger down the screen until he found Terry's name.

'Now, the interesting thing is that Sophie's dad was killed while protesting against forestry. A front-end loader fell on him and severed an artery in his leg. Sophie was reportedly very angry that he'd been killed while protesting, so I'm interested in knowing why she's gravitated that way. Here's a story from the *Farming Telegraph*, written by none other than Zara Ellison.' He handed over a print-out of the story.

Gerard Hooper was today found guilty of the man-slaughter of Colin Grawd. Mr Grawd was killed while trespassing and attempting to disable a front-end loader so it was unable to be used in logging.

Evidence was given that Grawd was under the bucket when it fell on him, pinning him to the ground and severing an artery, causing him to bleed to death at the scene.

It was stated that Gerard Hooper had been disabling the machine at the time in question; however, the *Farming Telegraph* has received information indicating Hooper might not have been responsible for the bucket falling and that it's believed there was another person involved.

Hooper continues to deny this.

Both men were members of Voices for Animals and had taken part in a small, peaceful protest prior to the accident. A spokesman for the group said it defied belief that the government would allow logging to take place in a pristine area that is the habitat of a diverse range of animals.

In a statement by his lawyer it was made clear Hooper would continue to fight for his innocence: 'Of course we'll appeal. Gerard Hooper is innocent of the manslaughter of Colin Grawd. They were friends and colleagues. In a democracy, everyone has a right to voice their opinion, so the trespassing charge is ridiculous. We intend to fight this.'

Colin Grawd's daughter, Sophie, made an emotional statement in response to Hooper's lawyer: 'The fact remains that I come home every day to a house that my dad isn't in anymore, so my mum gets into an empty bed every night. I don't care how or why or what happened that night. All I know is that Gerard was in the driver's seat when that bucket dropped on my dad, and now my dad's not here. He's in the ground.'

'She sounds like an angry young woman,' Dave commented. 'I'd better have a chat with her before I let them go. Now, Lee has just told me about an interesting development. Allegedly there was a report made to VFA about two properties with stock in poor condition. They were sent up to take footage—that's the whole reason they're here.' He went on to tell Jack as much as he knew. 'We'll have to find some way of verifying that. Can I leave that with you?'

'Sure. I'll get on it.'

Dave let himself into the interview room where Sophie was pacing the floor. 'Sorry to leave you so long, Sophie. Just got through a long chat with Lee.'

She smiled and sat down. 'That's okay.'

Not the response Dave was expecting.

'You don't seem to mind that you're here,' he observed.

Sophie shook her head. 'Not at all. We haven't broken any laws and we're very open about what we're doing, so we're never not going to answer your questions. The more people we speak to, the more awareness we raise.'

'So, Sophie, the question I have for you is, why are you involved with this group when it seems clear you blame them for your dad's death?'

'It's not the group I'm angry with. It's Gerard Hooper. Dad died standing up for something he believed in and so it's my job to keep his legacy going. I know Dad died during a logging protest, but he loved animals. That's what he was fighting for, the fact that animals would lose their homes if the forest was destroyed. I love animals too, that's why I joined Voices for Animals after Dad died. We're a peaceful protesting unit.'

Dave nodded. That made sense. 'Okay, you're free to go, but I want a talk with you all before you leave.'

Gathering the three together, Dave spoke severely to them. 'I can't charge you with anything. The dope—well, you're lucky there isn't enough there for me to charge you, and even if there was, it'd only result in a slap on the wrist. From what I've seen, you haven't done anything illegal. Firstly, because you're operating the drone from outside the farm boundaries, and secondly, you haven't filmed any people.

'What I need you to understand is that you are treading on very shaky ground. What you are doing is an invasion of people's privacy. I am telling you with as much force as I can that you must adhere to all the rules and regulations stated by CASA when operating that drone. If I hear so much as a whisper that you are breaking any of those laws, I will come down on you all like a ton of bricks.

'And I can't guarantee that any of the farmers around here will be as generous if they find you anywhere near their places. My suggestion is to get the hell out of town and go back to where you came from.' He paused for emphasis. 'All right?'

The three of them looked at one another and nodded.

'Good. Get out of here then.'

Chapter 19

Zara had wanted to turn her car around when she'd driven past Dave on the side of the road with the station wagon she'd seen near Rowberry Glen yesterday. But she couldn't. She needed to get back out to Will as quickly as she could.

She had smiled, thinking how quickly Jack had got to work.

Her smile had faded as she'd noticed the blonde girl standing alongside two men. She'd recognised her immediately. Sophie Grawd.

The journalist in her had badly wanted to turn around to find out what was going on, but the sister in her had needed to go home.

She'd made a promise to Will and she intended to keep it.

Bumping down the driveway, she registered that James's car was out the front of the house. She frowned, hoping that didn't mean bad news already. She wanted—no, needed—more time with her brother!

She parked the car and sat looking at her phone. How could she find Sophie's contact details? She hit the LinkedIn app on her phone and put in Sophie's name.

She was the first Sophie Grawd on the list.

She was listed as a student from Victoria, with a keen interest in raising awareness about unethical treatment of animals.

Zara couldn't believe her luck when she saw contact details listed. 'You little ripper,' she said, taking a screen shot and then tucking the phone in her bag.

Inside the house she found James and Lynda sitting at the kitchen table, holding hands. Her mum was crying.

'Oh no,' she said. 'No.'

James stood up. 'It's okay, Zara, he's still with us. But I do want to talk to you about Will's care from now on in.' His expression was sad and regretful, and Zara began to have an inkling of what he might say.

'I don't think Will'll regain consciousness. The medication he needs to suppress the pain will stop him from waking up, and the fever hasn't broken. The meds are keeping him comfortable and that's our priority now. Look, I know you've made a promise to him that he's able to die at home, but I think you should reconsider taking him into the hospital so we can care for him there. The nurses are skilled at palliative care and he'll be well looked after.'

'No,' Lynda said emphatically. 'We've talked about this, haven't we, Zara?' She looked towards her daughter for support. 'Both of us promised Will two things. One, that he would be able to die at home; and two, we wouldn't leave him alone. That's what's best for him and for us.'

'Yeah,' Zara chimed in. 'We've got to keep him here, James. Surely you understand?'

'I do, but I also know how tough it's going to be for you both and I wish I could change your mind. You both need to rest; at least, have some sort of respite. This may go on for days.'

Zara remembered something Lachy had said to her earlier. 'James, this isn't about us right now. It's about Will. He wanted to be here with us, and we'll have to make it work. And if it's days, then it's only a short time, isn't it?'

James held up his hands in defeat. 'Okay, okay. I'll be here as much as I can. And I can get a palliative care nurse to visit once a day, but you must try to get as much rest as you can, and make sure you eat and drink, even if you don't feel like it. There is no point in becoming ill yourselves. Will wouldn't want that either.'

Lynda nodded. 'We'll be fine, James, and knowing you're here is a really big comfort to us.'

'Absolutely,' agreed Zara.

James got up and kissed Lynda's head as he picked up his bag. 'I'll be back as soon as I can,' he promised.

～

The house was silent and the steady tick, tick of the clock in the spare room was beginning to annoy Zara. The afternoon sunlight trickled through a gap in the curtains and, when she opened her eyes, she could see the minute dust particles floating through the air. Her body ached for sleep, but every time she rolled over she found another reason to stay awake: listening for Will's call; the bed was lumpy; her mind wouldn't calm. It was frustrating, especially since she knew she'd have to take over from her mum in a few hours. Finally, she gave up and threw the covers off. Maybe a walk would make her feel better.

As she stepped onto the verandah and felt the heat hit her skin, she noticed dust coming up the drive. The dogs started to bark and ran out onto the road, their tails and hackles up.

'Sit down,' she growled, wondering who on earth would be bothering them right now. Surely people could just piss off and leave them with their grief. Then she recognised Kim's car.

'Hello, sweetie,' Kim said quietly as she got out. 'I hope I'm not intruding. I've brought more food. I'm sure you don't feel like eating, but you're going to need to. It's just easy stuff: chicken soup and some fresh rolls.'

'That's lovely, Kim, thanks. But you're right, we really don't feel like eating.'

'I've got no doubt. But it'll be here if you want it. Shall I just put it inside?'

She nodded. 'I've got to get out of the house for a while, so I'm going for a walk. Mum's in with Will, but it would be better if you didn't go down there.'

'Absolutely. Just ring if you need anything, okay?'

'We will.'

Zara left Kim to her own devices and started a brisk walk towards the shearing shed. Passing the chook pen, which had five chooks in it, Zara wondered when they'd last been fed. Maybe her mum had done it when she hadn't been here. Quickly she ducked in to check and saw the water trough was down slightly. Grabbing the hose, she turned the tap on and filled it up, before checking the layers' pellets and nesting boxes for eggs. There were none to be collected, so she shut the gate firmly behind her and kept walking.

She looked around and saw the dogs were following her; all three had their tails up in the air and looked happy to be going somewhere other than the house. 'I thought dogs knew when their owners were dying,' she said to them. 'You don't look like you do.'

Trixie broke into a run and danced around her feet as Zara walked up the steps into the shed. It had been a while since she'd been in here. The roof creaked as a gentle breeze ran through the openings and a chain hit the wooden pens with a thud.

She couldn't keep her mind off Will. What was he feeling now? Could he even feel anything? Was he still frightened; did he know that he didn't have long? Or was there just the blessing of a long, fuzzy darkness? The bliss of heavy sleep that gave him the ability to feel and know nothing?

There was an open bale of wool sitting in the wool bins, and fleeces on the floor next to it. She wondered why it hadn't been pressed properly. Sinking down, she ran her fingers deep into the wool and smelled the lanoline on them. In the quietness she closed her eyes and listened to the sounds of the wind and the rustling trees outside. Trixie flopped down next to her with a sigh, and Boof and Shadow walked around the board. She could hear the click of their claws on the wood.

Trixie put her head on Zara's chest and inched her nose along until it touched her chin.

'You dag,' she said, patting her head. 'Anyone would think you were a sook.'

Trixie sighed contentedly and shut her eyes.

It was late afternoon when Zara woke up. The dogs had gone and there was a rug over her. Someone had found her asleep in the wool. She'd been oblivious!

Her mind flew to Will, and she threw off the blanket and stood up quickly.

Next to her, the phone buzzed and Zara realised that was what had woken her. Grabbing it, she answered without looking at the screen.

'It's Jack.'

'Jack? Really?' She couldn't hide the surprise in her voice.

'I know. I know. But we did say we had a friendship until the next story . . .' He hesitated before asking, 'How are things out there?'

'The same, really. The doctor tried to get us to take Will into the hospital, but we won't do it. It's not right, since we promised him that he would stay at home.'

'Big ask.'

'It's what he wanted,' she answered simply.

'You're probably wondering why I'm ringing. Are you up for a chat? Or would you rather I left it for a while?'

'I'm a little curious. And I could do with a distraction. But let me check on Will first and I'll call you back. Is that okay?'

'Sure thing.'

Tucking her phone into her jeans, she jogged back to the house and found her mum sitting in the chair next to Will's bed. She'd opened the curtains and the setting sun was casting an orange glow across the room, falling on Will's face. He looked peaceful.

'Sleep okay?' Lynda asked when she saw her. 'You looked like you needed it.'

'You do too. Can I get you anything?'

Lynda shook her head.

'I'll be back in a sec.' Zara left the room and went to ring Jack. 'I'm back,' she said when he answered.

'Okay?'

'No change. So what did you want to chat about? I'm guessing that Dave has been busy.'

'Well, I can't comment on that. But what I can tell you is that we found the drone. I don't think it'll be a bother again.'

'That's great! What were they looking for?' she asked without thinking.

'I can't answer that either.'

'Right, so why are you ringing?'

Zara heard the smile in Jack's voice when he admitted, 'I wanted to see how you were going.'

'That's nice of you, thanks. I didn't mean to cry all over you today. Sorry about that.'

'It wasn't a problem.'

Zara stretched. 'Can I ask you something?'

'I don't promise to answer.'

Zara let out an exasperated breath. 'What you need to understand about me, Jack, is I'm a journo not a reporter. I find out the facts and I don't sensationalise things. I'm not going to hang you out to dry if you give me a snippet of information!'

'I'm not in the habit of doing that, but ask away. If I can answer, I will.'

Zara thought about that. 'Was Sophie Grawd in the car you pulled over today?'

There was a silence.

'I recognised her from the court case.'

'Then I guess you'd know her if you ran into her in the caravan park or the street, wouldn't you? And you'd probably be able to find out that she's an active member of Voices for Animals.'

Zara laughed. 'I guess I would. Thanks, Jack.'

The next twenty-four hours passed in a haze of grief, tiredness and doctors. Zara's phone call with Jack had been forgotten by the next day, with the care of Will overtaking everything. It was nearly dark when Zara heated up some of Kim's chicken soup and took it in to her mum. 'Here, I know you don't feel like it, but it's yummy.'

Lynda took the bowl and inhaled the steam rising up from the soup. 'Smells delicious.'

'Are you okay here for a little longer? I need to make a phone call.'

'Sure. I'm not going anywhere.' She looked over at Will, whose breathing had begun to be more erratic as time had gone on. The increased doses of morphine were making his eyes roll back in his head, and at one stage all Zara had been able to see were the whites of his eyes. It had unnerved her so much that she'd burst into tears. Her mum had followed and they'd spent a few moments holding each other and weeping, before they composed themselves and continued as they had been.

With another glance at Will, Zara crept out of the room and down into the kitchen. There were footsteps on the verandah and James came in.

'Do you want some soup?' she asked by way of greeting.

'I had tea before I came out, thanks anyway. Lynda down with Will?'

'She's nowhere else now,' Zara answered.

'I'll pop down.'

Nodding, she picked up her phone and saw Lachy had texted. *Thinking of you,* was all it said.

That reminded her of the screen shot she'd taken of Sophie's phone number and email address. Should she call? Did she even feel like it? Before she could contemplate it too much, she dialled the number and listened to it ring.

'Sophie speaking.'

'Hi, Sophie. It's Zara Ellison calling. I'm not sure if you remember me.' Somehow her professional self kicked in.

'You're the reporter I spoke to in the courtroom.' Her voice was flat. 'I remember.'

'That's right. How are you?'

'Fine. I'm not commenting on Dad's death. I told you that then, and I'm telling you again now. It's not something I want to talk about.'

'Sophie, I understand that, more than you'd know at the moment.' She paused, wondering how to start. 'I live in Barker now, and there have been reports of a drone being flown over farms. I just happened to drive past when you and your friends were pulled over by the police, and I've put two and two together. I also know from your LinkedIn profile that you're an active member of Voices for Animals. I wondered if I could talk to you about what your objective is? As a journalist, I like to get the facts from all sides of a story so I can report fairly.'

'What would you like to know?'

'What are you trying to achieve? What is your main objective?'

'The main objective is for people to understand what goes on behind the farm gate. We're putting the drone up in drought-affected areas to make sure the stock are being fed properly, that they have water and aren't sick or weak. As an environmental scientist, I also have an interest in how the land is looking throughout the drought, but primarily we just want to know that the animals are okay.'

'That's a great objective. And you do this with the use of a drone?'

'We're not breaking any laws. It's legal for us to stand on the road and put it up. If we're on the public road verge, we're still able to fly it over private property. And we also make sure we don't get any people in the footage.'

'So you don't feel as if that's trespassing in a different way?'

'Not if it's for the betterment of animals' lives.'

'Okay. Look, I'd like to write a really balanced story about this. Would I be able to contact you again for comment?'

'Any time.'

Zara put down the phone and smiled. Contact made and a distraction had.

Chapter 20

I hate the sound of that wind, thought Zara as she sat alone at the kitchen table clasping a lukewarm cup of coffee in her palms. *It feels like it's here to pick up Will's spirit and take him away.*

Her mum didn't want to leave Will's side tonight. Four days on from when Will had first come down with the infection, James had indicated it could be any time from now on. Lynda was dozing in a chair next to his bed. Zara had let Trixie in for company and the dog was sleeping under the kitchen table.

The wind had picked up since dark, which was strange because normally it dropped at night. But now it droned on, incessant in its drive to go nowhere in particular. Sometimes it tossed the leaves of the gum tree against the tin roof, making Zara jump every time. In between that, the kitchen was quiet, the only noise being the ticking of the old clock

Zara had given her mum for Christmas when she was eight. It sounded like the beat of Will's heart. But maybe it was too strong for that. The staccato beat reminded her that her brother's life was slipping away with every tick.

More than forty-eight hours had passed since he'd last spoken to them and they had come to the realisation they would never hear his voice again. That had brought a fresh round of tears. It made Zara want to ring him and hear his cheery voice on the message bank, but she was afraid she would break down altogether if she did that.

It was 2.33 am. The witching hour. She thought of a quote she'd read recently: 'Three am is the hour of writers, painters, poets, musicians, silence seekers and creative people.' At the time she'd thought that was beautiful. *But it's also the time people are waiting for loved ones to die,'* she thought.

Tick, tock, tick, tock. . .

'Oh, shut up!' She grabbed a chair and dragged it to the wall. She climbed up and took out the clock battery, throwing it on the floor. At once the kitchen was still. 'Thank fuck for that.'

Zara boiled the kettle and made two fresh mugs of steaming tea. In the bedroom the glow from the dim nightlight gave Will's shrunken face a ghoulish appearance. The cancer was eating him alive and there was nothing anyone could do. His handsome features had melted away down to the thin layer of pale skin now stretched taut across his bony face.

Putting down the drinks on the bedside table in among the bottles of pills and tissues, she gazed down at her brother. Perhaps it was time he let go. There was no coming back from here. She picked up his hand and held it close to her heart. 'It's time, Will,' she whispered. 'You don't need to stay any longer. I love you.'

Lynda was asleep in one of the comfortable lounge chairs. She was slumped forward, her face resting on the doona cover and her hand clasping the withered hand of her son.

'Mum, Mum,' Zara whispered as she gently shook her mother.

Lynda's eyes flickered before focusing. 'What time is it? Will?' She sat up in alarm, her voice croaky from sleep.

'He's still with us, Mum. Here, I've made you a tea.'

'Oh, thanks, love. Have you slept?'

'Yeah, I got a few hours earlier, but now I'm awake, so why don't you get some decent sleep in bed?'

'I can't leave him, Zara. I can't. He needs me here. I promised.'

Her mother's words pierced Zara's heart. She thought she could almost understand what it was to feel a mother's love when she heard Lynda's hurt, the fear, the need of a mother to do this last thing for her child.

'Okay, Mum. We can both stay together.'

Zara walked to the other side of Will's bed, pulling the second lounge chair closer so she could reach out and take her brother's other hand.

'I remember when he was a little boy,' Lynda said softly, staring at her son's face. 'He used to frighten me by climbing out of the window and escaping so he could be with Brian. He'd hear the noise of the sheep yards and just take off!' She smiled sadly. 'Do you remember that, Will? You just couldn't stay away.'

'What about the time he broke his arm going for a mark? He was still in boarding school then,' Zara said, squeezing his hand. She leaned forward and looked at his arm. 'The scar is still there from where they had to put in the plate.'

'Oh, Will, it's a wonder my hair didn't turn grey sooner with all the antics you used to pull,' Lynda said. 'From being such a terror when he was a toddler, he grew into such a beautiful, gentle man, didn't he?'

'Everyone loves him, Mum. There's no doubt about that.'

They sipped their tea in silence. No more words were necessary; they knew their task and waited for the inevitable.

❧

It was 4.32 am by the clock on the bedside table when Zara awoke to her mother's touch. Lynda was kneeling at her side and looking into her eyes. Instinctively Zara knew Will had gone.

'He's gone, Zara. He's gone.' Her mother's face dissolved as the grief rushed forth.

'No,' she whispered and reached for Will's hand to prove her mother wrong.

But there was no denying the fact: his rattling breaths had stopped, his chest had stopped rising. The cancer had finally claimed its victim.

Zara felt her heart close over and pinpricks of grief rise on her skin. 'Oh, Will,' she whispered and turned to Lynda. 'Oh, Mum.'

This time there was no restraint, only the pure pain of loss finally realised.

Chapter 21

It seemed like yesterday that Zara had been in the church in Barker, her brother's coffin at the altar covered in a wreath of gum leaves and native flowers. But it also seemed like a lifetime ago.

The tiny church had been packed and mourners had flowed out into the street as farmers, footy players and friends had joined Lynda and Zara in their grief. Zara had been grateful that Liz and Lachy had come up from Adelaide to support her. She'd needed the steadying hands of her friends as the footy club had formed a guard of honour at the front of the church and six pallbearers had carried the coffin out and placed it gently in the hearse. Everyone had gathered and watched as it drove away, towards the city, where he was being cremated.

Having Liz and Lachy with her during the wake at the footy club rooms near the oval, where Will had played, had been a comfort too, but somehow she'd found she'd spent a lot of time with Jack. His quiet presence had given her reassurance.

'Will would've been amazed at how many people he'd touched,' she'd whispered to Jack at one stage, looking at the throng of people. 'I don't think he could ever see himself through our eyes and know how much he was loved.'

In the past three weeks she'd fought the waves of grief that threatened to drown her, especially at night when she lay in her bed in Barker, tossing and turning, hearing the words '*I'm frightened*' replaying over and over in her head.

We kept that promise, Will. I hope you knew that. I hope you knew we were there until the end.

In the first week after Will's death, Zara had stayed on Rowberry Glen, sleeping in the spare room. Together she and Lynda had shared their grief and planned Will's funeral. They'd cried together and been strong when the other couldn't be.

After the funeral, Karl had visited and helped them make arrangements for the farm. There were a few sheep that could be sold and they'd opted not to put in any crops at all this season—it was still too dry. Rowberry Glen, Lynda decided, needed to be run very easily this year, until she got back on her feet.

On Karl's advice, Zara had talked to Mark Cullen and Doyley and found that one of the footy club boys who had come to see Will in his final days was looking for a job. Ray had settled in well and Lynda liked him. He didn't need to live on the farm—his parents had land about twenty minutes' drive from Rowberry Glen, so he could still stay there and come to work every day.

So far he'd proved worth his weight in gold, because Lynda hadn't been able to face going around the farm. There were too many memories.

Kim had suggested to Zara that perhaps her mother's grief wasn't only for Will. It probably brought all the old feelings from Brian's death to the surface. Zara thought she was right, because she'd found herself returning over and over to her dad's death in the aftermath of Will's. It dragged up all the old pain, the feelings of disbelief and injustice. Sometimes the empty space felt too enormous to comprehend.

Now she was on her way back to Adelaide. Not for good, but for a couple of weeks. The agreement she had with her mum and Lachy was that she would have two weeks in the office and two weeks in Barker, until Lynda felt she was able to cope by herself.

The excitement was building as she thought about her return to the office. She was craving normality, distraction, real life. Her phone rang and she smiled as she saw it was Liz.

'Hey,' she answered.

'Hi, where are you?'

'About thirty minutes away. Is my desk ready?'

'It's been ready since you left. So, you'll be in time for the editorial meeting?'

'Hopefully the traffic will be light and I'll get there.'

'I think Lachy will hold off until you're here, anyway.' There was a pause and Zara knew that Liz wanted to ask how she was.

'I'm fine.'

'I didn't ask!' Liz sounded indignant.

'But you want to. I'm learning to read people's pauses.'

'Everyone's really excited you're coming back, Zara. We've all missed you.'

Hanging on to the steering wheel tightly as a truck overtook her, Zara smiled. 'I've missed you all too. Has the mystery of Mr O'Grady been solved yet?'

There was a silence before she said, 'No, not yet.' Liz paused again. This time when she spoke, her voice was bright. 'But I've got some office gossip.'

'Oh, do tell!'

'We think Michael has been shagging the new journo, Claudia!' Liz's voice was full of glee.

'Nooo!' Zara said. 'Michael wouldn't mix work and personal life, would he?'

'Well, I saw them having dinner at the Boat Shed on Saturday and it didn't look like they were talking about work, if you get what I mean.'

'He's stupid!'

'You're telling me,' Liz lowered her voice. 'I think Lachy suspects something because he pulled both Michael and Claudia into his office separately today. And neither of them looked very happy when they came out. Lachy will have a fit if that's what's going on. He's always said that there shouldn't be office romances.'

'I know but, in reality, how can you stop them? You can't stop love. Apparently, that's a force not to be denied.'

'Can't say I'd know.'

And there it was again—that stabbing pain of grief just when she least expected it, because Will would never get to experience that kind of love either.

'You okay? Sorry, maybe I shouldn't have brought that up.'

Swallowing hard, Zara changed her grip on the wheel, wondering whether right now she had the energy to explain. 'It's actually not the conversation,' she said. 'It's knowing that Will missed out on falling in love and having children. All because of some stupid, cruel disease that has no right to exist!

'I don't know if that makes sense to you, but he died so young and missed out on so many things. And Mum misses out too. Will was the end of the family name. No more Ellisons coming from us.'

'There might be,' Lizzie said softly. 'You don't have to change your name if you marry.'

'But you know what I'm saying, right?'

'Yeah, and I'm just trying to make you feel better and I don't think that's what you need.'

'Give me a hug when I get to the office.'

'Ha! That I can do.'

❧

The office was just what Zara needed: noisy, busy and exciting. First of all she put her head into Lachy's office. He was sitting there as usual, with a cold cup of coffee in front of him and stains down his white shirt.

'Good to see things don't change,' she said, indicating his shirt.

He looked up and a broad grin spread across his face. 'Well, well, it's good to see you. Come here.' He pushed his chair back and stood up, holding his arms open. 'And I wouldn't want to disappoint you by having a clean shirt!'

Zara hugged him back. 'It's good to see you too,' she answered. 'It's good to be here!'

'How are you?' He looked down at her with such compassion that she had to take a second to gather herself.

'It's hard to explain. It's a bit like the ocean. Sometimes the waters are calm; that's when I feel okay. I never actually forget he's gone, but it feels like life could be normal again one day. Then, out of nowhere, this massive wave crashes over me and I feel like I'm drowning.' She shrugged. 'That probably doesn't make any sense, but that's how it is.'

'It makes sense.' Lachy gripped her upper arms and squeezed gently. 'It's going to take time and I think you nailed it when you said, "It feels like life could be normal again." It'll never be the way it was before, but there will be a time when feeling like life could be normal is the normal.' He let go of her and smiled sadly.

'I'll just dump my gear,' she said. 'And, Lachy, thanks. Thanks for everything.'

He gave her a wink and turned back to his desk.

'Oh my God, you're finally here!' Liz flew out from behind her desk and threw herself at Zara.

Laughing, Zara dropped the bag she was carrying and hugged her friend back. 'I am! And I'm so pleased to be here.'

Michael came over. 'Good to see you, Zara. I hope you're holding up,' he said softly, taking her hand and squeezing it.

'That's kind of you, Michael. I'm okay.' She glanced past him and saw a young woman she didn't know at the next desk. She raised her eyebrows and nodded her head towards the newcomer. Michael turned around. 'Claudia, come and meet Zara. She's the one I've been telling you about.'

Zara moved forward and held out her hand. Now she was the professional, not the grieving sister.

'Nice to meet you, Claudia. Zara Ellison. Look forward to working with you.'

'I've heard a lot about you, Zara. Seems you're respected far and wide.'

'That's a lovely thing to say, but I'm not sure if it's true.'

'Come on, you lot, are you coming to the meeting or not?' Lachy stood in front of the meeting room, hands on hips. 'Let's go, people.'

They all filed in and Lachy began talking. 'Okay, I need someone to take the stock-stealing story. We've had four reports of sheep and cattle theft and the Nationals' Grant Tann is calling for the reinstatement of the stock squad.'

Zara put up her hand. 'I can take that. His office is on my way home.'

'Good. Michael, are you happy to go to Landmark and talk to head of livestock about the Dublin sale prices? I know we ran the sale results last week, but I think we need some background on why they're so high and what the future for lamb is.'

'Sure thing.'

'Claudia, you can head to the wool stores this week and follow up on that story you did on the southern wool breeders' group that are exporting wool into China without an agent.'

'Okay.'

'Liz, there's a couple of late bull sales coming up in Meningie and Keith that you can get on the road and follow.' He ticked off the items on his list, then sat back in his chair and looked at them. 'Anyone got any stories they want to talk about?'

Zara put up her hand. 'I'm still following the story of the drone in Barker a few weeks ago. I've got a contact inside Voices for Animals—the group behind the drone—and I've spoken to a few of the farmers around there to get their views. Hoping to have that written by next week.'

'Okay, let me see it when you're done. Anything else?'

'The ABARES conference is in a couple of weeks. I'd really like to report on that,' Michael said. 'I've got a few sources in there who should give me the good oil.'

'Sure, but we'll need a couple more there with you. Perhaps Zara and Liz?' No mention of Claudia.

'No worries,' Zara said. She loved the big conferences. There was always so much to report on and so many interesting people to talk to. She'd struck solid-gold stories there a few times.

'Yep, I'm in too,' Liz answered.

She kicked Zara under the table and gave her a 'I told you so' wiggle of her eyebrows at the fact that Claudia wasn't going to get the gig with Michael.

Zara dropped her eyes to the table to stop herself laughing.

'Right, anything else? No? Okay, let's put this paper together.'

Zara went straight to her desk and checked her messages.

'*Zara. It's Jack. Ah, reckon today was the day you told me you were leaving town. Just wanted to wish you all the best with everything. Um. Yeah. Catch you sometime.*'

Somewhere in the distance a phone rang. Then Lachy yelled for Michael. And Zara knew she was back.

Chapter 22

'You sure you're cool with this?' Dave asked Jack as he loaded a suitcase into the ute. 'It's a big ask.'

'Nah, sounds pretty exciting, actually,' Jack answered.

'It's dangerous, not exciting,' Dave corrected. 'You'll have to be careful because, from my understanding, some of these protesters are violent. You're there to gather information, not to get yourself hurt.'

'I know, I know. Anyway, you'll be close by when it's time to go out in the field.'

'Yeah, mate, I will.' Dave clapped him on the shoulder. 'I'll be telling everyone you've gone on holidays. That you've gone overseas to meet a girl.'

Jack snorted. 'Reckon they'll all know that isn't true.' He rubbed at the beard he'd grown over the last three weeks. It had been incredibly itchy for the first week or so, but now it seemed to have settled on him, although he still got a bit of a shock when he looked in the mirror.

Dave had told him that was normal.

'Right-o, you'd better get going. Enjoy the academy. The undercover officer course is a good one. I'll be down there a day or so before you head out. Be safe.'

They shook hands and Jack climbed into the ute and started the engine. 'I guess the biggest risk is that someone will recognise me,' he said.

'Absolutely. But it's been a while since you lived in Adelaide. If you feel unsafe at any time, make sure you pull out.'

Jack nodded. 'Catch you later.' He let the clutch out and rolled forward, hearing Dave give the back of the ute a tap with his hand.

He'd spent the last weeks reading about the activists who Sophie, Lee and Terry had been involved with. To him, they didn't seem dangerous. Their signature protests were silent gatherings held outside farms, holding up placards. He couldn't find any reference to any violence. Empower Animals, another activist group, was a different story. They'd held loud, angry rallies outside ports where live export ships were being loaded, as well as in saleyards. There had been many arrests and a few people had been taken to hospital after being crushed in the crowd trying to break down the barriers and get to the animals.

Neither he nor Dave had been able to find out who had made the report about the two farms in Barker that supposedly had undernourished stock. In the end Dave had shrugged and said there were more important things to focus on. Like getting ready to go undercover.

Jack was looking forward to getting to the academy. It had been an age since he'd done anything but be a country copper. He'd often thought about doing a detectives' course, like Dave, but in the end he always decided against it. Dave had probably taught him more than any course would, and there could only be one detective in Barker. Dave.

Sometimes he'd toyed with the idea of moving towns. Maybe there'd be more opportunities to meet a girl in another town. He knew there wasn't anyone in Barker for him and, although he used to feel lonely, he was okay with it now. Plus, he really liked working with Dave. He guessed he was stuck at Barker.

Dave had insisted he make up some good bona fides for this undercover job, so he was now an ex-farmhand who'd become disenchanted with the industry. He was a vegan. That bit was going to hurt. No steak or milky coffee for a while. He'd worked on sheep farms in the mid-north of SA and on a cattle property in the south. He'd also had a short stint at a piggery in Victoria, but he'd really disliked that, so he'd left quickly.

Dave had told him that the cops had sent out 'the dogs'—cops who tailed some of the activists—to sniff out where their meeting places were and to build a dossier on them. Jack had received an email about it this morning and he was itching to get to Adelaide so he could read it.

Jack turned up the music in the ute and drove, his mind wandering to Zara. He wondered where she was now. He knew she'd gone back to Adelaide for a couple of weeks, for work. She'd told him that when he'd bumped into her at the roadhouse a few days before she was about to leave. He wondered if he should get Dave to contact her to make sure she knew that he wasn't to be approached as there was some chance she could turn up at a protest he was at. Still, maybe not. He didn't really know how it was going to play out. He hoped that with the beard and a hat pulled down over his face, she wouldn't recognise him, even if she did end up at the same protest.

He'd offered to do something to help her mum out, but Zara had said she thought they had it sorted. Then she'd given him a gentle punch on the arm.

'Thanks for the very vague info about Sophie Grawd.'

He smiled as he remembered the way he'd rearranged his face into a deadpan expression. 'I didn't give you anything you couldn't have found out yourself as a good journalist,' he'd said.

Zara had grinned widely. 'You keep telling yourself that.'

They'd said their goodbyes and Jack had driven away. As he'd looked in the rear-vision mirror he'd seen Karl pull up and get out. Then he'd seen them hugging and he'd looked forward again, not wanting to see more.

❧

Jack dumped his duffle bag in the room he had been allocated on the second floor of the police college and then went in search of the gym. It wouldn't hurt to go a few rounds with a boxing bag.

Gloving up, he tried a few test jabs then punched the bag hard. Pummel, pummel, pummel. He pretended he was in a protest and he had to defend himself. Sweat dripped off his forehead but he continued to punch.

After ten minutes his arms were aching and he slowed down, before getting on the treadmill and running a couple of kilometres. He realised he'd missed the gym. Training at footy with the boys or playing cricket during the summer didn't give him the workout he liked. He loved the hard physicality of boxing and weights. It made his blood pump and cleared his head. Maybe he'd get a home gym when he went back to Barker. The easy, slow country life had made a difference to his fitness.

Slowing down to a jog, he grabbed his towel and put it over his head to wipe the sweat away.

'You must be the new bloke?'

Jack got off the treadmill and draped his towel around his shoulders. 'Not sure about "new bloke", but here to do a bit of training.' He held out his hand. 'Jack.'

'Tony.' They shook hands.

'Guess I'll see you in the mess tonight.'

'See you then.' Jack followed the passageway back to his room, showered then settled at the desk. The dossier was thick and full of detail.

They'd followed four people: two men and two women. As far as the dogs could tell, they were the closest to being in charge.

> Josh Parker, 25-year-old, chiropractor. Not married, two foster dogs. Volunteers at the pound and specialises in rehoming abandoned animals. Member of Voices

for Animals for five years. Attended over twenty protests, none violent. Last one: Dublin saleyards.

Raymond Devlin, 30-year-old disability worker. Married with a baby, two months old. One dog, one cat. Member of Voices for Animals for three years. Last protest: a steakhouse in Melbourne where eight members stood quietly in the restaurant and held up placards telling the diners that animals had feelings.

Jack shook his head, feeling frustrated, but read on.

Amber Robinson, 22-year-old, student. Lives alone, no animals. Member of Voices for Animals for two years. Last protest: same steakhouse as Raymond Devlin.

Kristen Dunn, 28-year-old, cafe proprietor. Lives alone. Owner of Kristen Goes Raw (where meetings are held). Attended over one hundred rallies, focusing mainly on live export and piggeries.

Sounds like I'm going to be having a whole bunch of fun in the next little while, Jack thought as he turned the page.

Having followed Josh Parker for a week, we have seen him entering 32 Brock Road in Unley, Adelaide. Further investigations of records show this is his primary place of residence. He walks his dogs in the park a kilometre from his house and attends meetings for Voices for Animals weekly, at Kristen Goes Raw on Jamnut Street in Hunter.

Jack looked at the photos of Josh. He was a thickset man, going prematurely bald. There were pictures of him throwing balls to his dogs, in the park, walking to work. His workplace showed posters promoting Voices for Animals. The next one was of him sitting in Kristen Goes Raw with a group of other members of the group. Jack picked up the photo and looked closely. He recognised Sophie Grawd sitting next to Josh. So she was in there too. It was a good thing Dave had pulled him off the job when he'd impounded the car.

He flicked through the rest of the information then turned his attention to the computer and the links provided by the dogs.

First one was a video of a protest at the main saleyards on the outskirts of Adelaide. There were about forty men and women lined up against the pens with a man in the middle, talking through a loudspeaker. He was talking about the ethical treatment of animals and why saleyards made animals frightened. Jack watched closely, making sure he'd be able to recall details if he was asked. This video would have been of the protests Jack would've attended if he'd actually been who he was now saying he was. The auctioneer stopped halfway through a pen and told them to fuck off, they were interfering with a workplace. The activists ignored him. In the background the cattle were bellowing and there were the sounds of police sirens.

Jack rewound the video and watched it again and again, until he was sure he had all the details correct, then he started on the next one.

This one was of a live export rally. Hundreds of people were there and most of them seemed to be peaceful. There were three speakers: two women and a man. There were signs everywhere, saying: *Cooked alive*, *Ban live export* and *Live export equals cruelty*. The speakers were calling for the Prime Minister to ban live export. They said it wasn't about politics or economics, it was about the fact each and every animal had a right to life.

'Tell that to every poor bastard whose livelihood is affected if this industry is shut down,' Jack muttered.

Back when live export had been shut down without warning, there were reporters saying it wouldn't affect anyone other than the few hundred livestock producers in the northern part of Australia. They were very wrong.

Jack's mate, Peter, who was a truck driver, had lost his job and his truck because he hadn't been able to make the repayments on it. A mustering contractor Peter knew didn't have work for two years and had to shift his family down south to start again—and that wasn't even mentioning the people who had worked for him. The jillaroos and jackaroos were without jobs, and the land suffered because the animals that should have been sold weren't and feed was short. The impact of that decision had been much more far reaching than anyone could have imagined.

However, no one wanted animals to suffer. That bit was understood and agreed by everyone.

Jack started the next video and went back to his research.

Chapter 23

Zara grabbed her bag from the passenger's seat and locked the car before going into the office of Grant Tann. She signed her name and waited for someone to come and collect her.

She scrolled through her emails while she was waiting, then flicked across to Facebook to see what was happening. Tammy had put up a photo of five protesters camped outside her front gate. They had pitched tents and been there on and off for three weeks. *Sick of trying to get through this on the bus run,* she'd written. *Thought they'd gone but they've come back again.*

Far out, they don't give up, Zara thought. She enlarged the photos and tried to see if she recognised any of the faces of the protesters, but they were too blurry.

She imagined they'd be up in arms if their faces were shown, but it was okay for them to be camped outside a private residence, which happened to double as a business.

Then she mentally slapped herself. If she was going to be a good journalist, she couldn't let her feelings or opinions get in the way of writing a balanced story.

She tapped out a text to Tammy. *Looking like you've got permanent residents down there. Do you want me to come down and write a story? I can speak to Lachy if you're keen.*

'Zara, hi. Thanks for coming in,' Grant Tann appeared in front of her.

'Happy to help.'

They settled in his office and Zara took out her phone. 'Is it okay for me to record you?'

'Sure.'

'So, tell me why you think the stock squad needs to be reinstated,' she said once she'd set everything up.

'The recent price rises in both cattle and sheep have made it very attractive for people to steal stock and on-sell it, thereby making themselves a lot of money. Recently there have been thefts of hundreds of sheep from one property. Now, Zara, this isn't something that can happen without a lot of planning. There has to be organisation. Trucks, musterers, dogs. A place to put the stock once they've been stolen.'

Zara listened to him talk and made a few handwritten notes.

'I think farmers are feeling exposed right now. There's been reports of drones flying over farming land and—'

Zara interrupted. 'What about the protesters who are able to sit outside farm gates? They're not doing anything illegal because they're on public land, but their presence is intimidating for the people who live there, let alone their children.'

'Look, everyone has a right to feel safe in their own home. I believe this type of protest functions as harassment and there needs to be laws put in place to cover this type of protesting.'

After ten more minutes Zara wound up the interview. She had most of the story written in her head before she had left his office.

She drove home quickly, got out her computer and started to type before she lost what she wanted to say.

> Nationals Minister Grant Tann has called for the rein-statement of the Rural Crime Investigations Unit after a recent spate of stock thefts in rural South Australia.
>
> 'Why do we have Rural Crime Investigation Units in some states and not others?' he asks. 'Western Australia had an active squad for some time until the Labor Government decided it was a good idea to disband it. Queensland, on the other hand, has many squads that operate all across the state.'
>
> In recent years only nine people have been charged with stock stealing offences. However, this is not due to a downturn in theft, because there has been over two million dollars' worth of stock reported stolen in the past twelve months. It is because of the lack of manpower and dedicated squads investigating these crimes.

South Australia is not the only state calling for a rural crime unit to be reinstated, Western Australia echoes the call.

Responsibility for investigating rural crime fell to the Department of Agriculture after the stock squad was disbanded. However, Department of Agriculture employees do not have the authority or the skills to undertake detective work such as searching farms and conducting forensic investigations.

At the moment, local police detectives in the town closest to where the crime has occurred are investigating stock thefts. As skilled as these detectives may be, they are unlikely to have the same level of specialised skill and experience as the stock squad detectives. The detectives within any rural crime unit have to be able to ride motorbikes and horses, camp out and be stockmen. These detectives are a different breed altogether.

On 21 May 2018 there was a call by SA sheep producers to reinstate the Rural Crime Investigations Unit after sixty thousand dollars' worth of sheep were stolen from a property near Clare in the state's mid-north.

According to a police source, rural theft is no longer an opportunistic crime. Given the increasing numbers of sheep being stolen (such as the 1000 merino-cross ewes taken in December 2018 from a NSW property), the perpetrators clearly need to be highly organised. Thefts like this take a lot of planning.

There are sophisticated ways of casing farms— using drones, for example. And with the increasing number of animal activists coming onto or camping just outside private properties and causing mischief, farmers need to be able to call in professionals when needed.

Each theft has an impact on a farmer's bottom line. Then there is the additional expense of installing security equipment, not to mention locks and chains on gates and fences.

'I believe the police minister must act quickly and reinstate this specialised force before farmers are sent bankrupt,' said Minister Tann.

Zara sat back and reread her work. Grant Tann was being a little overdramatic with that last comment, but he'd said it and the quote was worth using.

She could probably add a few more details once she'd sought a comment from the police minister and found the most up-to-date rural theft figures. Her mind strayed to Jack. She wondered if she could get him to give her a quote for the story, then dismissed the idea. *There'd be no chance at all*, she thought.

Getting up, she stretched, before walking to the fridge and pouring herself a glass of wine. As the sun slipped below the horizon, the city lights started to twinkle through the sliding door that led out onto the balcony. She stood watching them for a while, wondering how her mum was coping tonight. She tried to see the stars, but to her disappointment the city lights blocked them out.

Zara had never seen herself as a country girl, even though she had a great love for the bush and had grown up on a farm. She loved the city's trendy little cafés, where she could get a latte any time of the day, and the cosy wine bars with live music where she could hang out in the evenings. But tonight she found herself longing for the silence of Rowberry Glen and the peace of the star-lit sky.

If she was sitting on the verandah, Trixie would be beside her, pressing her warm body against hers, while Boof and Shadow sat nearby, sighing with contentment. The silence she'd found so awful when Will had been dying had been replaced with serenity and solitude afterwards. Zara had enjoyed the quiet evenings with only the sound of sheep bleating or the wind rustling the trees. She felt closer to Will out there too. That was where his soul would be resting and she could chat with him quietly whenever she needed.

One night after Will's death, she'd gone back to the woolshed and sat on the board, her legs dangling over the edge, watching the moon rise. It had cast a white glow across the land, throwing long, dark shadows from the gum trees around the homestead. The freshness of the air had cleared her head, and she'd felt the life all around her and found some healing there.

Now she was back in the city, where she wanted to be, she found herself unable to stop thinking about her home.

Chapter 24

'How can you leave the town without a policeman?' Kim asked. 'Is it really that important?'

Dave nodded as he threw some clothes into a bag. 'I can't tell you what it is, but don't worry about the town. Steve is sending someone to cover. Hopefully I'll only be gone a week. Two at the most.'

Kim put her hands on her hips and stared at him. 'I didn't come down in the last shower, Dave Burrows. I bet this has got something to do with Jack and that horrible beard he grew just before he skipped town, supposedly on holiday.'

Dave stopped and put his hands on her waist. 'Absolutely nothing gets past you, does it, my love?'

Kim smiled. 'I try not to let it.'

'I can't tell you any more than I have already.'

'That's okay. I just need you to be safe.' She stretched her arms up around his neck and stood on tiptoe to kiss him.

'There won't be any problem with that,' he promised her. 'And I'll be able to talk to you most nights, I'd imagine. If not, I'll send you a text.'

She nodded. 'Now, at the risk of making you cranky before you go . . .'

'You never make me cranky.' He tightened his arm around her waist and pulled her to him. Looking down at her he felt his body respond the way it always did. How incredible to be in love with this woman since he was eighteen and still want—no, need—her the way he did when he was fifty plus. He dipped his head and kissed her, the urgency in his lips telling her of his desire.

'Don't you have to go?' she muttered against him.

'I can spare ten minutes.'

Kim giggled. 'Do you think it's going to take that long?'

He swotted her arse gently and pushed her onto the bed.

❧

Dave kissed Kim goodbye and got into the car.

'Please think about ringing Dean,' Kim said as she put her face through the window for another kiss.

'I know, I know, you've mentioned it once or twice before,' he answered good-naturedly.

'I wasn't sure you'd heard me.' Kim gave an impish smile and patted his arm. 'Love you.'

'Love you more. See you when I get back.'

He reversed out of the drive, gave another wave and headed towards the main road. The radio was playing, and he turned it up a little, before checking the clock. *The Country Hour* would be on pretty soon.

He hoped Jack had prepared himself well enough. It had been strange briefing him; it felt like only yesterday that Spencer Brown, his friend and work colleague when he'd been at Barrabine police station, had been briefing him about going undercover.

He remembered how he'd put a stone in his shoe to alter his gait and had worn contact lenses to change the colour of his eyes. Jack wouldn't need any of that—just a beard and long hair, and some sunglasses and a hat to hide his eyes. He hoped Jack had memorised his story well enough not to stuff it up. One little slip could mean real trouble for him.

'It's eleven forty-two on ABC Radio, the sounds of the north.' The radio announcer's voice cut through his thoughts and he realised half the trip had gone by without him noticing.

'And the play of the day is Rascal Flatts. We're featuring one song from their album of the same name, every hour for today,' the DJ informed him. 'Comin' up next is "I'm Movin' On". You're listening to ABC Radio, sound of the north.'

Piano strains came through the speakers and the hairs on Dave's arms rose just a little. He loved a good country song played with piano, fiddle and guitar. The voice of Gary LeVox started singing, and as Dave listened to the words, he felt as if the song had been written for him. Gary sang about being trapped in the past for too long and needing to make peace with it.

Kim flashed into his thoughts again. '*Please ring Dean.*' She'd said it more than once. And he'd ignored the request as he always did. It wasn't something he wanted to think about or deal with.

Dave agreed with the song's sentiment that he never thought he'd end up where he didn't belong. But he had. Once he'd realised that he couldn't be a farmer he'd had to choose another profession. He loved what he did now and he probably wouldn't change it, but back then it had been a heart-wrenching and difficult adjustment.

His thoughts turned to Dean and his mum. Trying to remember the last time he'd talked to his mother, he called her number on the car phone system.

'Dave?' The pleasure in his mum's voice made him feel terrible he hadn't rung earlier.

'Hi, Mum. How are you?'

'All the better for hearing your voice. Are you well?'

'All fine and dandy here. What are you up to?'

'Not a great deal. Sitting on the porch reading a book with a cup of tea.'

Dave could picture her doing just that, with the flowering potted geraniums lining the verandah and the tea-pot sitting on the wrought-iron table. She'd have her feet propped up on a stool and her sunglasses perched on her head.

He smiled at the vision. 'That sounds very peaceful.'

'It's lovely. The weather's started to cool down. The early mornings are soft and dewy, which is so nice. I get tired of the heat these days.'

'It can be draining. I find it hard sometimes at Barker, and Kim certainly does.'

'You have day after day of the heat, though, don't you? We're lucky enough to get a cool change now and then.'

There was a pause and Dave reached for something to talk about.

His mum beat him to it. 'We enjoyed having you and Kim over here, Dave,' she said quietly. 'But I know you found it difficult.'

The words came out of his mouth before he could stop them. 'I did. I don't know why, but I did. I thought I'd be fine, but I saw the city skyline as we flew in and something flicked inside of me.'

'I could see that,' she said softly.

'I don't understand why Dean never stood up for me, Mum. Or Adam. I could understand you—I mean, you weren't well when it all happened, and Dad was a controlling prick—but my brothers . . . we're supposed to have each other's backs. I would've if the boot had been on the other foot.'

'Dave, you're going to have to have this conversation with your brother. I'm your mum and I want you to deal with this because I can see it's eating you up. I don't hear from you often and you rarely call Dean, even since his accident.

'This type of anger can do a lot of damage to a body. Trust me, I know. I lived with stress for years. My hair fell out, my gums bled, and I used to get a rash on my elbows and on other parts of my body. All that stopped after your father died. Often I'd go to the doctor about the smallest of things and he'd say to me, "I think it's your stress levels." I have no doubt that your body could start to react the way that mine did after living with anger and hurt for such an extended period.'

Dave was silent as he thought back to all the times he'd seen his mum told off by his father—the tone of voice and the way she used to shrink when he started to shout.

'I never knew any of that.'

'Darling,' she chided him in her gentle way, 'you're my son. Of course I wasn't going to let you see those things. I dealt with it the way I thought was best—by hiding it from everyone. That's why I know that if you don't have this conversation with Dean, you will never find out what might be possible between the two of you.' She paused and Dave heard her take a sip of tea. 'So I'm going to suggest something to you, Dave. Why don't you hang up from me and ring Dean? Use this time to talk to him, because he's not sure where he sits with you.'

'I'll try,' Dave said, the words sticking in his throat.

'I don't want to point out the obvious, but it's always good to face things head on. Take care, Dave, speak soon.' She hung up the phone.

Dave was taken aback as the call was cut off. *Go, Mum,* he thought.

He turned up the radio for the next few kilometres, but his mum's words kept echoing in his head. *'He's not sure where he sits with you.'*

'Shit.' He punched in Dean's number and listened to it ring. He half hoped Dean wouldn't answer.

'Dave?' The hope in Dean's voice was evident and suddenly he couldn't say anything.

'Dave, is that you, mate?' The hope turned to uncertainty.

'Yeah,' he finally managed to get out. 'It's me.'

'Are you okay? You sound strange.'

'I'm . . . not sure. I've just been talking to Mum.'

'Is she okay?' Dean's voice was fearful now.

'Oh, yeah, she's fine. No worries with her.' Pause. 'She, uh, suggested I ring you.'

'I'm glad. It's great to hear from you. We don't speak often enough.'

Before he knew it, the words rushed out of Dave. 'Why didn't you stick up for me that night Dad kicked me off the farm?'

Now it was Dean's turn to be silent.

The humming down the interstate line seemed to grow louder as the silence stretched.

Finally Dean spoke. 'To be brutally honest, Dave, I don't think I have a clear reason. It all happened so quickly. One minute you were there and the next minute you weren't. And I guess I'd sound like a tosser if I told you I was frightened of Dad. But I was. He hit me when I was out in the paddock one day. I was fourteen and I hadn't shut the gate in between the rams and the ewes properly. Well, the flogging he gave me . . . I've never forgotten it and probably never forgiven him for it either.'

'I don't remember that.'

Dean made a sound that was half-snort, half-groan. 'You wouldn't. He made sure he hit my back, where my shirt covered me. No one ever saw the bruises and I never told Mum.

'And then when I saw him standing over you like that, I thought it wasn't a place for me to be. I didn't want to get in the middle. All these images flashed through my head—like when he hit me, like me being the boss, like being able to farm the way I wanted to. And then there was the horror of the situation. God, Dave, I can't tell you what it looked like from where I was.'

'Try being where I was,' Dave shot back, anger seeping into his voice.

Silence.

'I know. It was horrible on all accounts, but especially for you since no one stood up for you. Look, mate, I know I acted like a prat and you wouldn't believe the amount of times I've wished I could've acted differently, but I didn't and I'm sorry. I know my behaviour hurt you very badly.'

'Were you happy when I'd gone?' Dave wanted to know.

'I guess I'd be lying if I said I was unhappy. There's a difference, you know. A decision about the farm had to be made because that farm was never going to support all of us, it was just too small.'

Dave let out a strangled sound. His heart thumped through his chest. He'd been right all along. They'd all wanted him to go.

'It's not what you're thinking.'

Dave saw a parking bay ahead and flicked on his blinker. He wasn't in any fit state to drive.

'Adam and I . . . it wasn't like that. We'd been trying to talk the old man into buying more farming land . . .'

Dave slammed his foot on the brake and came to an abrupt halt. 'What?'

'We'd been trying to convince Dad to buy more acres so we could all stay. But he wouldn't have it. I guess when I saw how it all turned out, I figured it was the path of least resistance and went along with it. I was weak.'

So Dean had tried. He really had. And Adam too. Dave briefly wondered where Adam was now. His middle brother hadn't been heard of for years. Maybe he should search for him.

'I didn't know that.' He felt like he'd said that too many times today. There were so many things he really didn't know. That he'd assumed.

What had he drummed into Jack when they'd first started working together on investigations? Never assume anything. He should take some of his own advice.

Dave couldn't speak. His tongue was stuck to the roof of his mouth. He leaned over and grappled in the foot well of the passenger's side for the bottle of water he kept there. Frantically he gulped at it.

'Dave? Are you still there? Dave?'

'I'm here,' he managed.

'Are you all right?'

Staring out of the window, Dave tried to analyse how he was feeling. Shocked, for certain. A tiny glimmer of happiness. Maybe it would take a while to process exactly what had just happened. 'I'm fine,' he said eventually. 'Actually, I'm more than fine.'

Chapter 25

Jack was ready. His long hair was pulled back into a greasy ponytail and he was wearing a pair of ripped jeans and a tight T-shirt that had *Be the change* emblazoned across the front. He nervously patted his pockets to make sure he had everything and then shrugged into the bomber jacket that Dave had given him.

'All set?'

Jack nodded once.

Handing him two pens, Dave said, 'Slot these in your coat sleeves. They're cameras and a recording device. When you've finished, give them to us and we'll get the info downloaded. Or someone who knows how to will.' He gave a rueful smile. 'It won't be me.'

'I know that.'

Dave turned serious. 'Who are you again?'

'Jack, the ex-farmhand who got disillusioned with farming, turned vegan and wants to make change happen.'

'I'll be with you all the way, in the van outside. I won't be able to hear what's happening through the pens, but if you need help, we're right outside.'

Jack gave a brief nod and jiggled around.

'We're only looking for info about where the next rally is, okay? And for fuck's sake, don't go in too hard or too fast. It never ends well if you do that.'

'I'm good.'

Dave could see he'd lost Jack. He was already the vegan activist who wanted to create change.

'Go get 'em.'

~

Jack strutted down the street, keeping an eye out for anyone he might recognise from Voices for Animals.

Swinging open the door to Kristen Goes Raw, he took a seat towards the back of the café so he could watch everyone who came in and work out who was who.

Kristen herself came over with a menu and held it out to him. 'Nice shirt,' she said.

'Cheers. Got a tonic water?'

'Sure. Would you like anything to eat?' She smiled at him.

'I'll check out the menu. If I could get that drink straight up, that'd be great. Panting for something wet.'

'I'll be back.'

The door opened and Josh Parker walked in. He'd tied his two dogs outside by the front door.

'Hi, Josh,' Kristen called. 'You can grab the dogs some water from the kitchen, if you like. I just have to serve.'

'Thanks.' Josh clearly knew his way around Kristen's café because he walked into the kitchen without any hesitation.

Jack looked down at the menu and fought not to screw up his nose. All of the food looked really nice, but it wasn't steak or lamb chops.

Cauliflower hot wings with vegan aioli.

Southwestern pasta salad.

Quinoa stuffed peppers.

Rice paper rolls with mango and mint.

A girl he'd been through the academy with had talked about this quinoa stuff. He wasn't really sure what it was, but he was prepared to try it. Rice paper rolls didn't sound too bad either. He just hoped the servings would be big enough to fill him up.

He made a mental note to eat before he came next time.

The bell tinkled as the door opened again, and Amber and Raymond walked in with three other people Jack didn't recognise from his briefing. One was an older grey-haired man, his eyes hidden by sunglasses; the other two were women who looked to be in their thirties.

He angled his arm so the camera pen would catch the faces.

Kristen came back with his drink and looked at him expectedly. 'Ready to order?'

'What do you recommend?'

'The one-pot pasta Asian-style is really hearty if you're looking to refuel. If you're not too hungry then perhaps the rice paper rolls with mango and mint.'

Jack took a long swallow of tonic water and wanted to choke. A beer would've been much better. Finally, he said, 'I'll have the pasta.'

'No problem.'

The café was beginning to fill up and Josh looked like he was getting ready to take the floor.

'Is this seat taken?'

Jack had watched Sophie and Lee come in a few minutes before, but there weren't any chairs left.

'Be my guest,' he waved. 'Got a meeting on or something?'

Sophie nodded. 'We meet here every couple of weeks.'

'What do you meet about?'

'Hey, Lee, can you give me a hand with this PowerPoint, please?' Josh called out.

'Excuse me,' Lee said and went to help.

'We're called Voices for Animals,' Sophie answered.

'Sounds interesting. What do you do?'

'Raise awareness of animal cruelty.'

Jack leaned back in his chair and looked her. 'Is that right? Well, well, well.'

Kristen arrived with his meal. 'Let me know if you like it,' she said.

'Looks great,' he answered. He turned his attention back to Sophie. 'So what do you have to do to join Voices for Animals?'

'Pay a membership fee and be prepared to protest. We're non-violent; we don't make any trouble, just make people aware.'

'Hmm.' Jack didn't say anything else but picked up his fork and shovelled in a mouthful of the pasta. It was good.

'Right, ladies and gents, if I could have your attention,' Josh called out. 'I have some footage to show you of some saleyards south of Adelaide.'

Jack watched as a protester with a video camera on his hat walked through the yards. It was cold and raining, so it had to have been last winter. It hadn't rained at all this year as far as Jack knew.

The vision switched from one side of the race to the other, cattle on either side.

'Hey, who are you, what are you doing here?' A voice came from somewhere off camera. 'Mate, you're not allowed cameras in here. Didn't you see the signs?'

The cameraman didn't say a word, just kept walking, capturing footage of cattle. Most looked in pretty good nick to Jack, so he couldn't see what the problem was.

'Mate, you can't be here with that camera!'

Again, the protester didn't say a word, but the camera stayed on until the end of the saleyards, when he took off his hat and turned off the camera.

To Jack it seemed very strange, but the room went up in a loud roar of appreciation. A man whose face Jack didn't know was clapped on the back and people shook his hands. He stood up and raised his arm in thanks, then sat back down.

'Now, these cattle were sold to feedlotters and to abattoirs, so we know the ending for them all, unfortunately. We'll put this footage on our Facebook site and tell people of the animals' fate. I think we should target the abattoirs that are close to these saleyards next. They will have had some of these cattle go through the killing chain there.'

A few people clapped.

Jack looked around, then slowly stood up and looked at the people sitting around at the tables. 'You lot are fucking pretenders.' His voice was strong and clear.

The whole room swung around to look at him. Josh looked like he had just swallowed something nasty. His mouth curled up and his face went bright red.

'I'm sorry, sir,' he managed to say. 'I'm not sure I know you. Are you a member of Voices for Animals?'

'Nah, mate, and I don't wanna be part of a group who just gets around silently. You're like the silent army. Wave placards and say nothing. You're not achieving anything. Not friends of animals at all. What the fuck do you think you're going to achieve by wandering through the saleyards filming shit? That doesn't stop the sheep from getting on the boat. That doesn't stop the pigs from dying in piggeries. That doesn't stop the animals from being tortured before they're murdered for their meat!

'You need to get out there and make some noise!' He paused and then pointed his finger at Lee. 'And some of you,' his tone was disdainful, 'some of you are just uni students playing at being activists. You won't stick at it. This is just to fill the gap until something else takes your fancy— maybe you'll have kids, settle down, use that as an excuse to do nothing.' He pointed at his T-shirt. 'You actually have to *do* something. Animal activists have been peaceful for so long and it hasn't got them anywhere. Nothing's changed.'

Jack stopped as he noticed the older man with the sunglasses looking at him and he wondered what he was thinking. Jack wished he could see his eyes and read his expression.

Nobody seemed to know what to say. There was a general murmuring and people glanced his way, avoiding eye contact. Jack wanted to grin.

'Well, sir, thanks very much for your point of view. Clearly you love animals, just as all of us do here. Um,' Josh looked around worriedly, 'maybe we'll find you a membership form and you can join us at our rally at the abattoirs, if you think you can refrain from violence. We can't have you join unless you agree to that.'

Jack looked around with a smirk. 'Anyone know of any groups that want to pull some serious shit to help animals? That's the group I want to join.'

Most people looked at their hands.

'No? Well, I guess you're it then. What a fucking disappointment.' He stormed out of the room, letting the door bang shut behind him. Holding his breath, he stomped off down the street, waiting to see what would happen.

It didn't take too long. The man with the sunglasses followed him out the door.

'Hey you, angry man! Come back here.'

Jack stopped but didn't turn around. He could hear the man's footsteps clicking on the pavement as he walked towards him.

'What's made you so angry?'

'I don't like seeing animals suffer,' he said. 'Seen too much of it and I want it stopped. You're not going to stop it by sitting around.'

'Where you from?'

Jack turned around and faced him. 'Here and there.'

'Full of information.' The man crossed his arms and stared at him.

Jack shrugged. 'I worked on a few different farms when I first left school. You know, lured by the romance of sunsets and horseriding. I learned real quick that sheep stations and cattle farms aren't all they're cracked up to be. Got fed up with seeing animals get stuck in dams and eaten by maggots and dying through bad practices. Some of those animals suffered real bad, you know?'

He watched the man sizing him up.

'Yeah, I know.'

'If you understand that, then why the fuck are you hanging out with a mob of limp dicks like that?'

'We don't all have such passive approaches, you know.'

'What do you mean by that?'

He shrugged. 'How about you come back in and sign up and see what happens?'

'Why? Doesn't sound like you're going to be doing the short of shit I think is necessary.'

'Just get back in there and sign up.'

Jack regarded him carefully. 'What's your name?'

'Crumbs. We're on first-name basis only here. The less you know about us, the better.'

'Why's that?'

'You're full of questions. How about you answer one? What's your name?'

'Jack.'

'Well, Jack, come back inside and back yourself down a bit. Sign up and we'll take it from there.' Crumbs turned and, as he walked towards the café, he called out, 'By the way, when you're filling that form out don't put your real details on it. It'll just make you easier to find if the cops come looking for us.'

That sounded promising to Jack, so he followed Crumbs back into the café.

Back inside, Josh was showing the group another video. Jack stood at the door and waited until he was finished before saying, 'Sorry, all. Lost it a bit back there. I get worked up about this sort of stuff 'cause I want to make a difference, you know? Anyway, if you'll have me, I'd like to join.'

Amber held up a form and said, 'Fill this out and pay your membership.'

After the meeting Jack walked off down the now dark street. Out of the corner of his eye he could see the van Dave was in, but he kept his head down and walked on. He had a few kilometres to walk before he got back to the dingy unit that had been rented for him. He'd ring Dave when he got there.

His phone buzzed. *How'd it go?*

I'm in.

Fishing the key out of his pocket, he let himself into the unit and flicked on the light, before pulling a beer from the fridge and dialling Dave's number.

'All okay,' he said. 'You should've seen their faces when I let rip. I've got the pens to give to you.'

'I've left two new ones in the rubbish bin at the back. Put yours there and we'll grab them tomorrow. What's the plan?'

'Going to hit an abattoir south of Adelaide on Tuesday.'

'Right. Anything else?'

'They made me promise to be non-violent.'

'You'll have to work out how you're going to act if you want to gather info and draw out the extremists, which I think you need to do. Bit of a change in plans, I know, but if they're there, let's find them and stop them before they start.'

'I agree.' Jack paused. 'There was an old guy there, I haven't seen his face before. Not sure where he fitted in, but there's something about him. He didn't seem to be a leader or anything like that, but he had an air of authority. He was the one who came and found me when I stormed out. There's more to him than meets the eye. He implied that not everyone in the group is passive. If there's anyone who could get violent, I reckon it's him. Although I've got nothing concrete to base that on.'

'Get him on camera? Or a name?'

'I reckon I would've got him on the camera—I tried to angle it that way. His name is Crumbs but he told me not to put my real details on the membership form in case the cops came looking, so I'm guessing that's not his real name.'

'We should be able to work out who he is when we see the footage. Someone will know. Just keep your wits about you, okay?'

'I'd like to know who I'm dealing with there.'

'No worries. Leave it with me.'

Jack hung up the phone and drained his beer, suddenly feeling very tired. He'd had a massive adrenalin rush while he'd been at the meeting and now he was drained.

He'd had his tea, even if it didn't involve steak or chops, so maybe it was time for bed.

Chapter 26

It was a cold, clear morning as Max started up the tractor to warm the engine before he drove it to the silos. There he would start emptying the grain into the mixer so he could make the feed mix.

The cattle in the feedlot bellowed loudly and made their way over to the fence, knowing their feed would be there soon. A couple of them kicked their heels and pigrooted around the pen.

There was a mist coming down over the hills and everything was dewy to the touch.

The mixer was brand new—a Jaylor. His boss had told him that it was a leading machine in a variety of feed lot operations and he'd been working towards buying one for a couple of years.

'It's going to make the feed easier for the stock to digest. It delivers a much more consistent feed mix. That was the sales pitch anyway.'

Max was excited to be using it for the first time today. He felt it was a privilege to be the first. Getting out of the tractor, he walked around the machine to make sure there was nothing in its way and then checked the augers in the silos. It was much easier when you could pull up straight under the auger and get the barley into the machine.

Back in the tractor, Max threw the power takeoff shaft into gear and jumped out to check all the bearings and moving joints.

The sound of tearing steel made him spin around. As he did so, something flew out of the mixer and embedded itself in his skin. Letting out a scream, he ran towards the shed, blood streaming down his arm.

Zara's phone rang. Tammy.

'Hey, Zara, have you heard?'

'Heard about what?'

'Jantarna Feedlot. There was an accident there yesterday. I saw the cop cars as I was driving past. Thought you might want to do a little investigating.'

'Really? Tell me more.'

'I'm only putting two and two together, but I passed an ambulance on the way to town as I was coming home yesterday, then I saw a government car. I'm really not sure what's happened, but I'm guessing there was an accident and WorkSafe have got involved.'

'Oh no, I hope not. I hate it when people get hurt.'

'I know—it's like when I get an ambo call-out. I just hope it's not going to be a local. It's bad enough if it's someone you don't know, but if you know them and their family, it's just about unbearable.'

'I get what you mean. That's small towns for you. Look, thanks for the heads-up. I'll see what I can find out.' She was about to hang up but remembered the silent protestors. 'Have your friends left yet?'

'They packed up last night and went, thank God. I can't tell you how pleased I am. They've been there on and off over three weeks. But this time they've taken everything and I think they've gone for good.'

'Hmm, I wonder where they're going next.'

'I'm just glad they're not at my front gate.'

'Yeah, that's something positive. Take care, Tammy, and thanks for letting me know.'

Zara went into Lachy's office and told him about the call.

'You'd better get your skates on then,' he said.

She ran down the stairs and jumped into her car. As she navigated her way out of the city and weaved up through the Adelaide Hills and out onto the highway to Melbourne, she thought about what Tammy had said. There was something curious about the timing of the protesters leaving and a workplace accident nearby. If that's what it was. Maybe she was being cynical but it seemed like too much of a coincidence.

The country passed by quickly. Deep valleys that held trickling water and were green with grass during winter were the colour of sun-bleached wheat. Even though the feed had begun to break down, the cattle grazing on the sides of the hills looked content and fat.

Zara turned down a gravel road and pulled up at Jantarna's front gate. A large sign directed her to report to the office first. Biosecurity was important.

Slowly, she drove down the winding road and parked in the carpark, where another sign directed her to the headquarters. Before she could get out, a man flew out the door and down the steps of the portable office and jogged slowly towards her.

'Can I help you?' he called out.

Zara recognised him as Justin Hicks, the owner of the feedlot and the chairperson of the Lot Feeders Association.

'Hi, Mr Hicks, I'm Zara from the *Farming Telegraph*.' She opened the car door and got out, offering her hand so he could shake it. 'I'm wondering if I could ask you—'

'I'd like you to leave, thanks.' He stood in front of her and crossed his arms.

'Really? Why?'

'I've got nothing to say to a reporter.'

'Mr Hicks, I actually don't know what's happened here, but I was hoping you'd be able to help me with that.' She smiled encouragingly.

'My lawyer will be issuing a statement in due course. Now I'd like you to leave.'

Zara's mind went into overdrive. *Shit! This was serious stuff if the lawyers were involved.* 'Okay,' she backed away. 'I'll get going now. Thanks for your help.'

Justin Hicks stood there with his arms crossed and watched her exit the property. As soon as she hit the main road, she drove to the closest town and went to the pub.

❧

Zara ordered a squash and a chicken schnitzel and sat at the bar waiting for the publican to finish serving the other customers. Taking a bite, she listened to the conversations going on around her, hoping to hear a snippet of news about Jantarna.

'Another drink, love?' the bartender asked.

'No, thanks. Hey, did you hear the ambulance go through town yesterday? I hope something horrible hasn't happened.'

He leaned in as he nodded. 'Yeah, bloody awful.'

'What happened?'

'Young Max Carter who works at Jantarna got hurt out there. His mum works for me and got the call here. Pulled her apron off and threw it on the counter and said she had to go. Rang me a bit later to tell me what had happened.'

'Oh no! And what did happen?'

'Bit of metal got embedded in his arm somehow. Cut right through the tendons and ligaments. Not sure whether he'll ever be able to use his hand properly again. And he's got shrapnel-type injuries to his right leg.'

Zara shook her head. 'That's just tragic,' she said. 'How on earth did that happen?'

A group of young men came in through the door and he walked away to serve them. As he did, he tossed over his shoulder, 'Something about a mixer giving way.'

Zara ate half of her schnitzel and then left with a wave to the publican.

She picked up the phone as soon as she got into her car and called a source she had in the police force.

'Hey, it's me,' she said when he answered.

'To what do I owe this pleasure?' he asked. 'I'm pretty sure this is not a social call.'

'Jantarna Feedlot.'

'What about it?'

'There was an accident there yesterday.'

'Hmm.'

'And someone was hurt. Got some metal embedded in his arm.'

'Yes.'

'Anything else you can tell me?'

'It was a WorkSafe investigation, but now they've handed it to us.'

'And why would they do that?'

'Because we think it was sabotage. There is nothing to suggest a brand-new machine should disintegrate the way that one did.'

'Disintegrate?'

'There was a chunk of metal inside the mixer. It flew out the side when the victim started the machine. It's not the sort of metal that could have been left behind after it had been manufactured. We're alleging that someone deliberately put the metal in there.'

Zara was silent for a moment, taking in what he had said. 'So . . . you're telling me that someone set out to deliberately hurt the victim?'

'We don't know the reasoning behind it yet.'

'Is there anything else that you can tell me?'

'I've told you everything that I know.'

'Thanks very much, I owe you a beer.'

'You do. More than one.'

Zara hung up the phone and leaned back against her seat, sighing.

❧

Zara tapped on Lachy's office door before sticking her head around the corner.

'You free?'

'Yup.' He picked up his coffee cup and took a slurp before screwing up his nose. 'Yuck. Cold.' Then he glanced at his watch. 'No wonder. I made it hours ago.' He refocused on her. 'What's up?'

'I don't know, but I've got a feeling.'

Lachy peered over the top of his glasses. 'I've always told you to trust your feelings.'

'I know.' She came into the room and sat down opposite him, choosing her words carefully. 'I suspect there are animal activists involved in this so-called accident at Jantarna.'

'Why?'

'I don't think it's a coincidence that the protesters who have been camped outside of Tammy and Stu's piggery up and left yesterday. The source I spoke to inside the police department told me they believe it was sabotage.'

'Why are you thinking activists?'

Zara shook her head. 'I don't really know. All this non-violent stuff they're doing, it just doesn't sit well with me. I think there's something going in the background. That they're leading up to something big. But I admit, I have no evidence to base my suspicions on at all.' She crossed her legs and sat back in the chair. 'I can't help thinking back to Colin Grawd. He and Gerard Hooper were both members of Voices for Animals. I've noticed some protesters are the same people from when Colin was killed.

'Now the other interesting thing is that Sophie Grawd is a member of this group too, and she was one of the people involved in flying the drone around in Barker. I'm seeing a link here.'

'We can't report thoughts without fact.'

'I know! And that's what's so frustrating.'

Lachy fossicked around on his desk and found an email he was looking for. Passing it to Zara, he said, 'Why don't you go to this rally tomorrow. Voices for Animals has sent a media release out saying they'll be protesting at the abs down south.'

'What should I be looking for?'

'Shit, I don't know. There's a reason you're an award-winning journalist. Look for these familiar faces you're telling me about, ask if there are any other projects they've got coming up. Befriend them, make them trust you so they'll talk. You know the drill.'

Zara nodded. 'Righto, I'll be there tomorrow.'

Chapter 27

The pub that Crumbs had directed Jack to was down a narrow alleyway. Not the kind of place to be frequented by anyone other than locals.

Dave had sent Jack a message about the incident at the feedlot. It would give him ammunition when he talked to Crumbs. Apparently the detectives on the case were certain it wasn't an accident.

'They couldn't find any disgruntled employees, or any other reason the metal would've been in the mixer. Brand-new machine. Nothing had let go inside. Someone put a freaking large piece of metal in it. It's come through the wall of the machine when it was started up.' There was a pause down the line before Dave added, 'And on the inside of the mixer, there was a message spray-painted on the wall. *Don't kill them.*'

'A message? Jeez, that sounds like a serial killer leaving a calling card.'

'Sure does, but it's interesting that it was out of sight. Be careful with that piece of intel because we haven't released it to the media.'

'But what's the point in disabling a mixer? That doesn't do anything about saving the animals,' Jack said.

'No, but it stops them from being fed, doesn't it?'

At that point Dave was called away, leaving Jack puzzling over his words. Surely not feeding animals was cruel in itself. In small pens, where there wasn't any grass, there wouldn't be anything to eat unless the feed mix was delivered to them. Why would whoever stopped the machine think that not feeding them was a good idea?

He was still thinking about this when Crumbs slid into the booth. 'Got rid of all that anger today?' he asked as he signalled the waiter.

'No different to yesterday,' Jack answered. 'Twenty-four hours isn't going to change my feelings about protecting animals.'

Crumbs smirked a little and ordered a straight whiskey. Jack waved two fingers to indicate he wanted one too.

He waited for Crumbs to say more, but he just sat back in his seat and looked around the bar, sunglasses still firmly in place. Jack had decided they must be prescription glasses because Crumbs never seemed to take them off.

Jack's bomber jacket had the two new pens placed in either sleeve, so to get a better picture, he sat side on to Crumbs and stared out across the bar.

'Pretty girl,' Crumbs finally said as the waitress came back with two Scotches.

Jack shrugged. 'She's all right.'

'Got a girlfriend, Jack?' Crumbs suddenly asked, eyeballing him.

'I thought the less we knew about each other, the better,' he answered.

Again, Crumbs smirked. Taking a sip of his drink, he didn't answer or press Jack for details.

'I saw a post on the *Farming Telegraph*'s Facebook page yesterday.' Jack said. 'Do you follow it?'

'Why would I follow a farming page?' Crumbs asked disdainfully.

Jack leaned back and assessed his comment. 'Why wouldn't you? There's all sorts of info on there.'

Crumbs shrugged. 'I got better things to do with my time. Facebook is for the younger generation. I know it's got its place, but it's not for me.'

Jack got out his phone and pulled up the post that Zara had written about the Jantarna incident. Turning it around, he let Crumbs read it. He must've been right about the prescription glasses because Crumbs left them in place while he read.

'Why have you brought that up?'

Jack leaned forward. 'It's bloody genius, don't you see?'

'What, that someone has sabotaged the machine?'

'If the mixer isn't going, the animals aren't being fed.' As he said this, he realised what Dave had been alluding to in his phone call.

Crumbs took another sip but didn't say anything else.

'If the machine isn't working, the animals aren't being fed. If they're not being fed, then they're no closer to getting killed, are they? See, animals in feedlots lose weight if they're not fed every day. They go backwards, you get me? And then there's no point in sending them to the abattoirs. Whoever has done this has disabled the machine so the cattle have to be put back out on pasture or fed hay. They'd lose condition and bang! Shut down the whole feedlot for a little while. I realise it's only short-term, but it certainly throws a spanner in the works for them. Means they lose money too. Whoever did this is not just standing around, protesting peacefully.'

'Really?'

'Yes, really, this is the sort of shit I'm talking about. One piece of metal and it shuts the whole place down. Why can't we do this sort of thing?'

'I didn't read anything in there saying that it was done by activists,' Crumbs answered.

'That's even better, don't you think? It could be anyone—a pissed-off employee. Maybe the owner was fucking someone he shouldn't have been. There's a heap of reasons a person might want to do something like this.'

'But, Jack,' Crumbs leaned forward and stared at him through the darkened lens, 'what's the point in doing something like this if no one knows why it's done?'

'Because it's about the animals, nothing else. We'd know we'd stopped them from being killed.'

Nodding slowly, Crumbs leaned back again and watched Jack, before abruptly changing the subject. 'This protest tomorrow. You need to keep your anger under control. There's no negotiation with that.'

Jack banged his fist lightly on the table. 'Haven't you been listening to me?'

Suddenly Crumbs leaned forward again, this time reaching over the table and pushing his finger into Jack's chest. 'What you need to understand is that this is bigger than you. Don't you dare fuck up what we've been working towards for years. Just because you see silent protests doesn't mean there aren't other things going on. So, turn up tomorrow, keep your hands to yourself and do what I tell you, otherwise there's gonna be trouble. Hear me?'

'I'm not going to hang around just to play footsies with the media. It's gone beyond that, don't you think? Let's really get into some action.'

'I've told you. There are other things going on that you don't know about.'

Jack stared at him, his mind whirling. As he looked at Crumbs's face, the half-smile wasn't only arrogant but secretive.

'That wasn't your group causing that mixer to explode, was it? Did you guys do that?' His voice rose in excitement and he drummed his fingers on the table. 'And that arsehole got hurt too, so you got a double whammy! Good job!'

Again, Crumbs didn't answer, but the way he cocked his head to the side made Jack positive he was right.

'So, you do that sort of shit. When can I—'

'Calm the fuck down.' The anger returned. Crumbs's voice was low and mean. 'I never said that.'

'But—'

'I'm telling you once more. Turn up at the protest tomorrow, but be cool, okay? You can't let yourself get carried away. You've got to keep a lid on things, otherwise we'll get blackbanned. We still need to get our message out there. You stuff this up for us, then you'll find yourself in a whole new world of hurt.

'You're right,' Crumbs went on, 'the mixer was a great idea. Shame that someone had to get hurt in the process. Still,' he stood up and threw a twenty-dollar note on the table, 'it's all for the greater good. See you tomorrow.'

Jack held out his hand, but Crumbs left without shaking it.

❧

'He didn't confess, but I'm sure he organised it,' Jack said to Dave on the phone when he was back in the safety of the unit. 'I've got the recording and camera info, so I'll put that out back for you. Have you worked out who this bloke is yet?'

'Not yet. I've run his photo by most of the people who would know but haven't come up with a hit. Even when I put the nickname into the database, I got zero. I'll keep working on IDing him.

'I'm thinking he's either been involved with protesting for a long time and flown under the radar, or he's only just started, and I'm not getting the feeling from what you've told me that he's just started. I've got some people pulling up media reports on old protests—big ones—to see if we can link him to any of those and then get a lead on him that way.'

'He's been around for a long time,' Jack said with certainty. 'And there's a lot more to him than meets the eye.'

'Other than that, you going okay?'

'No problems. Except the bed is shit. Can you fix that?'

Dave snorted. 'First-world problem, you clown. Did I tell you when I first went undercover I slept on the floor of public toilets?'

'Excellent, one of the "back in my day" stories,' Jack said, before he took a swig from his beer.

Laughing, Dave said, 'Sounds like you're doing fine. What's the plan for tomorrow?'

'We're going to turn up and hold a silent vigil outside the abs.'

'You going to spice it up?'

'Play it by ear, I guess, but probably. I'm an angry fucker, remember? I've got to prove I'm capable of doing what I say I can.'

'Just be a little careful,' Dave cautioned. 'If he's told you to stay calm, then you probably should. But you read the play on the day.'

'Yeah, I'll do that. Read the play on the day.' They hung up and Jack walked over to the sliding door that opened onto a small patio, if it could be described as such. It was so tiny it would be a squeeze to fit two people in chairs out there.

He could hear the next-door neighbours arguing again. They seemed to do that a lot. And on the other side of his unit a lady was sitting outside having a cigarette. The smoke wafted into his place and Jack grimaced. Filthy habit. He wasn't staying outside to smell that. He couldn't see the stars anyway.

Going back inside, he shut the door and threw himself on the roughly made bed. Staring at the discoloured ceiling, he had an intense longing for the clear air and space of home. Then he reminded himself he had to get that thought out of his head, otherwise he might fuck it up tomorrow. With a burst of energy, he jumped off the bed and grabbed his computer. He didn't need to leave all the investigative work to Dave. He was pretty good at research too.

Dave had always taught him to be proactive. Jack googled 'big protests in Australia'. That didn't produce anything. He tried 'Animal activists clash'. Plenty of hits for that. He clicked on a video and watched a crowd of people move towards a supermarket, yelling and calling out. He didn't listen to what they were saying, he wanted to see the faces. Could he recognise Crumbs?

After two hours and five beers, Jack hadn't seen him and closed the computer in frustration, before turning out the light and falling back on the bed.

Just before he fell asleep, he had a thought. What if they were looking at this all wrong? Maybe it wasn't only animal protests they should be looking at. If Crumbs had been around for a while, maybe he'd been involved in other types of protests.

Chapter 28

Zara was worried about her mum. She'd tried to ring her daily for the past three days and she hadn't called back. On her way to the protest, she tried again.

'*You've called Rowberry Glen. Thanks for calling. Please leave . . .*'

Zara hung up. No point in leaving another message. Maybe she should ring James. She'd planned to go up there this weekend and stay for the fortnight. She still had the interview to do with Brock Doyle about the saltbush he'd planted.

The phone rang and she glanced down at the screen. Relief surged through her. 'Gee, I'm glad you've called me back, I was beginning to get worried,' she said by way of greeting.

'Bad few days,' Lynda answered. 'But I think I'm on the up and up now.'

Instantly Zara was on alert. 'Bad as in grief?' she asked.

'That and it's just so dry. Another one of the dams has run out of water. So we're having to cart it from one end of the place to the other. Not that it's a hard job, it's just time-consuming and soul-destroying.' She paused and Zara could hear the rattle of the ute in the background. 'And it's also soul-destroying burying one of your children,' she said in a low tone.

'Oh, Mum.' Zara glanced in the rear-view mirror and flicked on the blinker to change lanes. A truck in front of her was labouring up a steep hill. 'I was going to come home this weekend, would that help?'

'We're shearing on Friday and Saturday. I've got to get rid of stock. But don't let that stop you. And we . . .' Zara heard her mother suck in a deep breath as if trying to regain control of her emotions. 'We have to scatter Will's ashes.'

Her stomach lurched. When she'd left, the urn containing Will's ashes had been sitting on the kitchen window. She hadn't given much thought to scattering them; somehow she'd thought they'd just stay where they were. It would be like a funeral all over again.

'We don't have to do that until you're ready. It's not been that long, Mum, only six weeks.'

'I know, but I feel like I want to.'

'Do you know where?'

'I thought maybe in the creek. I know that sounds funny, because if there's a flood he'll be washed away, but he always loved the creek. Sometimes, after he got sick, I'd see him sitting down there on one of the fallen logs. I never knew what was going through his mind when he was down there—he never told me—but he and the dogs would stay there for hours. What do you think?'

'I think that sounds just like him, Mum. And it's a peaceful place. Among the wind and sunshine. Will would love the rain too, so I don't think you need to worry about him being washed away. He'd still be there in spirit.'

'Perhaps we could do that this weekend, when you're back?'

'I'm coming for a couple of weeks, so we can do it when we're ready. There's no hurry.'

'I started to clean out his room.'

'Ah.'

'There's so much gear in there. Stuff I didn't know about. Not that I needed to, I guess. I'm only his mum. But what are you supposed to do with five pairs of Rossi boots in various stages of wear?'

'Why don't you see if they'll fit Ray?'

Zara was sure her mum didn't hear her, because she kept right on talking. 'And all those brand-new R.M. Williams clothes he had—hardly ever worn. I can give them to the Red Cross, but then there's his phone and computer and watch.'

'You can't give everything away, Mum. You need to keep some things.'

Silence.

'I found something interesting in there, Zara. I don't really know what to do with it.'

Zara stayed quiet, but her heart kicked up a notch. Had her brother had a secret life?

'His diary. He wrote in it every day. You know, all the work we did on the farm. If we'd shifted a mob of ewes, he recorded it. If we drenched, he recorded it. You have to do that these days so we have records if we ever get audited by the Department of Ag.'

'Yeah, I know about that.'

'I read a couple of entries.'

'What was so interesting about them?'

'Will had been helping out old Terry Cook. He has land a couple of farms away from here. He was getting in a bit of a state because he couldn't afford to buy any more hay and his cattle were too poor to take to market. Will helped him out as much as he could, took a few loads of our hay over to him, but he couldn't get Terry to sell the animals.

'This was what he wrote in his diary: *Spoke to the Department about Terry today. They're going to investigate him. I feel like a traitor but something has to be done.*'

Zara didn't say anything, but her mind was whirling. Department of Ag?

'So he reported Terry for animal cruelty?'

'Well, I guess that was what it was. He obviously felt terrible about it, but Terry wouldn't listen to him. He would've felt he had to do something. Will hated any type of animal cruelty.'

'I know, but . . .' Zara stopped. 'I wonder if that had something to do with the drone turning up at Barker. Do you think he would've reported Terry to Voices for Animals?'

'No way, Zara! How could you even think that?'

'What was the date of this entry?'

'Eight weeks before he died.'

Zara nodded to herself. 'Timing fits with the drone turning up.'

'He wouldn't dob in a fellow farmer,' Lynda insisted. 'Not to an animal activist group. To the Department of Ag . . . well, I guess as farmers we all believe that if someone is mistreating their animals they should be held accountable. They're the people who give our industry a bad name.'

'So the question would be how did Voices for Animals find out?' Zara asked. 'And I totally agree. If someone is doing the wrong thing, the authorities should be notified so something can be done. You can't let people get away with mistreating their animals, Mum.'

'Like I said, I'm not disagreeing with the fact they should be reported. I'd encourage that! But I know Will wouldn't have said anything to an animal rights group.'

There was silence on the phone line. Zara changed the subject. 'How's Ray turning out? Is he as good as we thought he was going to be?'

'Yeah, he's great. Got a real knack with stock and he rides a motorbike! Actually, he looks like he was born on one. That's very helpful through the rocky hills.'

'Excellent. That's good to hear. Now, Mum, I've got to go.' The abattoirs had come into sight and she could see the protesters were there already. 'I'm covering a rally today, but I'll call you when I get home, okay?'

'Sounds good, honey.'

'Oh, by the way, how's James?'

'He's as solid as a rock.'

'I'm glad, Mum. See you.' Zara hung up and looked for a place to park.

Running her hands through her hair, she sighed. Maybe she'd left Barker too early. Her mum shouldn't be alone right now. And she could write from anywhere. Perhaps she needed to talk to Lachy about having some more time there. There were plenty of interesting stories in the mid-north and she wouldn't need to be with her mum all the time—just knowing Zara was nearby would probably help her. And maybe it would help Zara too. She'd been missing the sense of space since came back down to Adelaide.

As she drove by the protesters, she looked out for Sophie. There were about thirty people in the crowd, linked across the gateway into the abs. The trucks wouldn't be able to get in and out, if there were any coming. The police were there too.

That's not unusual, she thought. *Especially at a protest at an abattoir.*

Parking the car, she made sure she had her phone and it was fully charged, then walked over to the group.

'Hi, I'm Zara from the *Farming Telegraph*. Can I talk to you?' she asked the first person she came across.

'We're just trying to stop the animals from being murdered,' he said.

Zara nodded, knowing she wasn't going to get anything out of him other than the party line. She tried a policeman who was standing nearby instead.

'Everyone well behaved today?' she asked the officer.

'So far so good,' he answered.

With a half-smile, she left him alone, knowing he wouldn't say anything more either.

A man wearing a shirt proclaiming him to be the manager of the abattoirs came to the front gate and the crowd saw him and started to get restless. They shook their signs and pointed at them but didn't make any noise. Zara decided it was eerie to watch. People with so much passion not using their voices.

'I'm asking you to leave,' the manager called. 'You're disrupting our business.'

A general shuffle and, in among the crowd, Zara saw Sophie. Perfect; she'd grab her afterwards and talk to her.

She watched as the silent crowd continued to move restlessly and jiggle their signs up and down.

'We're not leaving.'

Everyone's head turned in the direction of the voice, including Zara's. She sucked in her breath when she located the speaker.

A dishevelled-looking man, with a beard and vivid blue eyes. Even with the beard, she recognised him immediately. Jack.

'What the heck?' she muttered, moving in and snapping some pictures. She zoomed in on his face. It was Jack, no question.

'How can you say we're disrupting your business when you're disrupting animals' lives?' someone else called out.

'There's need for change!' A woman's voice rang out this time and something flicked within the crowd. They became restless and started to chant: 'Need for change. Need for change. Stop murdering the animals!'

Zara watched as another protestor bumped into Jack and he stumbled. Another person came into view—the person who had pushed him.

Cloudy Eye. Oh my God! What is he doing here?

She frantically clicked the camera and took some close-up shots of him. He was wearing sunglasses as usual, but she knew they hid a cloudy left eye. It was the man who had sat in the courtroom all through Colin Grawd's case.

The protesters kept up their chants, stamping their feet and shaking their signs.

A truck rumbled into view. It was carrying a load of sheep and the protesters joined hands to form a human chain across the driveway.

The driver had to slow to a stop.

Zara watched as Jack banged on the door of the truck. 'And you're helping the bastards kill them,' he yelled, looking wide-eyed and out of control. Zara moved closer and took more photos. As Jack turned, he caught her eye and a look of shock crossed his face. Then he ducked into the crowd and disappeared.

The police started to move in and surround the protesters.

'We told you we wouldn't interfere unless things got rowdy,' one of the coppers yelled. 'Pull your heads in.'

But it seemed to Zara that Jack and the others who had called out had unleashed something within the protesters.

'Save our animals!' they chanted over and over. With their arms linked, they kept moving forward, surrounding the truck until the driver couldn't get out if he'd wanted to. One of them went to the back where the gate was and tried to unpin it, to let the animals out.

'Enough!' yelled the police and they forced their way through the human chain and stood in front of the gate, protecting it.

Zara's eyes were everywhere but a movement outside of the crowd caught her eye. She turned and saw that Cloudy Eye had left the group and skirted around the edge of the cars then disappeared. Clearly he didn't want to be caught up in any trouble.

Zara hurried after him. 'Sir!' she called to him. 'Sir, I'd really love to be able to tell your side of the story. Would you talk to me? Sir?'

He didn't stop until he got to a car, and yanked open the door. He started it and slowly pulled out onto the road and drove away. Zara tried to snap a photo of the car rego but it had all happened too quickly and the car was out of range by the time she managed to get the camera to her eye.

In the short time it had taken for Cloudy Eye to leave, the police had got everyone under control and the crowd had begun dispersing.

Zara made a beeline for Jack. Getting within a couple of metres of him, she was about to call his name when he looked at her with wide eyes and a small shake of his head.

She stopped. Had he just warned her off? *He's undercover*, she suddenly realised. *What's going on with this group to warrant putting a cop undercover?* Not wanting to put him in any danger, she turned, feeling a trickle of fear in her stomach. *Be safe, Jack*, she thought, and went in search of Sophie.

She was in deep conversation with a woman Zara didn't recognise.

'Sophie? Would you talk to me about what you're doing here today?' Zara asked when she was close enough.

Sophie glanced at the woman as if looking for permission. 'I guess so.'

'We'll both talk to you,' the woman said. 'I'm Kristen. Today's sort of rally isn't how we usually go about things.' She gave a rueful smile and shrugged. 'But I guess these things happen. Everyone has been getting a bit restless of late.'

'Do you mind if I record our chat?'

'That's fine.'

Getting out her phone, Zara quickly ran through some questions in her mind and jotted a couple of them on paper.

'Okay, I'm recording an interview on the . . .' She gave the date and time, then asked Sophie and Kristen to state their names, ages and occupations.

'Can you tell me about Voices for Animals? What you stand for and how you achieve it?'

Kristen began, 'We're an organisation that has been active for about ten years. We felt there was a need to get information out to the public about farming and the way animals are treated on farms. We believe in open and transparent industries and that people have a right to know how their food is farmed and gets to their plate. If it's cruel, then it shouldn't be allowed.'

'Sophie, let me ask you why you're here today supporting this cause.'

'Sure. I lost my dad in an accident earlier this year, as you know. At first I decided I didn't want to have anything to do with rallies, because my dad was killed while he was protesting. However, I've since thought his death shouldn't be in vain—he was fighting for something he raised me to believe in, so I needed to get involved in what I'm passionate about, which is animals—all sorts of animals, not just farming ones. So,' she shrugged her shoulders, 'here I am.'

'And you say that you're a non-violent organisation. How do you make sure of that?'

'We have very strict rules in place about violence,' said Kristen. 'It's not something we want to engage in. There certainly are people out there who like to take things further, but we believe we'll get more support by quietly stating our business rather than being extreme. Today was a little more rowdy than usual.'

Zara nodded. 'Two more questions: what's your end game? If you managed to get all the farmers to give up farming, how would you plan to look after all the animals?'

The two women looked at each other, lost for words. 'Ah . . . well, of course we'd make sure they were well looked after.'

'And how would you do that when you don't have any experience in caring for farm animals?'

'I think you're twisting what we're trying to do here. We raise awareness that some animals are treated in an unacceptable way and we want to see that changed.'

'But do you believe that animals can be farmed without cruelty?'

'This is my personal belief,' Kristen answered. 'If you kill an animal to eat it, I think that is cruel. If you kill an animal full stop, that is cruel. It's the killing part which is brutal.'

'One more question while I think of it: have either of you ever eaten meat?'

They both nodded. 'I used to until found out how they were killed,' Sophie said.

'Oh, that's made think of another question. Have you ever been to a farm and had farming practices explained to you? In other words, do you think you're well enough informed about the industry?'

'We know what we see.'

'Thanks for your time. I'll write this up as soon as I get back to the office.' Turning off the recording app, she smiled at both women. 'That was great. It's really good to get an understanding of what you're trying to achieve. I like to write really balanced articles and your comments are going to help with that. Awesome!'

They said their goodbyes and Zara made her way back to the car, her thoughts returning to Jack. He was nowhere to be seen, so she hoped he'd left and that no one had noticed his reaction to her.

As she was putting everything into the car, she heard a voice behind her.

'You and I need to have a talk. Now.'

Chapter 29

Zara froze. Slowly she turned and saw Dave standing behind her. Immediately she relaxed.

'Don't say a word,' he said. 'Get in your car and follow me.'

She opened her mouth to ask a question and then shut it quickly. The look on his face said he would brook no argument.

Dave was driving a nondescript white station wagon and Zara followed him closely, her heart beating fast. *What the hell was going on?*

Ten minutes later, he pulled into a side road and drove a little way down. That heightened Zara's anxiety. Still, she flicked on her blinker and followed him.

The car had barely stopped when she was out the door, walking quickly towards Dave. 'What the hell is going on?' Her voice was high with tension.

Dave walked towards her, his face set, and he was pointing at her. 'Give me your camera.'

'What?'

'Did you get photos of Jack? Give me your camera now.'

'Yeah, I got photos. You can't delete them, if that's what you're thinking. There's a freedom of information act, you know.' She was pissed off with his high-handedness.

He stopped in front of her and poked a finger at her. 'You will delete them, otherwise you'll be putting one of my men at risk. Give me your camera. Or I'll watch you delete them.'

'Risk from what?' Zara persisted. 'I'm not frightened of you, Dave. Pull whatever sort of shit you want to, but I'm not—'

'You listen to me, girlie. My only concern is for my officer. Jack is undercover, and if you blow that, you don't want to know what I'll do to you.'

That stopped her. She'd been in the right, but the fact that she might put Jack in danger—well, that was a sobering thought.

'How is a photo going to put him in danger? He's at the protest, and I assume doing what he should be doing. I'm not going to out him as an undercover cop.'

'If you put that in the paper and someone who knows him sees it, then he'll be in trouble. We don't want anything linking back to him. I want you to delete the photos.'

'All right, all right, I will,' Zara snapped. 'Stop the bad cop act. I know you better than that.'

'It's a serious thing he's doing, Zara. The bad cop act is so you are under no illusion as to what is going on. You need to forget you've seen him. If you go to another protest and he's there, don't even make eye contact with him. These people are not to be messed around with.'

'Has this got something to do with the feedlot accident the other day?'

'No comment. I just need you to do as I've asked.'

'Of course I will. I like Jack, he's a nice man. Unlike you when you want to be a prick.'

Dave looked at her. 'I've been called that more than once. Sorry if you think I was a bit heavy-handed. I needed to get my point across.'

'I'm deleting the photos now. Do you want to watch?'

'I wouldn't mind seeing what you've got.'

'Ah, so you need me now? How about a bit of quid pro quo?'

Dave had the good grace to look embarrassed, but finally he nodded. 'We'll see where that takes us,' he said. 'But I'll try.'

'Hang on.' She jogged back to the car and pulled her camera out of the bag and switched it on. Scrolling through the photos as she walked, she deleted the ones of Jack.

Cloudy Eye appeared in a shot and she stopped. 'There.' Her finger stabbed at the image. 'Do you know who this is?'

Dave took the camera and peered at the screen. 'Can you make this any bigger?'

'Not unless I download it to my computer and zoom in. Do you want me to?'

'Can you do it here?' He looked around at the dirt track. 'Don't you need to be back at the office or something?'

'I can do it here.' She put the computer on the bonnet of her car, opened it up, tapped a couple of buttons and set the camera next to it.

'How do you do that without an internet connection?' Dave wanted to know.

'I'm hotspotting from my phone,' she answered, looking at the screen. Tapping a couple of icons, she made the photo they had been looking at come up. A couple of clicks later and Cloudy Eye's face took up the whole screen.

'Why have you got an interest in him?' Dave asked.

'I've seen him before and I couldn't ever work out who he was. Do you know?'

Dave shook his head. 'I can't say I do.' He studied the photo. 'Where have you seen him? At protests?'

'What am I going to get in return?' she asked, crossing her arms. 'Come on, Dave, you know how this works. I give you what you want and you give me something I want.'

'You know, for someone so young, you drive a hard bargain.' He grinned as he said it.

'I learn quickly.'

'How about when this whole operation is over I give you an inside running on the story? Although there may not be any story. It'll just depend on what happens and how things go.'

'I understand that.'

Dave looked at her expectantly.

'I covered the Hooper manslaughter trial. I don't know if you remember it? Maybe you wouldn't, because it happened in Victoria. I was sent to cover it.'

'Refresh my memory.'

'It was Voices for Animals which started the protest—they were trying to stop logging and therefore the animals losing their homes.

'Actually, on a side note, these blokes weren't just members of VFA, it came up in the trial that they were on the membership list for a few different activist groups.

'But I digress. A couple of blokes broke in one night and started to muck around with the machinery—drain the oil so an engine would cook, cut the wires so a machine wouldn't start. Mischievous stuff, and bloody annoying for the operators. Anyway, they mucked it up. One guy—Gerard Hooper, allegedly—cut the hydraulic hoses at the back of the machine. The ones that hold up the bucket of the front-end loader. He cut the wrong ones,' Zara finished.

'I remember this. Sophie Grawd told me about it when I interviewed her. It was her father who was killed. Just refresh my memory.'

'Well, the hydraulics failed, and the bucket of the front-end loader crashed to the ground. Unfortunately, it pinned the other guy—Colin Grawd—underneath and he bled to death. The police charged Hooper with manslaughter.'

'How does this bloke fit in with all of that?'

'I called him Mr Cloudy Eye—his left eye looks as if it's been damaged somehow. He sat through the trial. Every single day he was there. He didn't sit with either family but I was very sure he wasn't there just because he had an interest in law. I couldn't link him to anyone, though.'

'Do you think he knew either of the men?'

'I couldn't be sure. I never saw the accused look at him, or him at the accused. But . . .' She stopped, remembering something. 'Oh my God! I found a photo while I was unpacking in Barker. It was one of those snaps that just happen—I didn't even realise what I'd taken—but as Hooper was being led away, it looked like he and this Cloudy Eye were staring at each other.'

Dave nodded. 'And where is this photo now?'

'Still back in Barker.'

'Maybe you could get it for me?'

'I might have a copy back at the office too. I'll check. Now,' Zara paused, 'I was talking to Mum a while ago and she mentioned that Will had rung the Department of Ag in relation to a farmer who didn't have enough hay to feed his stock but wouldn't sell them.'

Dave cocked his head and looked at her.

'I wonder if that's how the drone came to be in Barker.'

'That's a bit of a leap. Why would you say that?' Dave felt the thrill of adrenalin rush through him. And that would make sense of Will's cryptic comment that Dave had never got to ask him about before he died. But he couldn't let Zara know that, just as he couldn't let her know that he knew about the Hooper trial.

She shrugged. 'Will hated any type of cruelty to animals. It would be just like him to have reported the farmer if he refused to do the right thing. I wonder if he talked to VFA too. And that's why they turned up.'

'That's really good info, Zara. I'll look into that. It would be great to know why they suddenly started to target Barker. Thanks.'

She nodded. 'You know I'm back and forth between Adelaide and Barker, don't you?'

'Yeah, Kim told me about the arrangement. I think that's great for your mum.'

'Don't think I should leave her alone at the moment. I thought she'd be okay, but she didn't sound it today.'

'What about you? How are you?'

Zara thought for a moment. 'I keep very busy,' she answered.

'You haven't let yourself think about it very much then?'

'Not even that, I just need to be busy.'

'Can I give you a little word of advice?'

Zara smiled ruefully and slid her computer away. 'I think you're going to whether I want it or not.'

'It would be better to try to deal with your grief. I left something for way too long and it ate away at me for years. Finally, after Kim telling me over and over that I needed to face it head on, I did and I had no idea how much it was weighing me down.' He smiled. 'Anyway, I'm a middle-aged man, what would I know . . . but maybe have a think about it, hey?'

Zara nodded. 'Sure. And keep me in the loop with what's going on with this story, okay?'

'That I will. Right, you head out. I'll follow in a while.'

❧

Back at the hotel, he rang Steve, his boss, and asked him about the case. 'Do you know anything?'

'Look, I remember it vaguely, but not the details.'

'The journalist who covered the case told me this Crumbs bloke is the same guy who was at the trial. She said he was there every day and she couldn't link him to either of the families. I think it's strange he's turned up in another VFA protest. It also came to light he's got a cloudy eye. Now, that's something Jack hasn't mentioned.'

'Are you sure this is the bloke that Jack is talking to?'

'Same fella.'

'Well, if he's never mentioned that eye, how can we be sure it's the same man?'

'I've got photos of him from Jack and it's the same guy. He wears dark sunglasses all of the time.'

'And we still don't know who he is?'

'Nope. I'm not liking these coincidences.'

'No.' Silence. 'Well, we're just going to have to work out who he is. Maybe Jack could get him a drink and snatch the glass. We could run his fingerprints and see if we get a match.'

'We could try, just so long as it doesn't put Jack in any danger.'

'Dave, you know as well as I do that there is danger in what he's doing now. He'll just have to be careful how he gets hold of the glass. You've got a secure drop-off and pick-up point for the pens, haven't you? Get him to leave it there.'

'Okay. Will do.' Dave rang off and dialled Jack straightaway.

'You right?' he asked.

'Shit, what was Zara doing there? I thought she was back in Barker.'

'I thought she was too. Anyway, we got it wrong, but I think I've sorted it.'

'How do you know?'

'I keyholed her on the way out. Got her to come with me. Scared her a bit, then turned on the charm. She's pretty switched on. Happily deleted all the photos of you and promised not to make contact with you or write anything about you in the paper.'

'Once she understood the situation, I was sure she wouldn't compromise my position,' Jack said. 'She's straight down the line.'

'Well, she's all tucked in. Now, there's something else. I need you to be extra careful around Crumbs. I don't know what he's mixed up in, but it's something. Zara recognised him from a court case she was covering a while ago.'

Jack was silent, then said, 'I told you there was something off about him. Shit! Was that the Hooper case?'

'Yeah, anyway, I want you to try to lift something he's touched so we can get fingerprints. A glass, maybe.'

'Great idea. I had a thought last night—maybe he's been an activist in another industry. I googled everything I could think of but couldn't find anything on him.'

'Good point. If you can get a fingerprint sample, then we can see what the database turns up.'

'Sure.'

'Any other plans?'

'All's quiet on the western front.'

'Well, we'll just have to sit it out and see what they plan next.'

Chapter 30

Zara went straight to the office to type up her story and get it to Lachy before the deadline. She couldn't stop going over in her head what had just happened. *Jack was undercover!*

It gave her a squirmy, anxious feeling, knowing someone was in danger. She desperately wanted to pick up the phone and call him, but the idea was laughable. There was no way she could do that.

'Any goss?' Lachy asked her as he walked by her desk.

'Not a thing. The protestors got a bit rowdier than usual, but nothing crazy. Interviewed a couple of them afterwards and got some good quotes. I'd like to ring the abs manager, but the impression I got from him today was that he won't be talking to anyone. They disrupted a truckload of stock arriving today, so he's probably got a bit on his plate, making sure they catch up with the kill.'

'You'll still try?'

'Of course. Even if we run it next week, he still gets his side of the story across.'

'Sounds like a plan.'

Lachy kept walking and she heard him talking to the other journalists in the office. He ran a tight ship, Lachy did, and everyone loved working for him. He was a team player but pulled rank when he needed to. A uniter of people.

Focusing on her computer, Zara put in her headphones and started to type up the interview. When she'd finished the text, she went through the photos and worked out which ones would be best to go with the story. The one of Cloudy Eye caught her attention and she stopped scrolling through the file to have another look.

'Hey, Michael,' she called. 'Come and have a look at this bloke. Do you know who he is?'

'Flick it through on an email, yeah? I'm not going to make deadline otherwise.'

Deciding to write a group email, she sent it to all the reporters in the office, and Lachy for good measure, even though she was sure he'd already told her during the trial that he didn't recognise the face.

'Right, that's me for the day. I've got to go and do a few jobs,' she said to no one in particular.

'Hey, you up for a drink tonight?' Liz called.

The thought of having to go out for a drink made Zara suddenly feel exhausted. 'No, I don't think I am, sorry, Liz. I need to go home and put my feet up.'

And ring my mum, she thought.

Even though her mind was buzzing with the excitement and revelations of the day, what Dave had said to her about dealing with grief had filtered through too. As much as Will's death really wasn't something she wanted to talk or think about, perhaps she should. A quiet night at home might be just what she needed.

Collecting her things, Zara drove home in a bit of a daze and pulled up in her parking spot to find her mum's car parked next to it.

'What are you doing here?' she asked in surprise as she opened the car door. 'I only talked to you a few hours ago and you were carting water!'

'I know and I probably shouldn't be here, but I needed to get away. I haven't been off the farm or out of Barker since Will died. It felt like the walls were closing in on me.'

'Well, I'm glad you're here.' She hugged her mum. 'I'm feeling a bit out of sorts tonight too.'

Together they walked up the stairs and Zara fished out her key. Unlocking the door, they went inside, and after dumping her things on the couch, Zara poured them both a wine.

'I don't know what I have to eat,' Zara said, standing in front of the open fridge as if something was going to jump out at her.

'We can order takeaway, can't we? That's what you do in the city, isn't it?'

'I guess we can!'

'Close the fridge door, Zara. You're wasting electricity holding it open like that. Will used to do exactly the same thing. Stand there and gaze in as if something was miraculously going to make itself and he'd be able to eat it.'

Zara giggled and closed the door. 'Sorry. What did you do with James for the night?'

'He's on call.'

'What's the goss on him, Mum?' Zara asked, flopping down next to Lynda on the couch.

'There's no "goss", as you call it, at my age, Zara! Bloody hell, anyone would think I was a teenager. We met, started spending some time together and, I don't know, we just fell into a comfortable friendship. And a friendship is a great start to a relationship.'

'Is he going to move in with you?'

'The tricky thing about him being a doctor is that he needs to be close to the hospital in case of emergencies and it's a thirty-minute drive into town from our place. But the house is pretty lonely and quiet without Will.' Lynda looked down at the glass of wine in her hand and swallowed hard. Then she said, 'Zara, I know I've asked you before, but have you thought about coming home to work on the farm now that Will has gone?'

Zara had been expecting the question for a while now. 'No, Mum,' she said quietly. 'Not to work on the farm. Can you see me running around in the sheep yards and driving the tractor to put the crop in?'

'You used to.'

'Yeah, when I was a kid! I'd end up putting the rams in with the ewe at the wrong time of year or something.'

Lynda leaned back and looked at her daughter. 'You know, I always thought you'd come home at some stage.'

'Why? I love journalism.'

'I know you do, but the call of the country is usually pretty strong for a person who's grown up there. I guess . . . well, maybe I just hoped.'

'Don't get me wrong, you know I love the farming life—but writing about it, not actually doing it. I really enjoy getting out and talking to the people who are on the ground, and reporting on all the innovations, but as for actually doing it,' she shook her head. 'I think . . .' She paused, trying to find the right words. 'I think I love the adrenalin of deadlines and the buzz of the office. It's exciting trying to beat the clock, you know?'

Lynda laughed. 'No, I can't say I do! I would find that incredibly stressful. It's hard enough trying to battle with Mother Nature and to make it rain when we need it.'

'Yeah, well, hopefully it will come soon.' She paused for a minute and then said: 'I do miss home, though. The space and the dogs. The stars. But I love my job as well.'

'Can you have both, do you think?' Lynda asked.

Zara didn't answer for a while. 'Probably,' she said eventually. She thought about telling her mum that she had thought about shifting back to Barker, then decided against it. *Maybe not yet.*

They sat in companionable silence until Lynda said, 'Kim came to visit the other day. She's been an incredible support.'

'She seems really nice. And Dave does too. I had to laugh when I found I was going to be living next to a policeman in Barker! The trust between journos and coppers is pretty low. I thought it was a little ironic.'

'And Jack, he seems very nice too. I had a bit to do with him at the footy club when Will was still playing and I was helping out in the canteen.'

Zara looked at her mum out of the corner of her eye. 'And why would you be saying that, Mum?'

Lynda raised her eyebrows. 'No reason at all. I was just making conversation.'

'It sounded like matchmaking to me.'

'Not at all!'

'Really?' Zara's tone was dry. 'It's not like you haven't got priors on trying to set me up with other country blokes. And why did you mention Jack and not Karl? As far as I know Karl's footloose and fancy-free.'

'Do you like him? He's been such a help.'

'No, Mum!' Zara exclaimed in a loud voice.

Lynda's face became serious. 'I worry about you, Zara. You're always running here and there, chasing the next big news story.'

'No, I'm not. I only cover agriculture.'

'Don't split hairs. Just hear me out. You're getting older and I guess all I'm saying is that it would be nice if you found someone who made you happy. Like I have. Don't you get lonely living by yourself?'

'I've always enjoyed my own company, you know that.'

'And Will was the same. Do you remember, I don't know how old you both were—maybe nine and ten—when you packed up a saddlebag with enough food to last for the day, then you headed out along the creek and disappeared? If I remember correctly, you and he mustered a paddock of sheep and pushed them through to the next one without telling Dad! He didn't know until the next day, when he went out there and found they were in a paddock that didn't have much feed in it.'

'I remember the belting we got for doing that,' Zara said. 'The both of us thought we were being helpful! Will heard Dad talking about needing to shift the sheep and not having the time. It was just the wrong mob.' She sighed reflectively as she thought about Will and the fun they used to have together.

'Do you miss him?' Lynda asked.

'Of course I do. In some ways it doesn't seem real back here in the city.'

'It seems very real in the empty house at home,' her mum said quietly.

'Yeah. You know, I was here the other night, sitting out on the balcony trying to look for the stars, but I couldn't see them. All the lights and all. I did love being able to sit out on the verandah at home and look at the night sky.'

'There's something soul mending about seeing the stars.'

'Whatever happened to the trampoline we used to have at the back of the house?' Zara asked suddenly. 'I used to take my doona out there and sleep on the tramp so I could look up at them. I loved doing that.'

'Until there was a dewy night and you'd wake up with the doona all wet,' Lynda answered. Again there was silence.

'We had a lot of fun growing up on the farm.' Suddenly she changed her mind about telling her mum her thoughts on moving home. 'Mum?'

'Hmm?'

'I've been thinking about moving back to Barker. Not to the farm, but to Barker.' Zara thought she'd better clarify that.

Lynda turned to look at her. 'Really?'

'Yeah. I wasn't joking when I said I missed the stars. And even though being home while Will was dying was incredibly stressful, I still noticed how much I enjoyed being in a place where people genuinely care about each other. I wouldn't even know who my neighbours are here. I see the bloke from unit eight most mornings as I go to work, but I still don't know his name and I bought this place three years ago. The lady from unit two, we wave as we're coming back from the gym on Saturday mornings. And that's the only contact I have with them.'

'But, Zara, it doesn't have to be like that. I've never lived in the city, but I'm sure if you introduced yourself to your neighbours, you'd be able to start your own little community here. People are the same everywhere and someone has to make the first move.

'I'd love for you to come home, don't get me wrong, but don't do it for me. You need to do it for you and be happy with the decision; otherwise, you'll end up resenting me and I don't want that.'

'I didn't say anything about it being for you.'

Lynda smiled at her gently. 'You didn't have to. Anyway, let's get some dinner. It's been so nice just to sit and chat.'

Chapter 31

Jack's phone dinged at 2 am.

Meet me at the normal place in half an hour.

It was from Crumbs.

Adrenalin coursed through Jack as he threw the bedcovers back and dragged on a pair of jeans. What was this about? Had his scene at the abattoir given him entry into some other type of protest? He hoped so.

He typed out a quick text to Dave, telling him what was going on.

Make sure your phone is always on, Dave texted back. *We can track your location that way. Be safe.*

Checking that the two pens were in the bomber jacket sleeves and that he had everything, he let himself out of the unit and started to walk the dark streets to the meeting place.

He heard a van start up and felt the comfort of knowing the police were with him even though he wouldn't see them.

Entering the pub where he and Crumbs had met last time, he saw two other men. One he recognised as having been behind the bar during his last visit. Maybe he was the owner. Maybe that was why they were able to be in a bar in the middle of the night when it should be closed. He glanced behind him, hoping to see the unmarked police van, but there was nothing in sight. He refocused on what was happening inside.

Crumbs was pointing to a piece of paper on the table. He was wearing a different pair of glasses—still darkened but not sunglasses. He saw that Crumbs's eye had a cloudy look and suddenly realised the reason he wore sunglasses all of the time was that any type of light affected it.

Quickly, Jack walked over and saw he was pointing to a set of building plans.

'Phone,' Crumbs snapped, holding out his hand when he saw him.

Jack felt a sliver of fear trickle through. 'What?'

'Give me your phone. You can't have it on while we do this.'

Seeing no choice, Jack slid his lifeline from his pocket, turned it off and handed it to Crumbs.

'Right, take this.' Crumbs handed over a set of night-vision goggles, a pair of overalls, rubber boots and a jacket with a hood.

'What's the go?' Jack asked, taking what he was given and putting the night-vision goggles on to adjust them to his size.

'You wanted action? You're going to get action. This is Tonka and Blue. Make sure we all stay in sight of each other.' He folded the map and put it into a backpack, which he hoisted over his shoulder. 'Right, we good?'

The other men nodded, so Jack did the same.

'Let's go. This way.'

Crumbs led them down a dark passageway and out the back door. Jack felt his heart kick up a notch. His silent shadows wouldn't realise he'd gone out the back until it was too late, so the safety of the tail was now gone.

He was on his own.

❦

Jack rode in the back of a windowless van, sitting next to Blue, trying to work out what was happening. No one spoke and Jack wasn't going to be the one who broke the silence.

About an hour later, Crumbs brought the van to a standstill and opened the back door to reveal a track somewhere off in the bush.

Jack followed the lead of the other men, pulling on the overalls and boots and making sure the hood was over his head.

'Stick together,' was all Crumbs said, pulling down his goggles.

The world turned green as Jack followed suit, and the four men started to walk sure-footedly through the bush.

Jack smelled it before he saw it, and his stomach dropped. A piggery.

They were going to hit a piggery.

Silently Crumbs slid open the door into a shed, and Jack could hear the quiet grunting of the sleeping pigs and buzz of the cooling fan.

Jack didn't know much about pigs, but he did know they needed to be kept cool with the air circulating around them, otherwise they would overheat and die very quickly.

He would bet his last pay cheque that they were going to disable the cooling system.

Shit, shit, shit! He needed to get to Dave and warn him.

No phone and no tail.

No chance.

'Any security cameras?'

'Not that I can see.'

'You know what to do.'

Tonka and Blue had melted away into the darkness.

Crumbs handed Jack a bag. When he looked inside he saw some cameras and mounting equipment. 'Put these up around the place. Make sure you get the pens in the shot,' he instructed. Then he started to walk around the pens, taking photos with an infra-red camera.

'If you see any injured or hurt, let me know and I'll take a photo. We're gonna screw these bastards.'

'Right.'

Jack worked quickly, making sure the cameras were placed at the end of a row and could capture vision straight down the line of pigs. He checked the first one to ensure it was recording, then started on the next one.

As he strapped the last camera to the rafter, the fans stopped and the shed fell silent.

He'd been right. He looked around, wondering how many pigs would be in the shed. He knew the latest eco sheds could hold five hundred animals or more. *They were putting that many pigs in danger!*

'Let's go,' Crumbs said in his ear. Jack jumped; he hadn't heard the man come up behind him. Crumbs gripped Jack's arm forcefully and gave him a shove towards the entry.

'You wanted to be involved,' he said. 'How does it feel?'

'Fucking incredible.' Jack felt sick.

'Get a move on.'

The four men tracked back the way they had come, stripped off and placed everything in the boot.

Jack expected there to be some high-fives in celebration, but there was nothing. They didn't even speak; just got in the van in the same configuration and drove away.

This time Jack did speak. 'Are we done or doing more?'

'You'll know soon enough.'

When Crumbs opened the back door of the van, the first thing Jack saw was a red smudge on the horizon. They were facing east. There was an outline of a humpy to the left and Jack could smell the salty air of the sea. Not having known which direction they had driven in, he wasn't sure if they'd headed north along the Port Wakefield road or south towards the Coorong National Park.

What he did know was it wouldn't be long before the sun was up.

Jack looked around. The scrubland seemed to come very close to the walls of the humpy and the soil looked sandy. They must be very close to the coast but he had no idea where, only that the drive had taken an hour and a half according to his watch.

'Good job, boys,' Crumbs said and clapped Tonka and Blue on the shoulders. 'Now let the fun begin. Come on, let's get a feed.'

The shack was one room, the bedroom doubling as a kitchen. Jack couldn't see a toilet or shower, but he guessed they were outside. The toilet was probably the closest bush. A pot-belly stove stood in the middle of the room and Crumbs lit it with wood piled up next to it. The walls were lined with four beds.

'What are we doing here?' Jack asked.

'We go off grid every time we do a job. Stay here until the heat dies down,' Crumbs answered.

'What do you want me to do?' Jack asked, hoping he could get to the van and see where his phone was. He could only hope there was mobile reception out here.

Blue and Tonka seemed to know the routine and were pulling out sleeping bags from plastic tubs and throwing them on the beds.

'Grab a bit more wood from outside. Pile is out the door to the right.'

As he went to find the woodpile, Jack desperately cast around for something that would give him a clue as to where he was. There wasn't anything—not that he'd expected to see a town name but it would have been useful.

Jack felt very exposed out here by himself.

He put the wood down next to the stove and watched as Tonka fed the overalls into the fire. They fizzed and melted, and the orange flames burned up through them.

'What are you doing that for?' Jack asked.

'Don't want to risk having them lying around if something goes wrong.'

Jack had been toying with the idea of asking for his phone when Blue said, 'It's like the phones. They stay off until the heat has passed. Don't want anyone knowing where we are. The cops can track through phones, you know.'

'How would the cops know whose phone to track?' Jack asked. 'Are they following us?'

'Not that I know of, but we don't take risks.'

Crumbs opened a large can of baked beans and poured it into a pot. He put four slices of wholemeal toast under a gas grill then stirred the beans. 'There's water over there and the kettle. Fill it up and put it on the stove,' he instructed.

Tonka and Blue carted more wood in from outside then lay back on the beds, while Crumbs scooped up the baked beans and toast and put them on four plates. Jack boiled the coffee.

'Like I said, good job, boys. That'll teach the fuckers,' Crumbs said as he shovelled the food into his mouth. 'Those poor bloody pigs. Did you see the mess they were in? Shouldn't be allowed to keep them like that. An animal needs to be out in the open. Loved and cared for. Those poor things, sitting in their own shit and filth. We'll get that industry shut down if it's the last thing I do. Kinder for them to be out among nature.'

Tonka nodded his head. 'It's not natural them all being cooped up like that. The engine room was easy to kill,' he said. 'There was nothing sophisticated about the power board. Cut a few wires and I was done.'

'Yeah, get in and out real quick,' Blue agreed.

'Only way to do it.' Crumbs turned to Jack. 'So, Mr Angry Guy, are you satisfied now? This hardcore enough for you?'

'Bloody brilliant. Best thing I've done in a long time,' Jack said. 'That'll show everyone what really goes on. Talk about being pumped.' He clenched his fist.

'I'd love to see the fall-out,' said Crumbs. 'All of those cameras you put up, they're recording what's happening and the vision is going back to a bloke I trust. He's going to post it on Facebook when he's edited it. Everyone will see how bad pig farming really is then.'

Jack understood. It was a set-up. No one would know that the cooling system had been disabled. All people were going to see was animals panting and in distress. That in turn would cause an uproar about farming techniques and they would try to shut the industry down. Just like Crumbs had said before.

'Like I said . . .' Jack muttered, pushing his plate away. He couldn't eat any more. 'Bloody brilliant.'

'Not hungry?' Crumbs asked.

'Nah. Never eat too much this time of the day.'

'I always get a massive appetite after a job like this. All the adrenalin running through the system.' It was Blue who spoke then.

'How many jobs like this would you do in a year?' Jack asked.

'What, you want to do another real soon?' Tonka slapped Jack on the back. 'You found a keen one here, Crumbs!'

Jack turned to see Crumbs staring at him. 'Yeah,' he said. 'I did.'

'We do them when we think we're going to make an impact,' Blue answered as he put his plate in the plastic washing-up bowl and stretched. 'Well, that's me, I reckon.' He yawned and the others followed, slurping their drinks and scraping the last food from their plates.

Within ten minutes, the men fell into the beds and slept.

Jack didn't. He thought of all the pigs that would be suffering from heat stress. The fear and discomfort they would be feeling. His helplessness at not being able to alert anyone.

No one, not even Dave, had told him it could be like this when you were undercover. That you could be powerless to be able to put something right.

Of course, the farmer would find the heat-stressed animals first thing in the morning—he might even be there now. But it would be too late. It only took a short amount of time for pigs to overheat and die. He curled his hand into a fist and thumped at his pillow. Tonka gave a loud snore, before rolling over and muttering something unintelligible in his sleep.

Jack sighed, thumped his pillow again and rolled over. The bed was uncomfortable, and he felt as if there was a spring sticking into his back. After lying there for what he guessed was a good hour, he decided he had to get out. Quietly he threw back the bedcovers and tiptoed to the door.

He made it outside without anyone else stirring, but now what was he going to do? He didn't have any idea where he was—a bush humpy in the middle of the scrub. He had no way of knowing how far away from anywhere he was or even which direction to walk. Could he just disappear into the bush and risk it? He didn't think so.

Jack walked further down the track to see if he could identify any landmarks, but there was nothing that jumped out at him. The trees were growing on an angle, as if they had been battered by winds in their formative stages.

'Where the fuck do you think you're going?'

Jack spun around and saw Crumbs training a gun on him.

Instantly he put his hands in the air. 'For a slash, man. What's with the gun? You nervous or something?'

'You should be back inside sleeping.'

'I'm fucking wired! Bit hard to come down after what we've just done.'

'You better come back inside with me.'

Chapter 32

'Where's your man?' Steve asked Dave.

Dave had been frantically watching as the communications team tried to raise the GPS on Jack's phone. 'We don't know,' he admitted, running his hand over his head. 'The dogs lost him when he went into the bar early hours of this morning. They realised an hour later he hadn't come out, went in for a look and found the place locked up. On further investigation, they found a back entrance. They must've gone out that way.'

'Shit. What was the last communication with him?'

'He sent a text saying he had to meet them at the usual spot in half an hour. That was nearly eight hours ago.'

'Do we know of any protests or issues on farms?'

'Not that I've heard about.'

'We're just going to have to sit tight and hope like hell he's okay.'

'We need to get the STAR team and all the usual resources on standby.'

'I'll get them organised,' Steve said. 'Let you know when I've done it.'

Dave wanted to blame Steve for putting Jack in this position, but he couldn't. Jack had made the choice himself. And as much as Dave didn't want to admit it, Steve was right. They would just have to hope that Jack's training and wits kept him safe.

He stared at the screen, which had been tracking Jack, but there was nothing to see.

❧

Jack walked into the shack, his heart beating fast.

Blue and Tonka were still out to it.

'Mate, you've got this all wrong. I was just going for a piss.'

Crumbs put the gun down and grinned. 'I know, I just wanted to see your face.'

Jack frowned as he processed that. 'You sick fuck.' He gave a laugh, hoping it didn't sound forced. His heart was beating as though it was about to come through his chest wall.

'I know what it's like to be wired after something like this,' Crumbs said, going to a cupboard and pulling out a bottle of Scotch. 'I find it hard to sleep too. These guys,' he nodded at the sleeping men, 'they can sleep anywhere, at any time, after any job.' He sloshed some whiskey into a tin pannikin. 'Here, the sun's over the yardarm. Have a drink. It'll help you wind down.'

Jack took the cup, hoping that his hands weren't shaking too obviously. His heart hadn't slowed down yet.

'Cheers! To saving the animals.'

'To saving the animals.' Jack took a sip and put the cup back down. He needed to stay alert. Especially now he knew there were firearms around.

'I want to ask if you've done many of these jobs, but I guess you're not going to answer that.' Jack rearranged himself on the bed, trying to look relaxed. He talked in a low voice so as to not to wake the others.

'I've done a few.' Crumbs said, looking into his drink as if seeing some memory there.

'You're good at planning them. Coming up with a shock factor.'

Crumbs's face lit up. 'I wish I could see the footage. It'll go viral for sure. Someone will shut it down, but the damage will already be done. People will see it and they'll share it because they're horrified or incensed. Then we'll get an enquiry into pig farming and hopefully that'll be it. Bang! They'll shut the industry down.'

'But won't someone work out we cut the wires? Then they'll know it wasn't the farmers causing the stress, it was ac—' He stopped halfway through the word 'activists'. 'Us.'

'Oh, yeah, but by then it'll be too late. People online will have seen it. I'm sure the papers will report later that it was sabotage, but by then the images will already be in people's minds. And we can muddy the waters by denying we had anything to do with it. After all, don't forget, Voices for Animals is a peaceful mob. Some other organisation will get the blame. We don't need the glory of people knowing who did this; we just need the torture of these animals to stop.' There was a mad gleam in Crumbs's eye as he drained his cup of Scotch and poured another one. Jack sipped slowly. 'See, I told you there was a reason we kept all the VFA protests peaceful. They're a front for us. I don't want to be found by the coppers. If they ever come looking for me, well,' he shrugged, 'I'm only a peaceful protester. Method in my madness.' He took another sip.

Madness all right, thought Jack.

Crumbs continued talking. 'I worked on this one protest. Took months to plan it. I don't like it when people get hurt. I'm a bit pissed off that young lad lost the use of his hand. That was never meant to happen. Just bad luck. Anyway, this particular protest, me and a few guys, we let some foxes into a chook shed and filmed them attacking the chooks. Said that the owners hadn't made the shed fox proof. Trouble was, on the way out one of the blokes tripped over an electric fence and the shock sent his heart into funny rhythms and he had a fatal heart attack. It was really awful, but,' he looked up at Jack and toasted him, 'sometimes you can't make an omelette without breaking the egg.'

'Is the cause worth dying for?'

Crumbs stretched out on the bed as he thought about that. 'Lots of the animals do, so I guess we should put our lives on the line too. I had a mate once, when we were doing another protest in Victoria, he died, and I had to watch another mate go to jail for it. See, I promised the mate who died that I'd keep this going. Make sure that animals were always looked after. That's why my other mate took the fall. I had the skills and brains to think of things like this and make them work. He didn't.'

'What happened to your friend?' Jack said, twisting around on the bed to make sure the camera pen was focused on Crumbs. He hoped it was picking up what was being said.

'Got himself in between the ground and a front-end loader bucket. Didn't end well for the poor bastard. I swore that we'd always continue the fight. Like I said, I need Voices for Animals as a front. The peaceful protesters; the silent army, if you like. Sure, they don't get much done, but we make up for it behind the scenes.'

'Doesn't it bother you that you've hurt animals to make a point?'

He shrugged. 'Again, sometimes you have to do something outrageous for people to take notice. And sometimes the animals are better off dead than being where they are. Just like that piggery.' He filled his glass again and this time swallowed the whole lot in one gulp. 'Better get some shut-eye,' he said. 'We'll be here for a while, so there's not much else to do.' He lay back and pulled the rug over him. 'I just wish I could find out how people are responding to the video.'

Jack sat up. 'You could, you know.'

'How?' Crumbs's face looked eager. 'I haven't got a computer and I've only got one of those old brick phones.'

'I've got my phone. How about I see if I can find anything online?'

'Sounds good.' Crumbs got up, opened a box and looked through it, before taking out Jack's phone and throwing it to him.

Jack caught it and breathed a sigh of relief to hold it in his hands again. Quickly he turned it on and waited for it to start up. His phone pinged with a message. Not just once but five times. Each time he flicked the message away without opening it. It looked like Dave had sent him messages without any text in them. Obviously trying to get him to answer.

'Jeez, you're popular. Who's looking for you?' Crumbs asked.

'Mum,' he lied. 'I don't usually go away without telling her.' He kept his eyes on the screen.

Then he got onto the *Farming Telegraph*'s website and scrolled down.

'Is there anything there?'

Jack knew he needed to keep his phone on for as long as he could, so Dave would get the GPS signal. He couldn't risk sending a text, but he knew that the minute he'd come back live, the surveillance equipment would have kicked in and they'd have his location.

'Getting there, it's taking a while to load. I've only got one bar.'

Crumbs got up and came over, waiting like a schoolboy for a bar of chocolate.

'Here we go: *Pigs targeted in a deadly sabotage act* by Zara Ellison.'

'Interesting, they've got the sabotage thing already. Still, if it's that Zara Ellison, I'm not surprised. She covered the case where my mate was killed. She's an interfering little bitch, she is,' Crumbs said in a savage tone. 'I saw her trying to get my photo. That's one thing I'm proud of. I don't think there's a photo of my face anywhere in the media. I'm the silent assassin. You won't see me coming.'

Jack smelled the whiskey on his breath and realised he was drunk. He was surprised because he'd assumed Crumbs would have a high level of tolerance for alcohol. And he didn't like the fact Zara was on his radar, let alone the comments he was making about her.

'Why don't you want your photo in the paper?' Jack asked.

He shrugged. 'Better not to be a media tart if you're trying to stir up trouble.' He nodded as if to highlight his point. Then he grinned and gave a whoop. 'Hey, boys! Wake up and listen to news of our handiwork!'

Jack began to read as Blue and Tonka stirred, rubbed their faces and sat up.

'A piggery an hour south of Adelaide is the latest target of animal activists.

'Police are calling this a deliberate attempt to injure and kill the 500 pigs that were housed in this shed. Forensics have shown that the cooling system was disabled, rending the fans and air-conditioning useless.

'Out of the 500 sows, 30 have died and an undisclosed number will have to be euthanised. The rest are suffering from heat stress but should make a full recovery. A vet is on site.

'A spokeswoman for the animal rights group Voices for Animals, Sophie Grawd, said they didn't condone this act of violence. "Whoever has done this horrific act deserves to be punished to the full extent of the law. They cannot claim to love animals. We deplore this act. Our organisation raises awareness of cruelty to animals but does not cause it to make a point."

'The detective investigating, Peter Walker, hasn't made a comment yet, other than to say they will be investigating it thoroughly and hope to make an arrest soon.'

Crumbs snorted. 'Good luck with that. They won't find us here.'

'Nope, they won't, for sure,' Tonka agreed.

Crumbs shook his head, his smile wide. 'Well, well, didn't we get some attention?'

Jack put the phone in his pocket. 'Yeah, we did.' He frowned and spoke in a low, sad tone. 'But I still don't understand—they've got the story about the sabotage already. We haven't really done what we intended, have we? The public know that it was done deliberately.'

'Yeah, I wish they hadn't made that connection straightaway—or at least hadn't reported on it straightaway,' Crumbs said. 'But still, what's done is done. The footage that will have gone live a few hours ago will be shared by all our supporters. We should have a look at that. There won't be anyone on our sites saying that there was interference. What's wrong, boy, you sound dismal. Sorry it's over?'

Jack shrugged. 'Getting tired now, I think. The adrenalin has run out.' The last thing he wanted to do was see the footage. He pretended to tap at the phone. 'Can't get Facebook to load,' he said. 'Range mustn't be good enough.' He shrugged.

Crumbs stared at him a bit longer. 'Bugger. Can you get the story up again? Let me have another read.' He held out his hand.

Jack hesitated before handing the phone over.

Crumbs read the story again slowly, then handed the phone to Blue, who tapped on the screen and brought up the call log. 'Hey!' Jack said, reaching out to try to snatch the phone back. 'What are you doing? That's private.'

'I like to know who I'm dealing with.'

Jack's stomach constricted. He hadn't deleted the last few times he'd called Dave. *A fucking rookie mistake. Shit.*

There was a heavy silence in the hut.

After about ten minutes of horrible, heavy silence, Blue suddenly said what Jack knew he would. 'Look here, boss. There's a pattern here. Looks like every time you and our boy here have caught up, he's phoned a friend afterwards.'

'That's interesting,' Crumbs said, turning to look at Jack. 'Every time we have a catch-up, you ring a friend. Who is it? Your boyfriend?'

'A mate,' Jack shrugged. 'And I don't know what's interesting about that. I talk to him a lot. You guys are being suspicious over nothing!'

'But you only talk to him after our meetings?'

'I guess that's when I've got the time. I'm walking home. Anyway, if you look, I'm sure you'll find I talk to him at other times.' What Jack really wanted to do was reach over and grab the phone out of their hands, but he knew he had to play it cool. Like he didn't have anything to hide.

Tonka took the phone now and all three men closed in around him. 'Another interesting thing—all these text messages are blank. Strange someone is sending blank text messages, isn't it? And why isn't there a name attached to the number?'

'I thought you said they were from your mum?'

'Yeah, Mum's not too good with the mobile.' It didn't matter what Jack said now, he knew he was in trouble.

❧

'We got him!' Dave yelled. 'I've got a signal from his phone.'

Two officers ran to his side and looked at the laptop screen. Then they high-fived each other.

'Alert the STAR team, they've been on standby along with the air wing. We're going to need that chopper. Too far to go by car. GPS coordinates are . . .' He read them out and one of the officers ran to do his bidding, while the other stayed close by.

Over his shoulder, Dave snapped, 'Get Steve on the phone and tell him we're back in communication.'

The officer snatched up the phone, spoke quickly and then hung up.

Dave opened the internet browser, and typed in the

location on Google Earth. 'Come on, come on.' He tapped his fingers, frantically trying to speed up the search.

'Okay, this is what we've got.' He looked at the photos from Google Earth. A shack in the middle of nowhere. Trees, bushes, scrub. A two-wheeled track wound its way in from a main road. A safe house, that's what he was looking at.

Dave traced the track back to the main road. 'Get an outer cordon set up about five ks from those coordinates. The choppers will need to drop the STAR team on the beach, I reckon. We need ambulances on standby in the outer cordon. Let's go.'

'Sir, you're not supposed to be coming with us. That's not protocol. You should be coordinating from back here.'

Dave rounded on the young constable. 'You think I'm going leave my man out there while I stay safe here? I don't give a fuck about protocol.' Grabbing the laptop, he jogged out the door with the officer in tow.

After they got on the road towards the airport, Dave went back to Google Earth and looked closer. 'Okay, we want a drone up in the air. We don't know how many people are in there and whether there are firearms. We'll have to assume there are. If we get some aerial footage of the campsite, then we can work out how to go in and get him.' He couldn't let himself feel anything right now. Jack's life depended on him. All he hoped was they would get to Jack soon enough and it wasn't a booby trap.

Chapter 33

'Who are you?' Crumbs took another menacing step towards him, but Jack didn't flinch.

'You told me the less you knew about me the better. I'm Jack.'

'Cocky little smart arse.'

He held out his hands. 'I'm not trying to be smart, I'm just telling you. I'm Jack, a bloke who's on the same page as you. Trying to make change.'

'I thought there was something about you.' Crumbs threw a punch but Jack saw it coming and dodged. That seemed to infuriate Crumbs, who yelled, 'I'll ask you once more—who the fuck are you?'

Jack didn't see he had any choice now.

'I'm Senior Constable Jack Higgins from the South Australian Po—'

Crumbs let out a roar and charged at Jack, who ducked out of the way again. Blue came at him from the other side and managed to get him in a headlock and drag him to the chair. He held him down, strong hands on his shoulders, and Crumbs bent down to stare into his eyes. 'You're a fucking copper.'

'What the fuck are we going to do about that?' asked Tonka.

'Well, that's a good question,' said Crumbs. 'What do you think we should do about you, Jack?'

Jack stared back at him. 'I think you're in enough trouble as it is. So how about we talk about this?'

Blue ran his hands down Jack's arms to check him for weapons and drew out the pen from the coat sleeve. He looked at it then handed it to Crumbs.

'What's this? Looks like an interesting pen.'

Jack stayed silent. Tonka looked over. 'I've seen one of them before. On the internet. Throw it over here.'

Jack just shook his head and watched helplessly as Tonka pulled the pen apart to expose the camera and recording device.

'Well, what have we here?' asked Crumbs. 'Gathering evidence, are you?' He threw it on the ground and stomped on it.

'That's what policemen do,' said Jack as he heard the insides of the device crack.

Crumbs nodded at Tonka, who stepped forward and smashed his fist into Jack's face.

'Tie him to the chair,' Crumbs instructed.

Tonka went outside and came back with a handful of cable ties. It took only a minute to ensure Jack wouldn't be going anywhere quickly.

Fear was coursing through him, but Jack didn't let it show. He had to try to talk them down. 'You fellas are in a bit of trouble. We'd be better off talking about this.'

'That's what you think.'

'That's what I know. If you untie me, we can work out a deal.'

'Like hell. You're staying where you are.' Crumbs stared into Jack's face again and said, 'Mate, no one knows where you are. You're the one who should be worried, and after seeing what I did to those pigs, do you think I've got any qualms about burying you?'

Crumbs snapped his head towards the door, 'You two, get outside. We need to talk about this.'

Jack's head throbbed and he felt himself slipping into a dark abyss. He tried to stay with it and listen to what Crumbs, Tonka and Blue were talking about. He hoped that the phone had stayed on long enough for Dave to pick up the GPS signal. It seemed the men had forgotten about the phone sending out a signal. They were more concerned about what they were going to do with him.

He could feel the blood running down his cheek. His nose was already beginning to swell and he knew he was going to have a whopping shiner over his eye. He also knew that would be the least of his worries if Dave didn't get here soon.

'Come on, come on,' he muttered, straining to hear something that would indicate his rescue team were close by.

All he heard was Crumbs speaking. 'We're gonna have to bury him.'

'Jeez, mate, I don't know about that. That's cold-blooded murder. I don't want to be involved in that. Protesting and doing over a piggery is one thing, murdering a copper is different matter altogether,' said Blue.

'Well, he's got to disappear somehow,' said Tonka. 'Otherwise he's gonna dob us in. We can't just let him go.'

Jack could hear the crunching of boots outside as one of the men paced. He twisted his wrists, trying to loosen his hands, knowing it was futile against the cable ties.

It was Blue's voice that came next, but he used a different name: 'Clarry, you can't do it, mate. He's a copper. If we get caught, we'll never see the outside of prison again.'

'Don't you go getting cold feet on me. We're in this together and we have to decide what we're going to do with him.'

Who the hell is Clarry? Jack wondered.

Crumbs' voice: 'I know, Paul, but . . .'

They're using their real names, Jack realised. A wave of fog rolled through his head and he groaned. He wanted to be sick, but he breathed deeply through his nose and the feeling passed.

'. . . but he knows too much anyway. We've got more likelihood of being able to disappear with him dead. We'll have to go interstate or somewhere.'

Blue's voice again: 'John, listen to me. What about we just knock him out? The cops will find him at some stage, surely. He doesn't have to die.'

'Okay. Clarry. Paul. John. Stay with it, Jack,' he muttered to himself. 'Listen. Just listen.'

'We should have learned from the last time.' Jack thought that was Tonka aka John.

They've killed before? Jack strained to hear.

'That was different.' Blue aka Paul. 'That person was a nobody. This bloke here, he's a copper.'

'I know!' yelled Crumbs aka Clarry. 'I fucking know! The thing we have on our side is no one knows he's here. We can get rid of him and take off. What you blokes don't understand is that even if we don't do anything to him and they find us, we'll be done for abducting a copper. Sentences for either of those crimes aren't going to be real nice.'

'Why can't we leave him here alive and shoot through?' Paul wanted to know.

Jack heard a fist connect with bone and the heavy thud of a body hitting the ground.

'Hey, hey, hey,' Clarry's voice turned panicky. 'We can't go turning on each other now, John.'

'If it means you and I can get out of here and he stays to take the fall, then we can,' John answered.

'No, no, no, mate. We've done that once before. When Gerard Hooper went to jail. He took the fall for me then. Let's remember what our focus is here.'

'It's too murky now. Too many people have died. I think we walk away now.'

'Well, we have a difference of opinion then.'

❦

The STAR team deployed into the bush and surrounded the humpy. Dressed in camouflage gear, they moved like ripples through the land.

Dave was looking at the pictures the drone was streaming back to the computer and issuing instructions. 'Opening on the southern side. Two windows to the north,' he told them. 'Where's the infra-red camera view?' he snapped to the officer beside him.

'Here, sir.' The officer tapped at the keys and changed view.

'Okay, okay . . .' Dave peered at the screen and saw four images. Two bodies were moving and two bodies were still. He held his breath, hoping they would both move.

'We've got three inside, one out,' he said through the mike attached to his headset. 'Two moving, two not. One not moving is on the outside, the other is inside. Hold your positions.'

He waited a bit longer, but nothing changed. There were still two clearly moving, and two not. Dave didn't dare take the drone any closer in case it became audible.

As he watched he saw one person moving start to drag one who wasn't and knew it was time. It was beyond time; all he could do was hope that they weren't too late.

'All in position?'

'Affirmative.'

'Light them up.' Dave watched as red beams from their guns hit the moving targets.

'Righto, be on standby to go on my count. Three, two, one, go! Go! Go!'

From out of the bush streamed ten men with blackened faces, their guns trained on the shack.

'Get on the ground!'

'Police!'

'Stay where you are!'

'Get on the ground, get on the ground! Don't fucking move.'

Dave held his breath as he watched the screen. There were heat images of people swarming over the room. Dave could see a cluster of men bending over the body that was outside and the same images on the inside of the hut.

'Come on, come on. What's going on?' he muttered to himself.

Finally, after what seemed like a lifetime, a voice said through the headset, 'Cargo is secure. Your boy is okay,' and Dave let out a long, shaky breath.

Jack was safe.

'All clear!'

Dave threw down his headphones and left the van where he'd been stationed on the outer circle. He ran towards the hut and within seconds he was inside, his eyes taking everything in.

Three men on the floor, cuffed. Two yelling and one unconscious. 'Ambos,' he instructed.

'On their way.'

A STAR team member was guiding Jack out into the sunlight. In two steps, Dave was next to him.

'Okay?'

'Nothing that a bit of water and ice won't fix,' Jack said through a fat lip and swelling nose.

'Get him checked out,' Dave told the officer. 'I'll be right back.' He stood and looked around carefully. Something on the floor caught his attention and he walked over, hands in his pockets, and looked at it. The broken pieces of one of their surveillance pens. *Shit.*

'Dave?' Two Major Crime detectives had entered the house on the call of 'clear'.

He indicated the smashed pen on the ground. 'Jack had two pens. I can only see the remnants of one.'

'We'll take it from here.'

Dave nodded and stood back as he watched two members of the STAR squad lift up one of the blokes and shove him towards the door. One of the detectives called out, 'Make sure he gets checked out by the ambos.'

With nothing more to do, Dave left the shack and went back to the patrol car.

'How are you holding up?' he asked Jack as he got into the vehicle.

Jack had had the blood cleaned from his face and was leaning back against the seat with his eyes shut.

'Good meds, whatever the ambos gave me,' he answered. 'Feel great.'

'Don't get too used to them,' Dave said with a grin. 'They're probably some kind of narcotic—Endone or something full-on like that!'

'No wonder people take them. I feel like I'm sliding into a warm bath.'

Dave looked at Jack, who hadn't opened his eyes, and felt a rush of appreciation for the work of the STAR team. They'd done a quick and professional job of getting Jack out of there and he was grateful his mate was okay.

'We gotta have a bit of a debrief here, Jack. Did you get anything? And what did you have to do?'

'Put the cameras up in the piggery. They streamed live footage and then some bloke was going to edit it and put it up on Facebook. Has that happened yet?'

'Haven't heard about it but I imagine so.'

'The other two, Blue and Tonka, they just did as they were told. I didn't see them cut the wires at the piggery, but they must've, 'cause Crumbs didn't leave the pens. He took photos of everything. I think he was going to post them online too. Or get someone to. He's not good with technology.

'You need to go and talk to Zara. Crumbs knows about her. Said she was at a court case and she was . . . Can't remember . . .' He rubbed at his head and grimaced. 'Interfering or annoying, or something. But he also said that someone took the fall for him in that case.'

Dave nodded. 'Zara will be perfectly safe because this creep isn't going anywhere.'

As if on cue, Crumbs and Tonka were led out of the humpy, their hands behind their backs, and shoved into a waiting car. Blue was conscious now but waiting for an ambulance.

'You did good, Jack. Real good.'

'Still don't know who they are.'

'We will by the time we've finished with them,' promised Dave, then he clapped Jack on the back. 'How did you get back on the grid, though?'

Jack told him about having to give his phone up and then the brainwave of playing to Crumbs's ego. 'He couldn't wait to hear what was written about it all. I turned it on and all I could do was hope you'd know I was back online.'

'Egos get in the way every time,' Dave said. 'Anyway, mate, let's get you home.'

Jack pulled the remaining camera pen out of his sleeve and gave it to Dave. 'There might not be any pictures on that one. I pushed it all the way down in the side pocket of the jacket. I don't know how they didn't find it, but they didn't. But hopefully you'll get the conversation.'

'I'm proud of you,' Dave said.

Chapter 34

Zara pushed the drawer of her desk closed and looked around. She'd miss the office. The noise, the adrenalin rush and everything that went with working at the *Farming Telegraph*. Not that she'd miss it for good, but she had packed up her desk properly this time. Not like last time, when she'd sworn she'd come back.

She would stay writing for the paper; in fact, she was hoping to interview Jack and Dave about the piggery fiasco when she got back to Barker. She didn't know whether they would talk to her, but she could try.

Her stomach gave a little fizz of excitement at the thought of seeing Jack again. He'd been in her thoughts a lot since she'd realised that he'd been undercover.

She'd been so shocked when Kim had told her how they'd nearly lost Jack. The thought of not seeing his serious face around Barker had set her on edge until Kim had gone on to explain that everything was okay now and he hadn't been seriously hurt.

Zara hadn't understood her feelings then and she had decided she didn't want to delve into them too much right now. Lynda and she had talked about her returning to Barker and it had been clear that Lynda needed her, more than Lachy did. She just wanted to get back to Barker and set up her house, spend time at Rowberry Glen with her mum, and write her articles for the paper. Not exactly the life she'd planned, but for now the peace was necessary, as was time with her mum.

'Zara, got a moment?' Lachy asked from the doorway of his office. He indicated she should come in.

'What's up?' she asked as he shut the door behind her.

'Those items that were going missing from your desk?' He held out an envelope. 'Here's an apology from the person who was doing it. Brenton from advertising.'

'What?' A startled look came over Zara's face as she looked at the letter in her hand. 'Why?'

'I know,' Lachy frowned. 'It seems implausible—we never see the people from advertising up here—they stay down on the floor below. How all this happened, I still can't quite work out. Turns out he was sweet on you. Trying to get your attention but didn't know what was going on in your personal life. Don't worry. He doesn't work here anymore.'

'That's just creepy.' Zara dropped the letter back on to Lachy's desk. 'I don't need to read this.'

Lachy nodded. 'I've dealt with it, I promise you.'

Zara hugged Lachy. 'Thank you.'

She went back to her desk and it was only seconds before she heard Liz coming up behind her.

'I'm going to miss you so much,' Liz said, coming in and parking her butt on the edge of the desk. 'Are you sure you have to go?'

Zara smiled. 'Yeah, I am. I'll be back sometime, though. It's not like I'm not working for the *Farming Telegraph* anymore. I'm just doing it from another town. And we'll see each other. You'll have to come and stay—I've got room in the house.'

'You won't be able to keep me away.' Liz looked at her. 'What a crazy few months,' she said. 'Who would've thought your life could change so much with that phone call from your mum.'

Zara sighed and placed the last notepad from her desk into the box where she'd packed all of her things. 'I know. I can't believe Will's gone. Can't believe I'm leaving the city and I'm happy to do it!'

Michael came in through the door, his face hidden by a large bunch of flowers. 'I don't usually give flowers to deserters,' he said. 'But somehow, you're different!'

A delighted smile spread over Zara's face as Lachy and Claudia came in behind him. 'What's this?' she asked.

'Just a little something. We're all going to miss you, Zara,' Lachy said, pulling her into another hug. 'We know you're not going for good, and you'll still be working with us, but it's certainly going to be strange not to have you in the office every day.' He released her and handed her a small parcel wrapped in silver paper.

'Flowers and a present? Guys, you've gone overboard!' She unwrapped it to find a slim silver and gold pen with her name engraved on it, along with all of her work colleagues'.

'So you don't forget us,' Claudia said.

'As if I could!' Zara hugged each one of them, then stood back. 'Well, I guess I'd better go, if I'm going to get there by dark.'

'Don't forget you've got a deadline still. Wednesday by 11 am. If your story's not here by then, I won't run it,' Lachy said in a mock-stern tone.

'I know! It'll be in your inbox before then.' She gave each of them another hug, then drew a deep breath. 'Guess this is it.'

Zara looked around one last time, picked up her box and walked out to the waiting car.

Epilogue

Kim pulled a pan of roast beef from the oven and pierced a fork into the potatoes to see if they were cooked.

'That smells amazing,' Jack said as he sat down at the kitchen table with a beer.

'Feed the man meat,' Kim said with a chuckle.

'I gotta say, that vegan food I had undercover was really nice. I expected it to be horrible! And it was filling too. Not at all what I expected.'

'You gonna turn vegetarian?' Dave asked as he cut up the broccoli and put it in a container to go in the microwave.

'Not a chance; I'm just saying it was decent food.'

There was a knock at the door.

'You expecting someone?' Dave asked Kim with a frown.

'Can you answer the door, please, Jack?' Kim said, ignoring Dave.

Dave fixed his wife with a look. 'What are you doing?' he asked sternly after Jack had left the room.

'Zara, of course!' she whispered. 'Lynda and I have been talking.'

Dave rolled his eyes. His wife, the queen of match-making. He listened to Jack's surprised voice as he opened the front door.

'Oh my God, Jack, you're here! I didn't know.' Zara gave a happy laugh. 'How are you? I'm so sorry I almost outed you at the rally. I didn't put two and two together straightaway. Are you all right?'

'It's good to see you! I didn't know you were back in town. Are you here for long?'

'Gah! Too many questions,' Zara said. 'Tell me about you first.'

Kim tiptoed over to the doorway and peered around it. She turned and gave the thumbs-up. 'Hugging,' she whispered.

Dave gestured for her to come back to the bench. 'Leave them alone,' he hissed. 'Nosy. How about you just worry about you and me.' He leaned forward and kissed her.

'I'm fine,' Dave heard Jack say. 'Got a bit banged up around the face, that's all. Talk about an experience.'

'Will you tell me about it sometime?'

'Do you want to write a story about it?'

'Definitely! I could do a feature on you as the hero of the pig industry. You wouldn't expect anything less from me, would you? But I also want to hear about it because you're my friend.'

'I don't know about that,' Jack answered gruffly.

'Hmm, you might have something there,' Dave whispered as he wiped his hands on the tea towel. 'She was one of the first people he mentioned when we got him out of that humpy.'

'Look who I found,' Jack said, ushering Zara through the kitchen door. She held a bottle of wine and was dressed in jeans and a thick woollen jumper.

'Don't you look gorgeous,' Kim said, leaning forward to give her a hug. 'Doesn't she, Dave? Jack, what do you think?'

'Yes, Kim,' Dave answered in a henpecked voice, 'she looks very nice. It's cold out there, is it, Zara?'

'Yeah, it's just starting to rain again. Mum had thirty millimetres last week and now it's raining again! It's so exciting. They've got water in the dams and there's germination beginning to poke through. Everything looks lovely and fresh.'

'Such a relief for the whole farming community,' Jack said.

Kim and Dave exchanged glances. Jack had never shown much interest in the farming community before. Other than in his mates who played footy.

'Are you going down to cover the new trial for Gerard Hooper, Zara?' Kim asked.

'No, my colleague Liz is going to do that. I've been called as a witness. I guess to identify that Clancy was in the courtroom for all of the previous trial. I've got photos of him actually at the trial, which they're going to use for evidence.'

'I still think of him as Crumbs,' Jack said.

'Nasty piece of work, that bloke,' Dave said. 'I still can't understand why someone would deliberately hurt animals and think that was going to make people pay attention to their cause.'

Zara pulled out a chair and Dave took the wine, before pouring it into three glasses. 'I don't get that either. Another beer, Jack?'

'Please. One of the things that Crumbs said when we were in the safe house was that he felt the animals were better off dead rather than where they were.'

'Yeah, I know I've heard that argument before, but I can't understand why they did it in such a cruel way,' Zara said. 'I understand the need to raise awareness and all that, but not using such underhanded methods. As hard as I've tried to find a good reason for it, I can't.'

'You can't because there isn't one,' Dave said.

'I think you're right,' Zara said. 'It's really important to listen to both sides of the argument. That's what I've always tried to do in my reporting. I know there are activists who would happily talk to farmers and ask questions so they can understand what the farmers are trying to do. It's the extremists that cause the problems, as we saw this time. And I don't believe anyone is able to reason with them.

'Farmers also need to be open about how they produce. And most of the activists, that's all they're asking for. We know that most farmers treat their animals well, but the fact of the matter is that most animals are bred for eating, which straightaway causes a problem for some activists. Somehow both sides need to be more tolerant of each other.'

Kim was carving the roast. 'Absolutely right, Zara. Just because one person doesn't like someone else's point of view, doesn't mean they should force their own thoughts on that person. Everyone just needs to accept people are going to have differing opinions, without getting all uptight about it.' She put the knife down with a thud as if to emphasise her point.

Putting his arm around his wife's shoulders, Dave grinned. 'Sweetie, you'd have the whole world singing "Kumbaya" if you could.'

'And the world would be a much better place if I did.'

Dave laughed. 'Okay, okay! I shouldn't have even tried to start that argument! Now, I had word that John Spinner and Paul Crabb are going to trial in three months. They were denied bail at their hearing today.'

'I hope they throw away the key,' Zara muttered.

'And Crumbs has to face two charges. We're still trying to find evidence that he was the one who disabled the front-end loader in the Hooper trial. We're hanging our hats on Gerard spilling the beans, but we haven't managed to get him to talk yet. We're digging as hard as we can.' He paused. 'We also charged him with assault of a police officer, so he'll go away for a while. The other thing I have to tell you, Zara, is that I did a bit of digging on the drone.'

'Did you?' She leaned forward.

'Will did make the phone call to the Department of Ag. I spoke to the person who took the call. I couldn't find whether he'd got in contact with VFA. I don't think he did. My guess is that someone from the Department of Ag leaked it to VFA.'

The shock on Zara's face was plain. 'They can't do that!'

'Well, anyone can do anything just so long as they don't get caught. And in this situation it's not ideal, obviously. A government-based farming organisation leaking to animal activists. They're doing an internal investigation, but I can tell you that Will did not alert Voices for Animals.'

Jack touched Zara's hand. 'He was right to report Terry. It was an animal welfare issue, you know that.'

'I agree with you,' Zara said. 'And I'm glad he did it. As an industry we can't have people not doing the right thing by animals.' She looked over at Dave. 'What happened to Terry?'

'It's all been very hush-hush, but he's had his animals sold. They didn't charge him with anything, just made arrangements to sell the cattle. He's over eighty, you know.'

'Right,' Kim broke in. 'Enough talk of work. Come and sit down.' She raised her glass. 'Here's to good friends and neighbours,' she said.

They clinked glasses and started to eat.

'How's your mum holding up?' Kim asked Zara.

'She's much better. I think me being home for good is helping, and the rain is such a relief for her. She's still sad, of course, and I doubt that will ever leave her, but she's coping.'

'Oh, and what about James!' Kim leaned forward, glass of wine in hand, her face alight. 'Gosh, they kept that quiet, didn't they?'

Zara giggled. 'Yeah, they did. He's good for her. I like seeing them together.' She put down her knife and fork and looked at Dave. 'We spread Will's ashes today. That was tough. Final. I feel empty and sad,' she took a breath and looked around, 'but it's good to be here with friends, and Mum has James out there tonight, so I know she's okay. I've been thinking a lot about what you said, Dave, about not letting things fester. It was good to find Will a place where he's free.'

Dave nodded. 'Glad about that.'

'Did you say you were here for good?' Jack asked.

'Yeah, as of yesterday. I'm going to be hard to get rid of.'

'What about your work?'

'I'm still going to report for the paper. I'll have to travel a bit, but that's okay.' Zara stopped and excitedly put her hand on Jack's arm. 'Oh, I haven't told anyone yet! I've also got a new job.'

'Have you? What's that?'

'I'm going to be a mediator between activists and farmers. To try to raise awareness on both sides.'

'Jeez, good luck with that,' Dave said.

'I think it'll be challenging, but hugely rewarding.'

'That's a great job for you,' Jack said. 'You're really fair, so I think that's perfect.' He patted her hand. 'Maybe we could have a coffee and you could tell me about it?'

A smile split Kim's face, and she put her hand on Dave's leg under the table and squeezed.

Perfect.

Acknowledgements

Having to do acknowledgements twice a year is slightly difficult because I'm thanking the same people over and over and over again! Don't get me wrong, the people on Team Fleur need thanking every time! They keep me on the straight and narrow, but it's finding different words to thank them, every six months which is getting difficult! And just a little secret—I spend hours agonising over this part of the book, so this time, I'm not over thinking it, I'm just writing.

So, let's get started!

The Allen & Unwin and Agent Team Fleur: Tom, Annette, Christa, KM, Sarah, Laura and everyone else behind the scenes, with a special mention to Jenn Thurgate—what a power of work you do, without any of us authors even knowing! Gaby Naher, who I could not do without.

The WA Team Fleur: Carolyn, Heather, Robyn, Lauren and Graham, Ewin, Jan and Pete, Chrissy, Paul and Lee,

Al, Wal, Tom. Peter Fitzpatrick. And interstate: Carrie, Sarah, Bridget, Gillian (I never thought such tragedy could bring friendship), Bev.

The Plotting Team: DB—Never enough words to thank you. And Tanya.

And of course, all my family; human and canine.

None of what I do would be possible without any one of you. From the bottom of my heart, you have my thanks, appreciation and love.

Again, to all you readers; thank you for making my dream possible, for loving Detective Dave Burrows as much as you do and reading the words on these pages. It's quite incredible to think, as I sit in my office typing, some of you, somewhere, are waiting for the next book with anticipation. Thank you, thank you, thank you!

There's a name missing from this list, which I never thought I would have to leave out. Nineteen years of friendship; Starting from stock agent extraordinaire, to friend, confidant and safety blanket. When you left this world, Pete, you couldn't have known what a hole you left in so many people's lives. We miss you more than words could ever say, and it seems fitting that your name is the first words in this book and the last. Peter 'Windy' Gale.

With love,

Fleur x

The Shearer's Wife

FLEUR McDONALD

2020: When the Australian Federal Police swoop unheralded into Barker and make a shocking arrest for possession of narcotics, Detective Dave Burrows is certain there is more to the story than meets the eye. But the Feds insist that Dave is too invested in the town and its people to see the truth of what is happening there.

1980: Rose and Ian Kelly arrive in Barker for supplies before they begin shearing at Jacksonville Station. Rose, heavily pregnant with their first babies, worries that despite Ian's impending fatherhood he remains a drifter who dreams of the open road.

2020: After many months of grief over her brother's illness and death, journalist Zara Ellison is finally ready to begin a new chapter of her life and make a commitment to her boyfriend, Senior Constable Jack Higgins. But when she's assigned to investigating the Barker arrest, Jack begins to believe that Zara is working against him.

It takes a series of unconnected incidents in Zara's digging to reveal an almost forgotten thread of mystery as to how these two events, forty years apart, could be connected.

ISBN 978 1 76087 681 4

Chapter 1

1980

The beige Holden Kingswood wagon pulled to a stop next to the fuel pump at the Golden Fleece roadhouse.

Rose Kelly breathed a sigh of relief and rubbed her hands over her pregnant belly. She felt as big as an elephant and was desperate to get out of the confines of the car.

'All right then, sweet Rosie?' Ian, her husband, asked as he reached for his wallet sitting on the bench seat between them.

Rose smiled; she liked when Ian called her 'sweet Rosie'. His Irish lilt made her sound as if she were an exotic flower. His Irish rose.

'Not really. I'm really uncomfortable. How long until we get there?'

Ian threw the heavy door open. 'I'm not sure. Probably

half an hour. You'll be right. You're only pregnant, not sick. Many women have given birth in the back of a car.'

Rose groaned as she felt a solid kick from inside her, and reached for the door handle. 'That'd better not be me. I don't see *you* hauling around a stomach larger than the Opera House and getting kicked from inside!'

'Reckon I drag heavier wethers, though.' Ian grinned and leaned over, patting her leg. 'You'll be right, love.'

'Hmm. You only have to drag one sheep at a time. I've got two babies in here, Ian. Two! Could we stay here the night?' Rose asked, as she hauled herself out of the car. 'Barker looks like a nice little town. Surely they'd have a room at the pub. I'm really tired.'

Leafy trees lined the quiet street. Only two cars sat parked in front of the local shop. The voices of unseen men rose on the hot, still air: 'Catch! Catch!'

A cricket match on the oval, on Saturday afternoon, she thought. *Maybe there's a tennis club here*. Rose remembered playing tennis when she was at school. A sense of displacement hit her again. The nagging feeling of wanting to stay in one place had started a few months ago, as she'd felt her body swell. Travelling was increasingly awkward and the roads rough as her twin babies bounced inside her.

What she wouldn't do for a house and a garden, somewhere she could walk, potter and cook in a kitchen, instead of being pulled from one shed to the next. They hadn't been home since they were married twelve months before, on her nineteenth birthday, and it had been longer since she'd seen her family. Not that she was convinced they wanted to see her.

The irony of the situation was not lost on her: when she'd left her hometown, it had been to escape the confines of her strict, religious family, needing to taste freedom and space, and now all she wanted was a home. Somewhere to build a life. To raise her babies.

Her babies. Twins. She hadn't even known twins were possible. She hadn't known anything, so every part of this pregnancy was new and frightening. Ian had been so proud when she'd told him she was expecting.

'A baby! Well, it'll be a boy, for sure.'

Then there had been a bit of spotting and Ian had agreed to stop in a small town so she could visit the hospital. There, they'd found out she was having twins.

They'd driven in shell-shocked silence to the next shed. The next lot of shearers' quarters. The next lot of shearers. The shearing team—usually a dozen of them and all blokes—camped close to each other. She was sick of the constant travel, the weary men and the stench of sheep.

Their accommodation was the same as all the others: one small room for the two of them, nowhere private for a moment's peace. Rose had to share her new husband with everyone else and there were very few people for her to talk to. Sometimes she wondered how she'd ended up pregnant and on the road at twenty. But she loved and trusted Ian, and was still happy to sit beside him in the passenger seat.

She sighed, turning towards him as he spoke.

'Surely they do,' Ian nodded. 'But . . .'

The fuel attendant came out. 'How much would you like?' he asked, unscrewing the fuel cap.

'Fill her up. Thanks, mate.'

'Just passing through?' the man asked, as the smell of fuel rose into the air.

'Nah, be around for a few weeks. Got a bit of work out at a shed just north of here.' Ian walked away from the car and stretched. 'Out at Jacksonville.'

'Oh, yeah? Shearer?'

'Ian Kelly, at your service.' He held out his hand and the other man shook it.

'Stuart Martin. Good people out there at Jacksonville.' He glanced across at Rose. 'Long way to the hospital from there though. Nearly an hour's drive when the road's good. Get a thunderstorm and you'll be stuck for a while.'

'An hour, you say?' Ian answered. 'Thanks, I'll keep that in mind. Haven't been there before. Good to hear they're nice.'

'Can't go wrong with Ross and Ali Barton. Top shelf.' He looked over at Rose. 'Long to go?'

'A month or so yet. I wish they would arrive sooner,' Rose said, pushing her red hair away from her forehead. 'I'm sick of being fat and beaten up from the inside.' She paused. 'That sun's got some bite in it.' She fanned her face. Another kick and she clutched her belly, unable to stop from groaning aloud.

'Rose?' Ian took a step towards her.

An older woman, dressed in jeans and a shirt, walked out of the roadhouse, her blonde ponytail bouncing behind her. 'Hello! Oh, are you all right there?' She glanced at Ian as he put his hand on Rose's shoulder. 'Take some deep breaths now. That's right, in and out.'

Rose focused on the woman's voice and did what she was told.

The woman squatted down in front of her and smiled encouragingly. 'Well done. Keep breathing.' She turned to look up at Ian. 'Is she having contractions?'

'How the hell do I know? She was fine in the car a minute ago.' Ian took a couple of steps back, looking shaken.

Rose flapped her hands and shook her head. 'No,' she said when the pain receded. 'No, I'm fine. I get these cramps occasionally, and they go again.' She stood upright and looked at Ian. 'I'm fine, honest.'

'Come on, let's get you inside, out of the sun. I think a cold drink will do you wonders.'

'That would be wonderful, thank you,' Rose said, as the woman turned to walk inside. Rose planted her hand on her lower back as she plodded beside her, still marvelling at the change in her centre of gravity; her belly leading the way. 'I'm Rose.'

'I'm Evie,' the older woman smiled as she ushered Rose inside. 'How long to go?'

'Not soon enough! Twins, if you can believe it. Baptism by fire!'

'I can,' Evie replied. 'You're big enough. Those cramps you're getting are probably Braxton Hicks. And you're right, they come and go a bit.'

'Braxton what?'

'Hicks. It means your body is getting ready for labour.' Evie was silent for a moment while she opened the fridge and brought out an enamel jug. 'Haven't you heard about them before?'

Rose shook her head and tried to swallow the lump in her throat. 'We didn't talk much about this sort of thing in my family.'

Evie nodded with a kind smile. 'Did I hear you're on your way to Jacksonville?'

'Yeah, Ian has a stand at the shearing shed for a few weeks.'

'You're brave, going to stay out there. Away from the hospital.' She poured a glassful and handed it to Rose. 'Homemade lemonade. Sit down.'

Rose shook her head. 'I've been sitting all day. I need to stretch, but thank you.' She took a sip of the cold, sweet drink and smiled. 'This is just like my grandmother's. Lemon juice and sugar topped up with water?' she asked.

'Sure is!' Evie topped up her glass. 'Good old-fashioned, thirst-quenching drink. Plenty more where that came from.' She eyed Rose curiously. 'How long have you been on the road?'

'Feels like forever! Especially since I've got bigger. The car isn't as comfortable as it used to be. Every time we hit a pothole, I feel like the seat is coming up through my stomach!' She took another sip. 'We've come from Lucindale and before that Mount Gambier. I've forgotten where we were earlier.'

'Yep, I imagine the bubs are giving you a good kicking. Where are you from?'

'Ballarat.' She paused, suddenly and inexplicably wanting to pour out her heart to this woman. It had been so long since Rose had seen her mother, and there weren't many women to talk to on the farms and stations Ian worked. Sometimes the loneliness crept in. 'I'm a bit scared,' she said, the words tumbling out before she could stop them.

'Why's that, Rose?' Evie fixed her with such a sympathetic look, Rose thought she might cry.

'I don't know anything about this. Ian keeps saying I'll be fine. Women have had babies for generations.'

'And so they have.' Evie nodded.

'I don't even know if I'll realise when I'm in labour! I don't know anything, not even about these Braxtons—whatever you just said.' The anxiety that had been building in Rose over the months finally came to the surface.

'Oh, you'll know, all right,' Evie said dryly as she moved over to the bookshelf and started looking through the battered paperbacks and recipe books. 'How old are you?'

'Twenty.'

'Young and healthy. If you were having one baby, I'd say your Ian is right and you'd be fine. But having two is a whole different thing. You should be close to a hospital. Hasn't a doctor told you that already?'

'Last time I saw a doctor was three months ago.'

Selecting the book she was looking for, Evie handed it over to Rose. 'Here you go, have a read of this.'

Rose looked at the title: *All You Need To Know About Being Pregnant*.

'That'll give you a bit of an idea about what to expect.' Evie paused. 'I'd really have a hard think about going out to Jacksonville, Rose. It's a long way, and it'll feel even longer when the bubs decide they want to come.'

'You there, love?' Ian called out before Rose could speak. 'Let's get on the road.'

Trying not to frown, Rose took a couple of final deep gulps of her drink. 'Well, I guess that's me,' she said. She glanced around longingly. 'You've got a lovely home. Who would have thought this would be out the back of a road-house?' she said. 'I'd love a couch like yours.' She nodded towards the floral-patterned sofa, then turned to the door, and Ian. 'Coming!'

Evie put her hand on Rose's arm as they walked out to the car. 'Rose, I don't know you and this is none of my business, but I'm thinking those bubs could arrive very soon. If they're early, they'll need medical help.'

'What do you mean?' Rose glanced across at her, her eyes wide.

'Sometimes if babies are born early they need help to breathe. Lungs are the last organ to develop, and if your twins arrive prematurely, they'll need to stay in hospital for a while. We've got a good hospital here in Barker.'

'Oh.' Rose looked at Ian, then down at the ground, trying to ignore the butterflies in her stomach. The ones that weren't the babies or indigestion. They were getting harder and harder to ignore. She put her hand on her belly protectively and looked over at Ian. 'I'll need time to talk to my husband about that.' Her hands fell away as she moved towards the car.

'Of course. Still, if you decide you want to stop here, let me know. I have a little house just up the street, with no one living in it. Barker is a lovely, sleepy little town. Gets pretty warm in summer, but that's just like the welcome you'd get here.' She nodded. 'Off with you, then. But take care.'

'What are you two gasbagging about?' Ian held the car door open for Rose.

'I was just saying that being so far away from the hospital with twins on the way is quite dangerous,' Evie answered, her smile softened her firm tone. 'They might need medical help when they're born. I've just been telling Rose that you're welcome to use my other house if you need it. Just nearby, and it would easily fit your new family.'

Rose looked at Ian hopefully. 'A house sounds lovely.'

'Come on, sweet Rosie.' Ian bent to kiss her. 'You know the plan.' He turned to Evie. 'I want to get her back to Adelaide before the babies are born, but I need this shed to be able to do that.'

'Well, if you change your mind, the offer's there.'

Ian looked at her. 'Why would you do that when you don't know us?'

Evie shrugged. 'I like helping people.'

'Women have babies out in the bush all the time.'

'Yes, they do.' Evie paused, looking at Rose. 'Some survive and some don't. As I just said to Rose, twins are a different story.'

Ian gave a bark of laughter. 'In this day and age, you'd have to be pretty unlucky to have something go so wrong that you die.'

'If you're close to medical help,' Evie agreed.

Rose frowned as her middle tightened. 'Come on, Ian,' she urged. 'If we're going, let's go.' She reached her hand out to Evie. 'Thank you for your kindness. Country people and their compassion is one of the reasons I can cope being on the road.'

'Go well, you two,' Evie bade them farewell, smiling through the window to Rose as Ian started the car.

'She's a bit of an old busybody,' he said, pulling the column gear into reverse.

Rose looked out the window, tears unexpectedly filling her eyes. 'She was nice,' she said unsteadily as she looked down and opened the book to the first page.

What happens in the first trimester, she read. *Bit late for that.*

Ian glanced over at her. 'What have you got there?'

'Evie gave it to me.' She flicked the cover over so he could read the title, realising her voice shook a little as she spoke.

'Hmm.' Ian looked back at the road, silent for a while. 'Don't tell me you actually want a house and to be in one place all the time? You knew you weren't going to get that with me.'

'I know. I'm fine. Probably just tired.' She squeezed her eyes shut. What she really wanted to say was: Yes! Yes, she did want a house, with a pretty sitting room and a nursery for the babies. A bathroom she didn't have to share with men she didn't know and a pillow that wasn't lumpy.

Ian reached over and put his hand on her knee. 'Sweet Rosie, are you okay? Did the pains hurt that much?'

'They're pretty scary,' Rose admitted.

'You know I love you, don't you? This life on the road, going from shed to shed—it's the way it is. You know I don't want to be confined to one town. That's why I came to Australia. You didn't want that either.'

Rose glanced over at her husband—the tall, dark-haired Irishman she had fallen in love with the first day she saw him walk into the local pub in Ballarat, two years ago. He'd been working in a shed and come into town to let off a bit of steam. She'd been working behind the bar.

Ian had ended up sitting down one end of the bar that night, talking to her as much as he could. By the time the shed was finished, two weeks later, she'd handed in her resignation and said goodbye to her parents, leaving in the passenger seat of the Kingwood.

Her mother had been horrified. 'You've only just met him.' That was the first thing she'd said.

'Think of the family name—you leaving with him and not being married.' Her father had frowned deeply. With his role as a lay preacher in the Baptist Church, Rose could only imagine what he'd think this was doing to his Christian image, and he hadn't left her in any doubt of what he thought of her decision. 'Living together and not being married is against God's law, and no daughter of mine will be seen to be involved in such sin.'

And, finally, they had both agreed: 'Rose, you'll be back here begging us to take you in within weeks. Well, my girl, if you leave, don't think that will happen.'

That had been that. Rose, the daughter who had never rebelled, against her family or society, had picked up her bag and walked away from the tidy front yard, with its lilly-pilly hedge fence and green lawn that her father mowed every Saturday afternoon.

Her parents had stood in the doorway until she climbed into Ian's car, then turned and shut their door tightly, finalising the end of their relationship.

Their marriage had come eight months later, when they'd rolled into the sleepy town of Townsville. Rose had a photo of them standing on the town hall steps, both looking uncomfortable in their Sunday best. The registry office wedding had been followed by drinks at the Shamrock Hotel, where Ian had bragged to all who would listen that his Rose was the prettiest girl around. Their bed had been tiny and Ian's drunken snores had kept her awake. As had an annoying mozzie who seemed to know exactly where her ear was. Nothing like she'd imagined her wedding day would be.

The walk on the beach the next morning, the bouquet of flowers and gentle kisses and soft praises had made up for the flop of a wedding night.

Rosie hadn't given her family much thought, although from time to time the urge to speak to her mum was overwhelming, especially since she'd become pregnant. But that was a feeling she kept to herself.

As Ian swung the car onto the road and headed out of town, she thought about their life since she'd left. At first, she'd loved the nomadic lifestyle. She'd seen more of Australia than any of the girls she'd gone to school with. They were all back in their hometown, married or studying to be a nurse or a teacher. Their lives would emulate those of their parents. Never moving out of the same postcode, and perhaps only shifting a few streets away from where they were raised.

Rose had never wanted to be like that. She'd always yearned to get out of Ballarat, and that was why she'd taken the job at the pub—to earn enough money to be able to leave and start a new life.

But she had never counted on falling in love with Ian. And she had, quickly and hard. His accent had made her knees tremble as he whispered Irish words she didn't understand. He'd seemed wild and exciting and free.

Free. That was what she wanted to be.

Out of Ballarat and away from her parents' expectations and tight rules. The ones that would see her end up just like every other young woman in town: working for a year or two until she ended up married and pregnant. Again there was the irony, because that was exactly what Rose now was—married and pregnant.

She always found a smile on her lips when she remembered what Ian had said to her a couple of days before they left.

'Come with me, sweet Rosie. Life on the road with you will be perfect. We won't have much, but we'll have each other, and I want nothing more than you. Come with me, *A chroí.*'

Oh, how she loved the Irish endearments. They sounded so mysterious. Just like their travelling life had been meant to be.

The countryside now opened up to wide red plains, covered in golden swaying grasses and low olive-coloured shrubby trees. They looked prickly to Rose. A heat mirage shimmered at the end of the road and didn't get any closer as they drove towards it. The air felt as if it were burning as she breathed in, and the sunlight hurt her eyes.

'Rosie?' Ian was looking at her, concerned. 'I love you,' he repeated.

She touched his arm and tried to smile. 'I know.'

Chapter 2

2020

A cold wind blew through the Barker police station as the door opened; the missing-persons posters and other pamphlets and brochures flapped under the force of the breeze.

Joan, the long-standing receptionist, snatched at her paperwork and looked up, her smile turning to a frown.

Three men dressed in casual clothes but each wearing a vest declaring they were from the Australian Federal Police now stood in front of the desk. Dark sunglasses and stern looks were on their faces.

'Can I help you?' Joan asked, trying to reorganise the documents she'd been working on.

'Looking for the sergeant,' the one closest to her said, putting his sunglasses on top of his head. He held out a badge.

Joan looked at it. Jerry Simms.

'I'll get Dave for you,' she said, rising and walking casually towards the back of the office. Ducking through the doorway, she glanced over her shoulder and saw all three standing to attention, their hands clasped low in front.

'Dave!' she whispered, frantically indicating towards the front desk.

Dave looked up from his computer and over the top of the glasses perched on the end of his nose. Joan's hands were pointing, and she was making all sorts of hand signals that didn't make sense. He raised an eyebrow.

'AFP!' Joan finally managed to get out.

Both his eyebrows were near his hairline now and he leaned back in his chair for a moment before getting up and walking out into the front area.

'Detective Dave Burrows,' he said, holding out his hand to the closest man, who merely fixed Dave with a stern look.

'Can we go somewhere private?' the nameless man asked, glancing at Joan.

'Right through here,' Dave answered, gesturing in the direction he'd come from.

The three men walked past him and found chairs in his office. Dave glanced over his shoulder at Joan and gave a wink, before following them through.

Settled in the office, the ringleader, his face still serious, introduced his team.

'I'm Jerry Simms and these are my colleagues, Allan Taylor and Rob Cooper.' They all shook hands this time, though the remaining stern-faced men still didn't speak.

'What can I do for you fellas?' Dave said. 'Pretty unusual to get a visit from the AFP out in a quiet country town like Barker.' He sat and crossed his legs, ready to listen.

'We're here to intercept a package that will be arriving at the post office today. I'm only letting you know out of courtesy that we're in town. Although we'd appreciate your assistance in "doing the door" when we go in to take control of the package.'

Dave was quiet for a moment. 'Whose door?'

'We won't tell you anything more until the parcel has been delivered.'

Frowning, Dave steepled his fingers as he looked at the men. 'That doesn't sound very friendly.'

'It's not a negotiation point. We can't compromise this transaction—it's integral to a larger operation,' Jerry said, as he leaned forward. 'Detective, we require your assistance. You'll have to trust us until the procedure is finished.'

Dave narrowed his eyes and thought about his answer. 'It's the local show today. I'd hope that if you're chasing someone, they won't be a local. But if they are, it would be better if I knew who the person of interest is. You forget, Jerry, that my partner and I will probably know this person. We've both been in this town a long time. We have local knowledge that might assist you.'

Jerry shook his head before Dave had finished speaking and kept it moving until there was silence. 'No. No, we're not forgetting. What you need to understand is we haven't worked with either of you before. Both you and Senior Constable Higgins come with high recommendations, and we understand you're both competent and dedicated to the police force. But you're also very entrenched in Barker. This is a small town and the walls have ears.' He looked out towards where Joan sat, then leaned back and shook his head. 'No go.'

'Have you got a time frame? I'm going to need to talk to Jack. Let him know what's going on. He's out taking a statement from a burglary victim.'

Jerry glanced at his watch. 'At zero eleven hundred.'

The office door banged shut as Jack Higgins' voice filtered through from reception.

'Perfect timing,' Dave said.

'That bloody wind!' Jack could be heard declaring to Joan. 'It's straight off the snow. Pity it hasn't got any rain in it. Whose car's out the front?'

There was a muffled answer from Joan and silence from Jack. Dave could imagine the mimed conversation as Joan tried to tell Jack who was in the office. Maybe she'd even written him a note saying who it was. He almost grinned as he envisaged the look of surprise on Jack's face when he worked out the car belonged to Feds.

'That's Jack now.' Dave nodded towards the front. 'I'll brief him and then introduce you.'

'There's no need,' Jerry said. 'I can do that.'

Dave ignored him and met Jack as he was about to walk into the offices. 'Back out here,' he said quietly, pointing towards the front door. Jack reversed out and Dave saw Joan watching them. He gave her a thumbs up. *Everything's okay.*

Dave and Jack bent their heads together. 'What the hell is going on?' Jack asked.

'The plastic police are in there. Need our help with an operation. Got some good grass on someone expecting a package. They want us to help with the door. Don't know if its drugs or what.'

'The Feds? Whose door? What package?' The words tumbled out of Jack's mouth as Dave saw his excitement rise.

'You know as much as I do. They're not exactly forthcoming with information. Come on, I'll introduce you. Guessing it's something to do with the imports who've come into town with the ag show. I certainly hope it's no one local.'

Jack sobered. 'Yeah, good point. So, no indication?'

'Nothing.' Dave stopped and looked at Jack. 'Where's Zara today?' he asked.

'Being ever the good journalist and covering the agricultural show, but you know she'll sniff this out quick enough. Just the strange car will be enough.'

'Let's hope she stays on the showgrounds for a while, then.'

Dave pushed open the door and went back into his office, where the three men were leaning close together, talking in hushed tones.

'This is my partner, Jack Higgins,' Dave said. He resisted the urge to introduce the three AFP coppers as Huey, Dewey and Louie, dressed as they were in an unofficial uniform of beige chino pants and pale blue shirt, open at the neck.

An air of serious confidence, and perhaps arrogance, radiated from each face. Still, Dave had come across that type of attitude before.

'G'day,' Jack said, shaking hands with them all. 'Sounds like there's something interesting in the pipeline.'

'We've got intel that a parcel will be delivered today and we want to intercept it,' Jerry confirmed. 'Do you have experience on the video camera, Senior Constable?'

'Yeah, I do.'

'Good. We need everything from the moment we knock on the door until we walk out again to be filmed. You can work with Allan here, both filming from different angles. Rob, Dave and I will get the door open. Got that?'

Dave cast a glance at Jack to see how he was taking the high-handed instructions.

'Sure, whatever you need,' Jack said, to Dave's surprise.

'Right, let's move out, boys,' Simms said to his men.

'Hold on, don't you think it's going to raise some eyebrows, three strange blokes dressed in AFP vests? Let alone a different car parked in a quiet street where all the residents know everything about everyone?'

Jerry turned to Dave. 'That's why we're taking your vehicles. We'll be back in an hour and a half.'

Dave watched them leave and raised his eyebrows at Jack.

'They can be tossers, can't they? No such thing as flexibility.'

Jack laughed and rubbed his hands together. 'But they've given us some excitement for the day.'

'Hmm. Like I said before, just so long as it isn't someone local they're chasing. I would hate to charge someone who lives here.'

'Depending on who it is,' Jack replied.

❧

Dave, Jerry and Rob sat in Dave's unmarked police car, opposite the post office. There hadn't been much conversation, which suited Dave. He'd been too busy watching all the locals who weren't at the show, walking up and down the street, dressed in heavy jackets, trying to keep the biting wind from their bodies. Who were the Feds after? The only way to guess that was to see who was going to the post office, apparently.

Dave was in the front seat, while the other two were in the back behind the tinted windows. The locals would have to look closely to realise there was anyone else in the vehicle with him.

He'd seen Mrs Hunter stop and chat with the young girl, Beattie, from the chemist shop, and Jamie Flemming had pulled up in his muddy farm ute, run in to the deli and come out with an iced coffee and sausage roll.

His wife wouldn't be too happy if she knew that's what her husband was up to, Dave thought. Jamie was supposed to be on a diet—diabetes, or so he'd told Dave last time they'd run into each other.

Everyone Dave had seen was a local, and surely whoever was supposed to have this package—whatever might be inside it—was not a local. He knew his town. Or so he hoped.

'What are we waiting for?' Dave asked. 'A delivery or a pick-up?'

'The postal delivery truck,' Rob said. They were the first words he'd spoken, other than to say hello.

'The truck would have been here at ten o'clock this morning.' Dave looked at his watch. 'It's now nearly twelve-thirty.' As he said that, he saw Joan walking towards the post office, her keys in hand. She'd be getting the police station mail, and her own, he knew. 'You've missed it.'

'No, we haven't. There had to be time to sort the mail. She'll be getting it from her mailbox soon.' There was a pause. 'Look.'

The two men leaned over the seat towards the wind-screen, then Jerry muttered, 'There we go.'

Dave stared at his receptionist, Joan, as she walked towards the post office, dread filling his stomach. 'What? Who?'

'She's coming now.' Rob pointed, his hand coming from between the seats, aimed at Joan.

Not able to find any words, Dave sat and waited. No. It couldn't be Joan they were after.

'Over there, in the green coat. Behind your receptionist.'

Dave glanced away from Joan and saw Essie Carter in a green coat. The relief was instant but replaced with scepticism. 'Who? Essie?'

'Estelle Carter of 10 Fifth Street, Barker,' Rob said. He held the page with Essie's information on it, over the back seat for Dave to take.

Reaching out, Dave kept his eyes on Essie. 'You're wrong. Essie's been here in Barker forever; rarely leaves town. She goes to church every Sunday, and volunteers at the hospital and at the Red Cross op shop. Raises her granddaughter on her own. Bloody hell, Essie must be sixty-odd. I can't imagine she's doing anything illegal.'

'You don't think? Look at her. Checking out her surroundings, looking over her shoulder,' Jerry said. 'Got all the hallmarks of guilt to me.'

'What's she supposed to have done?' Dave said. 'What's in the package?'

The two men didn't answer.

Essie had stopped briefly to talk with Joan, then hurried on to the post office. As she stepped into the alcove, where the mailboxes were, she cast a glance over her shoulder. Dave got his binoculars out and watched as, with shaking hands, Essie tried to insert the key into her box, but dropped the set. Joan was next to her and bent down to pick up the keys before Essie could.

The elderly lady snatched the keys back and then gave Joan a quick smile. She said something that looked like, 'Clumsy me.'

Joan collected the mail and turned to go, putting a hand on Essie's shoulder before she left. Dave thought he could lip read through the binoculars: 'See you at church on Sunday,' and Essie nodded without smiling.

Dave continued to observe, his eyes fixed through the lenses, his heart sinking. It was like watching a slow-motion train wreck. Essie took another look around, then a deep breath. Dave had to admit Jerry was right. This wasn't the behaviour of a person without something to hide.

She inserted the key into the lock and ducked down to look inside. As she withdrew the contents, Dave got a glance of a small yellow padded envelope before she quickly stuffed it in her jacket pocket. Then she turned and walked out onto the street again, head down.

'Guilty as sin,' Rob said. 'Hope those boys got her behaviour on video.'

'What do you think, Dave?'

Dave watched Essie walk with purpose towards the corner. 'I think there's more to this than you know.'

His mind was racing. This was the Essie who had decorated the church with flowers for Dave's wedding to Kim. The Essie who was so grateful for what Dave had done to save her daughter. The Essie who was always the first to pop into the station with a birthday cake and a smile. What he was seeing here couldn't be right.

Except he knew what he'd seen: something was happening and Essie was involved.

There's got to be more to this, he thought. *I've got to find out what.*